P9-DWW-098

Praise for *Forever, Interrupted*

"Touching and powerful . . . Reid masterfully grabs hold of the heartstrings and doesn't let go. A stunning first novel."

—*Publishers Weekly* (starred review)

"You'll laugh, weep, and fly through each crazy-readable page."

—*Redbook*

"A moving novel about life and death."

—*Kirkus Reviews*

"A poignant and heartfelt exploration of love and commitment in the absence of shared time that asks, what does it take to be the love of someone's life?"

—Emma McLaughlin and Nicola Kraus,
#1 *New York Times* bestselling authors

"Moving, gorgeous, and at times heart-wrenching."

—Sarah Jio, *New York Times* bestselling author

"Sweet, heartfelt, and surprising. These characters made me laugh as well as cry, and I ended up falling in love with them, too."

—Sarah Pekkanen, internationally bestselling
author of *The Opposite of Me*

"This beautifully rendered story explores the brilliance and rarity of finding true love, and how we find our way back through the painful aftermath of losing it. These characters will leap right off the page and into your heart."

—Amy Hatvany, author of *Safe with Me*

Praise for *After I Do*

"As uplifting as it is brutally honest—a must-read."

—*Kirkus Reviews*

"Written in a breezy, humorous style familiar to fans of Jane Green and Elin Hilderbrand, *After I Do* focuses on Lauren's journey of self-discovery. The intriguing premise and well-drawn characters contribute to an emotionally uplifting and inspiring story."

—*Booklist*

"Taylor Jenkins Reid offers an entirely fresh and new perspective on what can happen after the 'happily ever after.' With characters who feel like friends and a narrative that hooked me from the first page, *After I Do* takes an elegant and incisively emotional look at the endings and beginnings of love. Put this book at the top of your must-read list!"

—Jen Lancaster,
New York Times bestselling author

"Taylor Jenkins Reid delivers a seductive twist on the timeless tale of a couple trying to rediscover love in a marriage brought low by the challenges of domestic togetherness. I fell in love with Ryan and Lauren from their passionate beginning, and I couldn't stop reading as they followed their unlikely road to redemption. Touching, perceptive, funny, and achingly honest, *After I Do* will keep you hooked to the end, rooting for husbands and wives and the strength of true love."

—Beatriz Williams,
New York Times bestselling author

"Taylor Jenkins Reid writes with ruthless honesty, displaying an innate understanding of human emotion and creating characters and relationships so real I'm finding it impossible to let them go. *After I Do* is a raw, unflinching exploration of the realities of marriage, the delicate nature of love, and the enduring strength of family. Simultaneously funny and sad, heartbreaking and hopeful, Reid has crafted a story of love lost and found that is as timely as it is timeless."

—Katja Millay,
author of *The Sea of Tranquility*

MAYBE IN
ANOTHER LIFE

Also by Taylor Jenkins Reid

Forever, Interrupted
After I Do

MAYBE IN ANOTHER LIFE

~ A Novel ~

TAYLOR JENKINS REID

WASHINGTON SQUARE PRESS
New York   Toronto   London   Sydney   New Delhi

W

Washington Square Press
An Imprint of Simon & Schuster, Inc.
1230 Avenue of the Americas
New York, NY 10020

This book is a work of fiction. Any references to historical events, real people, or real places are used fictitiously. Other names, characters, places, and events are products of the author's imagination, and any resemblance to actual events or places or persons, living or dead, is entirely coincidental.

Copyright © 2015 by Taylor Jenkins Reid

All rights reserved, including the right to reproduce this book or portions thereof in any form whatsoever. For information address Washington Square Press Subsidiary Rights Department, 1230 Avenue of the Americas, New York, NY 10020.

First Washington Square Press trade paperback edition July 2015

WASHINGTON SQUARE PRESS and colophon are registered trademarks of Simon & Schuster, Inc.

For information about special discounts for bulk purchases, please contact Simon & Schuster Special Sales at 1-866-506-1949 or business@simonandschuster.com.

The Simon & Schuster Speakers Bureau can bring authors to your live event. For more information or to book an event contact the Simon & Schuster Speakers Bureau at 1-866-248-3049 or visit our website at www.simonspeakers.com.

Manufactured in the United States of America

10 9 8 7 6 5 4 3 2 1

Library of Congress Cataloging-in-Publication Data

Reid, Taylor Jenkins.
  Maybe in another life : a novel / Taylor Jenkins Reid. —First Washington Square Press trade paperback edition.
      pages ; cm
  1. Chick lit. I. Title.
  PS3618.E5478M39 2015
  813'.6—dc23
                                                            2014039873
ISBN 978-1-4767-7688-0
ISBN 978-1-4767-7689-7 (ebook)

To Erin, Julia, Sara, Tamara,
and all of the other women I feel destined to have met.
May we know each other in many universes.

MAYBE IN ANOTHER LIFE

It's a good thing I booked an aisle seat, because I'm the last one on the plane. I knew I'd be late for my flight. I'm late for almost everything. That's why I booked an aisle seat in the first place. I hate making people get up so that I can squeeze by. This is also why I never go to the bathroom during movies, even though I always have to go to the bathroom during movies.

I walk down the tight aisle, holding my carry-on close to my body, trying not to bump anyone. I hit a man's elbow and apologize even though he doesn't seem to notice. When I barely graze a woman's arm, she shoots daggers at me as if I stabbed her. I open my mouth to say I'm sorry and then think better of it.

I spot my seat easily; it is the only open one.

The air is stale. The music is Muzak. The conversations around me are punctuated by the clicks of the overhead compartments being slammed shut.

I get to my seat and sit down, smiling at the woman next to me. She's older and round, with short salt-and-pepper hair. I shove my bag in front of me and buckle my seat belt. My tray table's up. My electronics are off. My seat is in the upright position. When you're late a lot, you learn how to make up for lost time.

I look out the window. The baggage handlers are bundled

up in extra layers and neon jackets. I'm happy to be headed to a warmer climate. I pick up the in-flight magazine.

Soon I hear the roar of the engine and feel the wheels beneath us start to roll. The woman next to me grips the armrests as we ascend. She looks petrified.

I'm not scared of flying. I'm scared of sharks, hurricanes, and false imprisonment. I'm scared that I will never do anything of value with my life. But I'm not scared of flying.

Her knuckles are white with tension.

I tuck the magazine back into the pouch. "Not much of a flier?" I ask her. When I'm anxious, talking helps. If talking helps her, it's the least I can do.

The woman turns and looks at me as we glide into the air. " 'Fraid not," she says, smiling ruefully. "I don't leave New York very often. This is my first time flying to Los Angeles."

"Well, if it makes you feel any better, I fly a fair amount, and I can tell you, with any flight, it's really only takeoff and landing that are hard. We've got about three more minutes of this part and then about five minutes at the end that can be tough. The rest of it . . . you might as well be on a bus. So just eight bad minutes total, and then you're in California."

We're at an incline. It's steep enough that an errant bottle of water rolls down the aisle.

"Eight minutes is all?" she asks.

I nod. "That's it," I tell her. "You're from New York?"

She nods. "How about you?"

I shrug. "I was living in New York. Now I'm moving back to L.A."

The plane drops abruptly and then rights itself as we make our way past the clouds. She breathes in deeply. I have to admit, even I feel a little queasy.

"But I was only in New York for about nine months," I say. The longer I talk, the less attention she has to focus on the turbulence. "I've been moving around a bit lately. I went to school in Boston. Then I moved to D.C., then Portland, Oregon. Then Seattle. Then Austin, Texas. Then New York. The city where dreams come true. Although, you know, not for me. But I did grow up in Los Angeles. So you could say I'm going back to where I came from, but I don't know that I'd call it home."

"Where's your family?" she asks. Her voice is tight. She's looking forward.

"My family moved to London when I was sixteen. My younger sister, Sarah, got accepted to the Royal Ballet School, and they couldn't pass that up. I stayed and finished school in L.A."

"You lived on your own?" It's working. The distraction.

"I lived with my best friend's family until I finished high school. And then I left for college."

The plane levels out. The captain tells us our altitude. She takes her hands off the armrest and breathes.

"See?" I say to her. "Just like a bus."

"Thank you," she says.

"Anytime."

She looks out the window. I pick up the magazine again. She turns back to me. "Why do you move around so much?" she says. "Isn't that difficult?" She immediately corrects herself. "Listen to me, the minute I stop hyperventilating, I'm acting like your mother."

I laugh with her. "No, no, it's fine," I say. I don't move from place to place on purpose. It's not a conscious choice to be a nomad. Although I can see that each move is my own decision, predicated on nothing but my ever-growing sense that I don't belong where I am, fueled by the hope that maybe there is, in fact, a place I do belong, a place just off in the future. "I guess . . . I don't know," I say. It's hard to put into words, especially to someone I barely know. But then I open my mouth, and out it comes. "No place has felt like home."

She looks at me and smiles. "I'm sorry," she says. "That has to be hard."

I shrug, because it's an impulse. It's always my impulse to ignore the bad, to run toward the good.

But I'm also not feeling great about my own impulses at the moment. I'm not sure they are getting me where I want to go.

I stop shrugging.

And then, because I won't see her again after this flight, I take it one step further. I tell her something I've only recently told myself. "Sometimes I worry I'll never find a place to call home."

She puts her hand on mine, ever so briefly. "You will," she says. "You're young still. You have plenty of time."

I wonder if she can tell that I'm twenty-nine and considers that young, or if she thinks I'm younger than I am.

"Thanks," I say. I take my headphones out of my bag and put them on.

"At the end of the flight, during the five tricky minutes when we land, maybe we can talk about my lack of career choices," I say, laughing. "That will definitely distract you."

She smiles broadly and lets out a laugh. "I'd consider it a personal favor."

When I come out of the gate, Gabby is holding up a sign that says "Hannah Marie Martin," as if I wouldn't recognize her, as if I wouldn't know she was my ride.

I run toward her, and as I get closer, I can see that she has drawn a picture of me next to my name. It is a crude sketch but not altogether terrible. The Hannah of her drawing has big eyes and long lashes, a tiny nose, and a line for a mouth. On the top of my head is hair drawn dramatically in a high bun. The only thing of note drawn on my stick-figure body is an oversized pair of boobs.

It's not necessarily how I see myself, but I admit, if you reduced me to a caricature, I'd be big boobs and a high bun. Sort of like how Mickey Mouse is round ears and gloved hands or how Michael Jackson is white socks and black loafers.

I'd much rather be depicted with my dark brown hair and my light green eyes, but I understand that you can't really do much with color when you're drawing with a Bic pen.

Even though I haven't visited Gabby in person since her wedding day two years ago, I have seen her every Sunday morning of the recent past. We video-chat no matter what we have to do that day or how hungover one of us is feeling. It is, in some ways, the most reliable thing in my life.

Gabby is tiny and twiglike. Her hair is kept cropped close in a bob, and there's no extra fat on her, not an inch to spare. When

I hug her, I remember how odd it is to hug someone so much smaller than I am, how different the two of us seem at first glance. I am tall, curvy, and white. She is short, thin, and black.

She doesn't have any makeup on, and yet she is one of the prettiest women here. I don't tell her that, because I know what she'd say. She'd say that's irrelevant. She'd say we shouldn't be complimenting each other on our looks or competing with each other over who is prettier. She's got a point, so I keep it to myself.

I have known Gabby since we were both fourteen years old. We sat next to each other in earth science class the first day of high school. The friendship was fast and everlasting. We were Gabby and Hannah, Hannah and Gabby, one name rarely mentioned without the other in tow.

I moved in with her and her parents, Carl and Tina, when my family left for London. Carl and Tina treated me as if I were their own. They coached me through applying for schools, made sure I did my homework, and kept me on a curfew. Carl routinely tried to persuade me to become a doctor, like him and his father. By then, he knew that Gabby wouldn't follow on his path. She already knew she wanted to work in public service. I think Carl figured I was his last shot. But Tina instead encouraged me to find my own way. Unfortunately, I'm still not sure what that way is. But back then, I just assumed it would all fall into place, that the big things in life would take care of themselves.

After we went off to college, Gabby in Chicago, myself in Boston, we still talked all the time but started to find new lives for ourselves. Freshman year, she became friends with another black student at her school named Vanessa. Gabby would tell me about their trips to the nearby mall and the parties they went to. I'd have been lying if I said I wasn't nervous back then, in some small way, that Vanessa would become closer to Gabby than I ever could, that Vanessa could share something with Gabby that I was not a part of.

I asked Gabby about it over the phone once. I was lying in my dorm room on my twin XL bed, the phone sweaty and hot on my ear from our already-hours-long conversation.

"Do you feel like Vanessa understands you better than I do?" I asked her. "Because you're both black?" The minute the question came out of my mouth, I was embarrassed. It had seemed reasonable in my head but sounded irrational coming out of my mouth. If words were things, I would have rushed to pluck them out of the air and put them back in my mouth.

Gabby laughed at me. "Do you think white people understand you more than I do just because they're white?"

"No," I said. "Of course not."

"So be quiet," Gabby said.

And I did. If there is one thing I love about Gabby, it is that she has always known when I should be quiet. She is, in fact, the only person who often proves to know me better than I know myself.

"Let me guess," she says now, as she takes my carry-on bag out of my hand, a gentlemanly gesture. "We're going to need to rent one of those baggage carts to get all of your stuff."

I laugh. "In my defense, I am moving across the country," I say.

I long ago stopped buying furniture or large items. I tend to sublet furnished apartments. You learn after one or two moves that buying an IKEA bed, putting it together, and then breaking it down and selling it for fifty bucks six months later is a waste of time and money. But I do still have *things*, some of which have survived multiple cross-country trips. It would feel callous to let go of them now.

"I'm going to guess there's at least four bottles of Orange Ginger body lotion in here," Gabby says as she grabs one of my bags off the carousel.

I shake my head. "Only the one. I'm running low."

I started using body lotion somewhere around the time she and I met. We would go to the mall together and smell all the lotions in all the different stores. But every time, I kept buying the same one. Orange Ginger. At one point, I had seven bottles of the stuff stocked up.

We grab the rest of my bags from the carousel and pack them one after another onto the cart, the two of us pushing with all our might across the lanes of airport traffic and into the parking structure. We load them into her tiny car and then settle into our seats.

We make small talk as she makes her way out of the garage and navigates the streets leading us to the freeway. She asks about my flight and how it felt to leave New York. She apologizes that her guest room is small. I tell her not to be ridiculous, and I thank her again for letting me stay.

The repetition of history is not lost on me. It's more than a decade later, and I am once again staying in Gabby's guest room. It's been more than ten years, and yet I am still floating from place to place, relying on the kindness of Gabby and her family. This time, it's Gabby and her husband, Mark, instead of Gabby and her parents. But if anything, that just highlights the difference between the two of us, how much Gabby has changed since then and how much I have not. Gabby's the VP of Development at a nonprofit that works with at-risk teenagers. I'm a waitress. And not a particularly good one.

Once Gabby is flying down the freeway, once driving no longer takes her attention, or maybe once she is going so fast she knows I can't jump out of the car, she asks what she has been dying to ask since I hugged her hello. "So what happened? Did you tell him you were leaving?"

I sigh loudly and look out the window. "He knows not to contact me," I say. "He knows I don't want to see him ever again. So I suppose it doesn't really matter where he thinks I am."

Gabby looks straight ahead at the road, but I see her nod, pleased with me.

I need her approval right now. Her opinion of me is currently a better litmus test than my own. It's been a little rough going lately. And while I know Gabby will always love me, I also know that as of late, I have tested her unconditional support.

Mostly because I started sleeping with a married man.

I didn't know he was married at first. And for some reason, I thought that meant it was OK. He never admitted he was married. He never wore a wedding ring. He didn't even have a paler shade of skin around his ring finger, the way magazines tell you married men will. He was a liar. A good one, at that. And even though I suspected the truth, I thought that if he never said it, if he never admitted it to my face, then I wasn't accountable for the fact that it was true.

I suspected something was up when he once didn't answer my calls for six days and then finally called me back acting as if nothing was out of the ordinary. I suspected there was another woman when he refused to let me use his phone. I suspected that *I* was, in fact, the other woman when we ran into a coworker of his at a restaurant in SoHo, and rather than introduce me to the man, Michael told me I had something in my teeth and that I should go to the bathroom to get it out. I did go to the bathroom. And I found nothing there. But if I'm being honest, I also found it hard to look at myself in the mirror for more than a few seconds before going back out there and pretending I didn't know what he was trying to do.

And Gabby, of course, knew all of this. I was admitting it to her at the same rate I was admitting it to myself.

"I think he's married," I finally said to her a month or so ago. I was sitting in bed, still in my pajamas, talking to her on my laptop, and fixing my bun.

I watched as Gabby's pixelated face frowned. "I told you he was married," she said, her patience wearing thin. "I told you this three weeks ago. I told you that you need to stop this. Because it's wrong. And because that is some woman's husband. And because you shouldn't allow a man to treat you like a mistress. I told you all of this."

"I know, but I really didn't think he was married. He would have told me if he was. You know? So I didn't think he was. And I'm not going to ask him, because that's so insulting, isn't it?" That was my rationale. I didn't want to insult him.

"You need to cut this crap out, Hannah. I'm serious. You are a wonderful person who has a lot to offer the world. But this is wrong. And you know it."

I listened to her. And then I let all of her advice fly right through my head and out into the wind. As if it was meant for someone else and wasn't mine to hold on to.

"No," I said, shaking my head. "I don't think you're right about this. Michael and I met at a bar in Bushwick on a Wednesday night. I never go to Bushwick. And I rarely go out on a Wednesday night. And neither does he! What are the odds of that? That two people would come together like that?"

"You're joking, right?"

"Why would I be joking? I'm talking about fate here. Honestly. Let's say he is married . . ."

"He is."

"We don't know that. But let's say that he is."

"He is."

"Let's *say* that he is. That doesn't mean that we weren't fated to meet. For all we know, I'm just playing out the natural course of destiny here. Maybe he's married and that's OK because it's how things were meant to be."

I could tell Gabby was disappointed in me. I could see it in her eyebrows and the turn of her lips.

"Look, I don't even know that he's married," I said. But I did. I did know it. And because I knew it, I had to run as far away from it as I could. So I said, "You know, Gabby, even if he is married, that doesn't mean I'm not better for him than this other person. All's fair in love and war."

Two weeks later, his wife found out about me and called me screaming.

He'd done this before.

She'd found two others.

And did I know they had two children?

I did not know that.

It's very easy to rationalize what you're doing when you don't know the faces and the names of the people you might hurt. It's very easy to choose yourself over someone else when it's an abstract.

And I think that's why I kept everything abstract.

I had been playing the "Well, But" game. The "We Don't Know That for Sure" game. The "Even So" game. I had been viewing the truth through my own little lens, one that was narrow and rose-colored.

And then, suddenly, it was as if the lens fell from my face, and I could suddenly see, in staggering black-and-white, what I had been doing.

Does it matter that once I faced the truth I behaved honorably? Does it matter that once I heard his wife's voice, once I knew the names of his children, I never spoke to him again?

Does it matter that I can see, clear as day, my own culpability and that I feel deep remorse? That a small part of me hates myself for relying on willful ignorance to justify what I suspected was wrong?

Gabby thinks it does. She thinks it redeems me. I'm not so sure.

Once Michael was out of my life, I realized I didn't have much else going for me in New York. The winter was harsh and cold and only seemed to emphasize further how alone I was in a city of millions. I called my parents and my sister, Sarah, a lot that first week after breaking up with Michael, not to talk about my problems but to hear friendly voices. I often got their voice mails. They always called me back. They always do. But I could never seem to accurately guess when they might be available. And very often, with the time difference, we had only a small sliver of time to catch one another.

Last week, everything just started to pile up. The girl whose apartment I was subletting gave me two weeks' notice that she needed the apartment back. My boss at work hit on me and implied that better shifts went to women who showed cleavage. I got stuck on the G train for an hour and forty-five minutes when a train broke down at Greenpoint Avenue. Michael kept calling me and leaving voice mails asking to explain himself, telling me that he wanted to leave his wife for me, and I was embarrassed to admit that it made me feel better even as it made me feel absolutely terrible.

So I called Gabby. And I cried. I admitted that things were harder in New York than I had ever let on. I admitted that this wasn't working, that my life was not shaping up the way I'd wanted it to. I told her I needed to change.

And she said, "Come home."

It took me a minute before I realized she meant that I should move back to Los Angeles. That's how long it's been since I thought of my hometown as home.

"To L.A.?" I asked.

"Yeah," she said. "Come home."

"You know, Ethan is there," I said. "He moved back a few years ago, I think."

"So you'll see him," Gabby said. "It wouldn't be the worst thing that happened to you. Getting back together with a good guy."

"It *is* warmer there," I said, looking out my tiny window at the dirty snow on the street below me.

"It was seventy-two the other day," she said.

"But changing cities doesn't solve the larger problem," I said, for maybe the first time in my life. "I mean, *I* need to change."

"I know," she said. "Come home. Change here."

It was the first time in a long time that something made sense.

Now Gabby grabs my hand for a moment and squeezes it, keeping her eye on the road. "I'm proud of you that you're taking control of your life," she says. "Just by getting on the plane this morning, you're getting your life together."

"You think so?" I ask.

She nods. "I think Los Angeles will be good for you. Don't you? Returning to your roots. It's a crime we've lived so far apart for so many years. You're correcting an injustice."

I laugh. I'm trying to see this move as a victory instead of a defeat.

Finally, we pull onto Gabby's street, and she parks her car at the curb.

We are in front of a complex on a steep, hilly street. Gabby and Mark bought a townhouse last year. I look at the addresses on the row of houses and search for the number four, to see which one is theirs. I may not have been here before, but I've been sending cards, baked goods, and various gifts to Gabby for months. I know her address by heart. Just as I catch the number on the door in the glow of the streetlight, I see Mark come out and walk toward us.

Mark is a tall, conventionally handsome man. Very physically strong, very traditionally male. I've always had a penchant for guys with pretty eyes and five o'clock shadows, and I thought Gabby did, too. But she ended up with Mark, the poster boy for clean-cut and stable. He's the kind of guy who goes to the gym for health reasons. I have never done that.

I open my car door and grab one of my bags. Gabby grabs another. Mark meets us at the car. "Hannah!" he says as he gives me a big hug. "It is so nice to see you." He takes the rest of the bags out of the car, and we head into the house. I look around their living room. It's a lot of neutrals and wood finishes. Safe but gorgeous.

"Your room is upstairs," she says, and the three of us walk up the tight staircase to the second floor. There is a master bedroom and a bedroom across the hall.

Gabby and Mark lead me into the guest room, and we put all the bags down.

It's a small room but big enough for just me. There's a double bed with a billowy white comforter, a desk, and a dresser.

It's late, and I am sure both Gabby and Mark are tired, so I do my best to be quick.

"You guys go ahead to bed. I can get myself settled," I say.

"You sure?" Gabby asks.

I insist.

Mark gives me a hug and heads to their bedroom. Gabby tells him she'll be there in a moment.

"I'm really happy you're here," she says to me. "In all of your city hopping, I always hoped you'd come back. At least for a little while. I like having you close by."

"Well, you got me," I tell her, smiling. "Perhaps even closer than you were thinking."

"Don't be silly," she says. "Live in my guest room until we're both ninety years old, as far as I'm concerned." She gives me a hug and heads to her room. "If you wake up before we do, feel free to start the coffee."

After I hear the bedroom door shut, I grab my toiletry bag and head into the bathroom.

The light in here is bright and unforgiving; some might even go so far as to describe it as harsh. There's a magnifying mirror by the sink. I grab it and pull it toward my face. I can tell I need to get my eyebrows waxed, but overall, there isn't too much to complain about. As I start to push the mirror back into place, the view grazes the outside of my left eye.

I pull on my skin, somewhat in denial of what I'm seeing. I let it bounce back into shape. I stare and inspect.

I have the beginnings of crow's-feet.

I have no apartment and no job. I have no steady relationship or even a city to call home. I have no idea what I want to be doing with my life, no idea what my purpose is, and no real sign of a life goal. And yet time has found me. The years I've spent dilly-dallying around at different jobs in different cities show on my face.

I have wrinkles.

I let go of the mirror. I brush my teeth. I wash my face. I resolve to buy night cream and start wearing sunscreen. And then I turn down the covers and get into bed.

My life may be a little bit of a disaster. I may not make the best decisions sometimes. But I am not going to lie here and stare at the ceiling, worrying the night away.

Instead, I go to sleep soundly, believing I will do better tomorrow. Things will be better tomorrow. I'll figure this all out tomorrow.

Tomorrow is, for me, a brand-new day.

I wake up to a bright, sunny room and a ringing phone.

"Ethan!" I whisper into the phone. "It's nine o'clock on a Saturday morning!"

"Yeah," he says, his gritty voice made grittier by the phone. "But you're still on East Coast time. It's noon for you. You should be up."

I continue to whisper. "OK, but Gabby and Mark are still sleeping."

"When do I get to see you?" he says.

~

I met Ethan in my sophomore year of high school at Homecoming.

I was still living at home with my parents. Gabby was offered a babysitting job that night and decided to take it instead of going to the dance. I ended up going by myself, not because I wanted to go but because my dad teased me that I never went anywhere without her. I went to prove him wrong.

I stood at the wall for most of the night, killing time until I could leave. I was so bored that I thought about calling Gabby and persuading her to join me once her babysitting gig was over. But Jesse Flint was slow-dancing with Jessica Campos all night in the middle of the dance floor. And Gabby loved Jesse Flint, had been pining away for him since high school began. I couldn't do that to her.

As the night wore on and couples started making out in the dimly lit gym, I looked over at the only other person standing against the wall. He was tall and thin, with rumpled hair and a wrinkled shirt. His tie was loose. He looked right back at me. And then he walked over to where I was standing and introduced himself.

"Ethan Hanover," he said, putting out his hand.

"Hannah Martin," I said, putting out my own to grab his.

He was a junior at another school. He told me he was just there as a favor to his neighbor, Katie Franklin, who didn't have a date. I knew Katie fairly well. I knew she was a lesbian who wasn't ready to tell her parents. The whole school knew that she and Teresa Hawkins were more than just friends. So I figured I wasn't hurting anyone by flirting with the boy she brought for cover.

But pretty soon I found myself forgetting anyone else was even at the dance in the first place. When Katie did finally come get him and suggest it was time to go, I felt as if something was being taken from me. I was tempted to reach out and grab him, to claim him for myself.

Ethan had a party at his parents' house the next weekend and invited me. Gabby and I didn't normally go to big parties, but I made her come. He perked up the minute I walked in the door. He grabbed my hand and introduced me to his friends. I lost track of Gabby somewhere by the Tostitos.

Soon Ethan and I had ventured upstairs. We were sitting on the top step of the staircase, hip to hip, talking about our favorite bands. He kissed me there, in the dark, the wild party happening just underneath our feet.

"I only threw a party so I could call you and invite you," he said to me. "Is that stupid?"

I shook my head and kissed him again.

When Gabby came and found me an hour or so later, my lips felt swollen, and I knew I had a hickey.

We lost our virginity to each other a year and a half later. We were in his bedroom when his parents were out of town. He told me he loved me as I lay underneath him, and he kept asking if it was OK.

Some people talk about their first time as a hilarious or pathetic experience. I can't relate. Mine was with someone I loved, someone who also had no idea what we were doing. The first time I had sex, I made love. I've always had a soft spot in my heart for Ethan for that very reason.

And then everything fell apart. He got into UC Berkeley. Sarah got into the Royal Ballet School, and my parents packed up and moved to London. I moved in with the Hudsons. And then, one balmy August morning a week before the beginning of my senior year of high school, Ethan got into his parents' car and left for Northern California.

We made it until the end of October before we broke up. At the time, we assured each other that it was just because the timing was wrong and the distance was hard. We told each other we'd get back together that summer. We told each other it didn't change anything; we were still soul mates.

But it was no different from the same old song and dance at every college every fall.

I started considering schools in Boston and New York, since

living on the East Coast would make it easier to get to London. When Ethan came home for Christmas, I was dating a guy named Chris Rodriguez. When Ethan came home for the summer, he was dating a girl named Alicia Foster.

When I got into Boston University, that was the final nail.

Soon there was more than three thousand miles between us and no plan to shorten the distance.

Ethan and I have occasionally kept in touch, a phone call here or there, a dance or two at mutual friends' weddings. But there has always been an unspoken tension. There is always this sense that we haven't followed through on our plan.

He still, all these years later, shines brighter to me than other people. Even after I got over him, I was never able to extinguish the fire completely, as if it's a pilot light that will remain small and controlled but very much alive.

"You've been in this city for twelve hours, according to my calculations," Ethan says. "And I'll be damned if I'm going to let you be here for twelve more without seeing me."

I laugh. "Well, we'll be cutting it close, I think," I say to him. "Gabby says there is some bar in Hollywood that we should go to tonight. She invited a whole bunch of friends from high school, so I can see everybody again. She's calling it a housewarming. Which makes no sense. I don't know."

Ethan laughs. "Text me the time and place, and I will be there."

"Awesome. Sounds great."

I start to say good-bye, but his voice chimes in again. "Hey, Hannah," he says.

"Yeah?"

"I'm glad you decided to come home."

I laugh. "Well, I was running out of cities."

"I don't know," he says. "I like to think you've just come to your senses."

I am pulling things out of my suitcase and flinging them around the guest room. "I swear I will clean this up," I say to Gabby and Mark. They are dressed and standing by the door. They have been ready to go for at least ten minutes.

"It's not a fashion show," Gabby says.

"It's my first night back in Los Angeles," I remind her. "I want to look good."

I had on a black shirt and black jeans, with long earrings and, of course, a high bun. But then I thought, you know, this isn't New York anymore. This is L.A. It was sixty degrees out this afternoon.

"I just want to find a tank top," I say. I start filtering through the clothes I have already thrown across the room. I find a teal shell tank and throw it on. I slip on my black heels. I look in the mirror and fix my bun. "I promise I will clean this all up when we get back."

I can see Mark laughing at me. He knows I sometimes don't do exactly what I say I'll do. No doubt, when Gabby asked him if I could stay here, she prepared him by saying, "She will probably throw her stuff all over the place." Also, I have no doubt he said that was OK. So I don't feel too bad.

But I don't think that is why Mark is laughing, actually. He says, "For someone so disorganized, you look very pulled together."

Gabby smiles at him and then at me. "You do. You look, like, glowy." She grabs the doorknob and then says, "But looks aren't the measure of a woman." She can't stop herself. This political correctness is just a part of who she is. I love her for that.

"Thank you both," I say as I follow them to their car.

When we get to the bar, it's fairly quiet. Gabby and Mark sit down, and I go up to get our drinks. I order beers for Mark and me and a glass of chardonnay for Gabby. The bill comes to twenty-four dollars, and I hand over my credit card. I don't know how much money I have in my account, because I'm afraid to look. But I know I have enough to live for a few weeks and get an apartment. I don't want to be a person who nickels-and-dimes, especially when Mark and Gabby have been sweet enough to give me a place to stay, so I just put it out of my head.

I bring the two beers to the table and turn back to get Gabby's wine. By the time I sit down, another woman has joined us. I remember meeting her at Gabby and Mark's wedding a couple of years ago. Her name is Katherine, I believe. She ran the New York City Marathon a few years ago. I remember faces and names really well. It's easy for me to remember details about people I have only met once. But I learned a long time ago not to reveal this. It freaks people out.

Katherine extends her hand. "Katherine," she says.

I shake her hand and say my name.

"Nice to meet you," she says. "Welcome back to Los Angeles!"

"Thanks," I say. "Actually, I think we've met before."

"We have?"

"Yeah, at Gabby and Mark's wedding. Yeah, yeah," I say, as if it's coming back to me. "You were telling me about how you ran a marathon somewhere, right? Boston or New York?"

She smiles. "New York! Yes! Great memory."

And now Katherine likes me. If I'd come right out with it, if I'd said, "Oh, we've met before. You were wearing a yellow dress at their wedding, and you said that running the New York Marathon was the hardest but most rewarding thing you've ever done," Katherine would think I was creepy. I have learned this the hard way.

Soon some of my old friends from high school start trickling in, the girls Gabby and I hung out with: Brynn, Caitlin, Erica. I scream and shout at the top of my lungs when I see each of them. It is so nice to see familiar faces, to be somewhere and know that the people who knew you at fifteen still like you. Brynn looks older, Caitlin looks thinner, Erica looks just the same.

Some of Mark's friends from work show up with their spouses, and soon we are crowding around a table too small for us.

People start buying other people drinks. Rounds are on this person or that person. I nurse my beer and a few Diet Cokes. I drank a lot in New York. I drank a lot with Michael. Change starts now.

I'm up at the bar again when I see Ethan walk in the door.

He's even taller than I remember, wearing an untucked blue cotton button-down and dark jeans. His hair is short and tousled, his stubble a few days old. He was cute in high school. He's handsome now. He will only get more handsome as he ages, I suspect.

I wonder if he has crow's-feet like I do.

I watch as he scouts around, searching for me in the crowd. I pay for the drinks in my hand and walk toward him. Just when I worry he'll never see me, I finally catch his eye. He lights up and smiles wide.

He moves toward me quickly, the gap between us almost instantly reduced to zero. He throws his arms around me and squeezes me tight. I briefly put the drinks down on the edge of the bar so I don't spill them.

"Hi," he says.

"You're here!" I say.

"*You're* here!" he says.

I hug him again.

"It's really great to see you," he tells me. "Beautiful as ever."

"Thank you kindly," I say.

Gabby makes her way toward us.

"Gabby Hudson," he says, leaning in to give her a hug.

"Ethan!" she says. "Good to see you."

"I'm going to grab a drink, and I'll meet you in a minute," he says to us.

I nod at him, and Gabby and I turn back toward our table.

She raises her eyebrows at me.

I roll my eyes at her.

An entire conversation without a word spoken.

Soon the music is so loud and the bar is so crowded that conversation becomes difficult.

I'm trying to hear what Caitlin is saying when Ethan gets to the table. He stands next to me, resting with his arm up against mine without a hint of self-consciousness. He sips his beer and turns to Katherine, the two of them trying to hear each other over the music. I glance over for a moment to find him looking intently at her, gesturing as if he's making a joke. I watch as she throws her head back and laughs.

She's prettier than I realized. She seemed plain before. But I can see now that's she's quite striking. Her long blond hair is blown out straight. Her sapphire-blue dress flatters her, hanging off her body effortlessly. It doesn't even look as if she needs to wear a bra.

I can't go anywhere without a bra.

Gabby pulls at my hand and drags me onto the dance floor. Caitlin joins us and then Erica and Brynn do, too. We dance to a few songs before I see Ethan and Katherine come over to join us. Mark hangs back with the others, nursing his beer.

"He doesn't dance?" I ask Gabby.

Gabby rolls her eyes. I laugh as Katherine, twirling, catches my eye. Ethan is spinning her.

I wonder if he'll take her home. I am surprised at how much this idea bothers me, just how unsubtle my feelings are.

He laughs as the song ends. They break apart, and he high-fives her. It seems like a friendly gesture, as opposed to a romantic one.

Looking at him now, recalling what it used to be like between us, how I liked myself around him, how I felt good about the world and my place in it with him by my side, how I ached when he left for college, I remember what it feels like to truly love someone. For the right reasons. In the right way.

Gabby taps my shoulder, bringing me back to reality. I turn to look at her. She is trying to tell me something. I can't hear her.

"Some air!" she yells, pointing to the patio. She waves herself off like a fan. I laugh and follow her out.

The moment we step outside, it's an entirely different world. The air has cooled, and the music is muted, contained by the building.

"How are you feeling?" Gabby asks me.

"Me?" I say. "Fine, why?"

"No reason," she says.

"So Mark doesn't dance, huh?" I ask, changing the subject. "You love dancing! He doesn't take you dancing?"

She shakes her head, scrunching her eyebrows. "Definitely not. He's not that kind of guy. It's fine. I mean, nobody's perfect but you and me," she jokes.

The door opens, and Ethan walks through. "What are you guys talking about out here?" he asks.

"Mark doesn't like dancing," I tell him.

"I'm actually going to go see if I can get him to cut a rug once and for all," Gabby says. She smiles at me as she leaves.

It's just Ethan and me alone out here now.

"You look a little bit cold," he says as he sits down on the empty bench. "I'd offer you my shirt, but I'm not wearing anything underneath."

"Might break the dress code," I say. "I thought since I'm in L.A., I should wear a tank top, but . . ."

"But it's February," he says. "And this is Los Angeles, not the equator."

"It's crazy how new this city feels to me, even though I lived here for so long," I tell him as I sit down next to him.

"Yeah, but you were eighteen when you left. You're almost thirty now."

"I prefer the term *twenty-nine*," I say.

He laughs. "It's nice to have you back," he says. "We haven't lived in the same city for . . . I guess almost thirteen years."

"Wow," I say. "Now I feel even older than when you called me almost thirty."

He laughs again. "How are you?" he asks me. "Are you well? Are you good?"

"I'm OK," I say. "I have some things to work out."

"You want to talk about them?"

"Maybe," I say, smiling. "At some point?"

He nods. "I'd love to listen. At some point."

"What's going on with you and Katherine over there?" I ask. My voice is breezy. I'm trying to sound as if this is casual, and I'm pulling it off.

Ethan shakes his head. "No, no," he says. "Nothing. She just started talking to me, and I was happy to entertain her." He smiles at me. "She's not who I came to see."

We look at each other, neither one of us breaking the gaze. His eyes are on me, focused on my eyes, as if I am the only other person in the world. And I wonder if he looks at every woman that way.

And then he leans over and kisses me on the cheek.

The way it feels, his lips on my skin, makes me realize I have spent years looking for that feeling and never finding it. I have settled for casual flings, halfhearted love affairs, and a married man, searching for that moment when your heart jumps in your chest.

And I wonder if I should really kiss him, if I should turn my head ever so slightly and put my lips on his.

Gabby and Mark come through the door.

"Hey," Gabby says, before staring at us. "Oh, sorry."

"No," I say. "Hey."

Ethan laughs. "You're Mark, right?" he says, getting up and shaking his hand. "Ethan. We didn't formally meet earlier."

"Yeah. Hey. Nice to meet you."

"Sorry," Gabby says. "We have to head out."

"I just found out I have an early-morning thing," Mark says.

"On a Sunday?" I ask him.

"Yeah, it's this thing at work I have to do."

I look at my watch. It's after midnight.

"Oh, OK," I say as I start to rise.

"Actually, I could take you home," Ethan says. "Back to Gabby's place later. If you want to stay for a while. Whatever you want."

I catch a coy smile come across Gabby's face for a split second.

I laugh to myself. It's so obvious, isn't it?

By coming back to L.A., I'm not just trying to build a better life with the support of my best friend. I've also reopened the question of whether Ethan and I have unfinished business between us.

We've spent years apart. We've gone on to live two very different lives. And we're right back here. Flirting off to the side at the party, while everyone else is dancing.

Will we or won't we? and *If I let him take me home, will it mean more to me than it means to him?*

I look at Ethan, and then I look at Gabby.

Life is long and full of an infinite number of decisions. I have to think that the small ones don't matter, that I'll end up where I need to end up no matter what I do.

My fate will find me.

So I decide to . . .

S o I decide to go home with Gabby.
    I don't want to rush into anything.

I turn and give Ethan a good-bye hug. I can hear, through the door, that the DJ just started playing Madonna's "Express Yourself," and for a moment, I sort of regret my decision. I love this song. Sarah and I used to sing it in the car together all the time. My mom never let us sing the part about satin sheets. But we just loved the song. We'd listen to it over and over.

I consider taking my good-bye back, as if the universe is telling me to stay and dance.

But I don't.

"I should go home," I say to Ethan. "It's late, and I want to get on West Coast time, you know?"

"I totally understand," he says. "I had a great time tonight."

"Me, too! I'll call you?"

Ethan nods as he moves to give Gabby a hug good-bye. He shakes Mark's hand. He turns to me and whispers into my ear, "You're sure I can't convince you to stay out?"

I shake my head and smile at him. "Sorry," I say.

He smiles and sighs ever so subtly, with a look that says he's accepted defeat.

We walk back into the bar and say good-bye to everyone— Erica, Caitlin, Brynn, Katherine, and the rest of the people I've met tonight.

"I thought for sure you were going home with Ethan," Gabby says as we are heading back to the car.

I shake my head at her. "You think you know me so well."

She gives me a doubting look.

"OK, you know me perfectly. But I just feel like if things with Ethan and me are going to happen, they will happen on their own time, you know? No need to rush anything."

"So you do want something to happen?"

"I don't know!" I say. "Maybe? Eventually? It seems like I should be with an honest, stable, nice guy like him. He seems like a move in the right direction, men-wise."

When we get to the car, Mark opens the doors for us and tells Gabby he's just going to take Wilshire Boulevard home. "That seems easiest, right? Less traffic?"

"Yeah," Gabby says, and then she turns around and asks me if I've ever heard of the Urban Light installation at the Los Angeles County Museum of Art.

"No," I say. "I don't think so."

"I think you'll really like it," she says. "They installed it a few years ago. We're gonna end up driving by it, so I'll point it out. This is all part of my campaign to make you fall in love with L.A. again, by the way."

"I'm excited to see it," I say.

"People always say that Los Angeles has no culture," Gabby says. "So, you know, I'm going to prove them wrong in the hopes that you'll stay."

"You do remember that I lived here for almost twenty years," I tell her.

"I meant to ask you." She turns toward me as Mark looks ahead, driving. "How are your parents and Sarah?"

"Mom and Dad are good," I say. "Sarah's at the London Ballet Company now and living with her boyfriend, George. I haven't met him, but my parents like him, so that's good. My dad's doing well at work, so I think my mom is considering only working part-time."

They don't send me money in any traditional sense. But for years, they have given me such a large amount of money every Christmas that I almost feel like I'm getting a Christmas bonus. I don't know how much money my family actually has, but it certainly seems like a lot.

"Your family doesn't come to the U.S. anymore?" Mark asks.

"No," I say. "I always go over to see them."

"Any excuse to go to London, right?" Mark says.

"Right," I say, although that's not really true. They've never offered to come back to the U.S. And since they are the ones buying the ticket, I don't have a lot of say in the matter.

I turn toward the car window and watch the streets go by. They are streets I didn't frequent as a teenager. We're in a part of town I don't know that well.

"Did you have fun tonight?" Gabby asks me.

"Yeah, I did," I tell her, my gaze still on the sidewalks and storefronts we're passing. "You have a lot of great friends out here, and it was awesome to see the girls from high school. Did Caitlin lose like thirty pounds?"

"Weight Watchers, I think," Gabby says. "She's doing really well. She was doing well before, though, too. Women don't need to be thin to be valuable."

I can see Mark smile into the rearview mirror, and I smile back at him. It is a small intimacy between us, our mutual eye-rolling at Gabby's political correctness. I start to laugh, but I hold it in. Gabby's not wrong. Women don't have to be thin to be valuable. Caitlin was the same person before she lost the weight as she is now. It's just funny that Gabby always feels the need to spell it out all the time. She can't take it for granted.

Gabby's phone dings, and she picks it up. I watch as she reads the text message and immediately hides her phone. She's terrible at keeping things from me.

"What is it?" I ask.

"What is what?"

"On your phone."

"Nothing."

"Gabby, c'mon," I say.

"It's not important. It means nothing."

"Hand it over."

She reluctantly puts the phone in my hand. It's a text message from Katherine.

Going home with Ethan. Is this a terrible idea?

My heart sinks in my chest. I look away and hand the phone back to Gabby without a word.

She turns back to look at me. "Hey," she says softly.

"I'm not upset," I say back, but my voice is thin and high-pitched. Upset is exactly how I sound.

"C'mon," she says.

I laugh. "It's fine. He can do what he wants." I'm glad I didn't stay out late with him, looking to see if there was something between us. "I specifically did not stay out with him tonight because I didn't want it to be a one-night thing. If it was anything. So there you go. Spares me the embarrassment."

Gabby frowns at me.

I laugh defensively, as if the harder I laugh, the harder I can push her pity off me and out the window. "He's a great guy. I'm not saying he's not, but, you know, if that's how it gonna be with him, I don't need that."

I look out the window again and then immediately back at Gabby.

"I like Katherine, actually," I say. "She seems great."

"If I may," Mark interjects. "I don't know much about the history between the two of you, but just because he's sleeping with someone else doesn't necessarily mean . . ."

"I know," I say. "But still. It makes it clear to me that he and I are best left in the past. I mean, we dated forever ago. It's fine."

"Do you want to change the subject?" Gabby asks me.

"Yes," I say. "Please."

"Well, should we go to breakfast tomorrow while Mark goes into work?"

"Yeah," I say, turning away from her and looking out the window. "Let's talk about food."

"Where should I take her?" Gabby asks Mark, and the two of them start rattling off names of restaurants I've never heard of.

Mark asks me if I like sweet or savory breakfasts.

"You mean, do I like pancakes or eggs?"

"Yeah," he says.

"She likes cinnamon rolls," Gabby answers at the exact same time I say, "I like places with cinnamon rolls."

When I was a kid, my dad used to take me to this dough-nut shop called Primo's Donuts. They had big, warm cinnamon rolls. We'd go get one every Sunday morning. As I got older, we got busier. Eventually, a lot of my parents' time was spent shuttling Sarah to and from various rehearsals and recitals, so it became harder to find time to go. But when we did, I always ordered a cinnamon roll. I just love them so much.

When I moved in with Gabby's family, Tina used to buy the cans of raw cinnamon rolls and bake them for me on the weekends. The bottoms were always burned, and she had a light hand with the prepackaged icing, but I didn't care. Even a bad cinnamon roll is still a good cinnamon roll.

"With a lot of icing," I tell Mark. "I don't care if it's a day's worth of calories. Gabby, if you're up for it, I can try to find Primo's, and we can go there tomorrow."

"Done," she says. "OK, we're almost at the museum. Up on the right here. You can sort of see the lights now, just right there."

I look forward, past her head, and I think I see what she's talking about. We breeze through the green light, hitting a red in front of LACMA, and now I see it perfectly.

Streetlight after streetlight, rows of them, tightly lined up and lit. These are not the streetlights that you see today, the kind that shoot toward the sky and then curve over above the street. These are vintage. They look as if Gene Kelly might have swung on them while singing in the rain.

I look at the installation, staring with purpose out the window. I suppose there is something very simple and beautiful about it. City lights against a backdrop of a pitch-black night does have a sense of magic to it. And maybe there's a metaphor here, something about brightness in the middle of . . . Oh, hell. I'm lying. The truth is, I don't get it.

"Actually," Gabby says, "why don't we get out? Is that cool, Mark? Can we park and take a quick picture by the lights? Hannah's first real night back in L.A.?"

Mark nods, and when the light turns green, he pulls up to the curb. We get out of the car and head to the center of the lights.

We take turns taking pictures of each other, round robin–style. Gabby and I stand between two rows of lights, and Mark takes pictures of us with our arms around each other. We wear oversized grins. We kiss each other on the cheek. We stand on either side of a lamppost and mug for the camera. And then I offer to take a picture of Mark and Gabby together.

I switch places with Mark, getting out my own phone to take the photo. Gabby and Mark tuck themselves together, holding each other tight, posing underneath the lamps. I back up just a little, trying to frame the picture as I want.

"Hold on," I say. "I want to get all of it." I can't get far enough away from them to get the top of the lights in the shot, so I walk to the edge of the sidewalk. It's still not far enough away, so I push the walk button and wait for a signal so I can stand on the street.

"Just one sec!" I call out to them.

"This better be good!" Gabby yells.

The light turns red. The orange hand changes to a white-lit pedestrian, and I step down into the crosswalk.

I turn around. I frame my shot: Mark and Gabby in the middle of a sea of lights. I hit the shutter. I check the photo. I start to take another for good measure.

By the time I hear the screeching of tires, it's too late to run.

I am thrown across the street. The world spins. And then everything is shockingly still.

I look at the lights. I look at Gabby and Mark. The two of them rush toward me, mouths agape, arms outstretched. I think they are screaming, but I cannot hear them.

I don't feel anything. Can't feel anything.

I think they are calling to me. I see Gabby reach for me. I see Mark dial his phone.

I smell metal.

I'm bleeding. I don't know where.

My head feels heavy. My chest feels weighed down, as if the entire world is resting on it.

Gabby is very scared.

"I'm all right," I tell her. "Don't worry. I feel fine."

She just looks at me.

"Everything is going to be OK," I tell her. "Do you believe me?"

And then her face blurs, and the world mutes, and the lights go out.

So I decide to stay out with Ethan.

I'm eager to spend time with a good man for a change.

I turn and say good-bye to Gabby and Mark. That very second, "Express Yourself" comes on in the bar, and I know I've made the right decision. I absolutely love this song. Sarah and I used to make our parents listen to it over and over in the car, singing at the top of our lungs. I've got to stay and dance to this.

"You don't mind, right?" I say as I hug Gabby. "I just want to stay out a bit longer. See where the night takes me."

"Oh, please, go for it!" she says as I hug Mark good-bye. I can see a sly smile on her face, visible only to me. I roll my eyes at her, but a small grin sneaks out at the last minute. Then Gabby and Mark head for the door.

"So," Ethan says as he turns to me, "the night is ours for the taking." The way he says it, with a little bit of scandal in his voice, makes me feel as if we're teenagers again.

"Dance with me?" I say.

Ethan smiles and opens the door to the bar. He holds it for me to walk through. "Let's do this," he says.

We only get a minute or so before the song ends and another starts playing. This new one has a Spanish feel to it, a Latin beat. I feel my hips start to move without my permission. They sway for a moment, back and forth, just testing the waters. Soon I just let go and allow my body to move the way it wants to. Ethan slips his arm around the lowest part of my back. His leg just barely grazes the inside of mine. He moves back and forth and then pulls me quickly against him. He spins me. We forget about everyone else around us, and we stay like this, song after song, moving in tandem. Our faces stay close together but never touch. Every once in a while, I catch him looking at me, and I find myself blushing ever so slightly.

By the end of the night, when the dancing is over and the bar is thinning out, I look around and realize that everyone else in the group has gone home.

Ethan grabs my hand and leads me outside. As our feet hit the sidewalk, away from the din of the bar, I feel the effects of a night spent in a small place with loud music. The outside world feels muted compared with the bar. My eyes feel a bit dry. The balls of my feet are killing me.

Ethan's leading me down the street as the rest of the bar funnels out.

"Where's your car?" I ask him.

"I walked. I live only a few blocks from here. This way," he says. "I have an idea."

I stumble to try to keep up with him. He's going too fast, and my feet are killing me. "Wait, wait, wait," I say.

I bend over and take my shoes off. The sidewalk is grimy. I can see wads of gum so old they are now black spots in the concrete. Up ahead, a tree has rooted itself so firmly into the ground that it has broken up the sidewalk, creating jagged edges and crevices. But my feet hurt too much. I pick up my shoes and follow Ethan.

Ethan looks down at my feet and stops in place. "What are you doing?"

"My feet hurt. I can't walk in these. It's fine," I say. "Let's go."

"Do you want me to carry you?"

I start laughing.

"What's so funny?" he asks. "I could carry you."

"I'm good," I say. "This isn't the first time I've walked barefoot through a city."

He laughs and starts walking again. "As I was saying . . . I have a great idea."

"And what is that?"

"You've been dancing," he says as he pulls me forward.

"Obviously."

"And you've been drinking."

"A bit."

"And you've been sweating up a storm."

"Uh . . . I guess so?"

"But there is one thing you haven't been doing."

"OK?"

"Eating."

The second he says it, I am suddenly ravenous. "Oh, my God, where do we eat?" I say.

He quickens his pace toward the major intersection up ahead. I start to smell something. Something smoky. I run with him, my feet hitting the gritty concrete with every step, until we make our way to the crowd forming on the sidewalk.

I look at Ethan. He tells me what I'm smelling. "Bacon. Wrapped. Hot dogs."

He cuts through the crowd and walks up to the food cart. He orders two for us. The cart looks like a glorified ice cream wagon that you might see someone pushing at the park. But the woman running it is keeping up with the orders of all the tipsy people out on the street.

Ethan comes back with our hot dogs nestled in buns. He puts one under my nose. "Smell that."

I do.

"Have you ever smelled anything that good this late at night in any other city you've been to?"

Right now, this second, I honestly can't think of a time. "Nope," I say.

We walk around the block and find ourselves on a residential street. The sounds of the crowd and the smoke of the cart are gone. I can hear crickets. *While standing in the middle of a city.* I forgot that about Los Angeles. I forgot how it's urban and suburban all at once.

The street is lined with palm trees so tall you have to throw your neck back to see their full scope. They continue on up and down this block, up and down the blocks to the north and south. Ethan walks to one of the trees and the surrounding grass. He sits down on the thin curb that separates them from the street. He puts his feet on the road, his back up against the tree. I do the same next to him.

The bottoms of my feet are black at this point. I can only imagine how dirty I will make Gabby's shower tomorrow morning.

"Dog me," I say, holding my hand out, waiting for Ethan to give me the one he has decided is mine.

He does.

"Thank you," I say. "For buying me dinner. Or breakfast. Not sure which this is."

He nods, having already taken a bite. After he swallows, he says, "Ah, I made a rookie mistake. I should have gotten us water, too."

The world is starting to come into focus a bit more now

that we have left the bar. I can hear better. I can see better. And maybe most important, I can taste this delicious hot dog in all of its bacon-wrapped glory.

"I know it's become a cliché now," I say. "But bacon really does make everything else taste better."

"Oh, I know," he says. "I don't want to sound pretentious, but I really feel like I knew that before everyone else. I have loved bacon for years."

I laugh. "You were into bacon when it was just a breakfast food."

He laughs and adopts an affected tone. "Now it's changed. It's so commercial."

"Yeah," I say. "You probably put bacon on a doughnut back in oh-three."

"All kidding aside," Ethan says, "I really do think I figured out candied bacon first."

I start laughing at him between bites.

"I'm not joking! When I was a kid, I would always put maple syrup on my bacon. Maple syrup plus bacon equals . . . candied bacon. You're welcome, America."

I laugh at him and put my hand on his back. "I'm sorry to break it to you," I say, "but everyone's been doing that for years."

He looks right at me. "But no one told me about it. I came up with it on my own," he says. "It's my own idea."

"Where do you think people got the inspiration for maple bacon doughnuts or brown sugar bacon? All around the country for years and years, people have been putting maple syrup on their bacon and loving it."

He smiles at me. "You have just ruined the only thing I've ever considered a personal achievement."

I laugh. "Oh, come on. You're talking to a woman with no

career, no home, barely any money, and no potential," I say. "Let's not bring up personal achievements."

Ethan turns to me. His hot dog is long gone. "You don't really think that," he says.

Normally, I would make a joke. But jokes take so much effort. I wave my head from side to side, as if deciding. "I don't know," I say. "I sort of really think that."

Ethan shakes his head, but I keep talking. "I mean, this is just not where I thought my life was going, at all. And I look at someone like Gabby or someone like you, and I mean, I sort of feel like I'm behind. It's not a big deal," I say, finally realizing that I'm complaining. "Just something for me to work on. I mean, I guess I am just hoping to find a city and stick with it one of these days."

"I always thought you should be back here," Ethan says, looking at me directly.

I smile, but when Ethan doesn't break his gaze, I get nervous. I slap my hands on my thighs lightly. "Well," I say, "should we get going?"

Ethan stares forward for a moment, his eyes focused on the ground underneath his feet. Then he sort of comes to, snaps out of it. "Yeah," he says. "We should head back." He stands up as I do, and for a moment, our bodies are closer together than either of us anticipated. I can feel the warmth of his skin.

I start to back away, and he lightly grabs my hand to stop me. He looks me in the eye. I look away first.

"Something I've been wanting to ask you for a while," he says.

"OK," I say.

"Why did we break up?"

I look at him and feel my head cock to the side ever so slightly. I'm genuinely surprised by the question. I laugh gently.

"Well," I say, "I think that's what eighteen-year-olds do. They break up."

The tension doesn't dissipate.

"I know," he says. "But did we have a good reason?"

I look at him and smile. "Did we have a good *reason*?" I say, repeating his question. "I don't know. Teenagers don't really have to have good reasons."

He laughs and starts walking back in the direction we came from. I walk with him.

"You broke my heart," he says, smiling at me. "You know that, right?"

"Excuse me? Oh, no, no, no," I say. "I was the heartbroken one. I was the one who got dumped when her boyfriend went to college."

He shakes his head at me, smiling despite himself. "What a load of crap," he says. "*You* broke up with *me*."

I smile and shake my head at him. "I think we're dealing in revisionist history here," I tell him. "*I* wanted to stay together."

"Ridiculous!" he says. His hands are buried deep in his pockets, his shoulders hunched forward. He is walking slowly. "Absolutely ridiculous. A woman breaks your heart, comes back to town a decade later, and pins it on you."

"OK, OK," I say. "We can agree to disagree."

He looks at me and shakes his head. "Nope!" he says, laughing. "I don't accept."

"Oh, you're being silly," I say.

"I am not," he says. "I have proof."

"Proof?"

"Cold, hard evidence."

I stop in place and cross my arms. "This should be good. What's your proof?"

He stops with me, comes closer toward me. "Exhibit A: Chris Rodriguez." My senior-year boyfriend.

"Oh, please," I say. "What does Chris Rodriguez prove?"

"You moved on first. I came home from Berkeley for Christmas ready to knock on your door and sweep you off your feet," he says. "And the minute I get into town, I hear you're dating Chris Rodriguez."

I laugh and roll my eyes just a little bit. "Chris didn't mean anything. I wasn't even with him by the time you came home from school for the summer. I thought, you know, maybe you'd come home for those three months and . . ."

He moves his eyebrows up and down at me, the visual version of *hubba hubba*.

I laugh, slightly embarrassed. "Well, it didn't matter anyway, right? Because you were with Alicia by then."

"Only because I thought you were with Chris," he says. "That's the only reason I dated her."

"That's terrible!" I say.

"Well, I didn't know that at the time!" he says. "I thought I loved her. You know, I was nineteen years old at that point. I had the self-awareness of a doorknob."

"So maybe you did love her," I say. "Maybe it was you who moved on from me."

He shakes his head. "Nah," he says. "She broke up with me when we got back to school that year. Said she needed someone who could tell her she was the only one."

"And you couldn't do that?"

He looks at me pointedly. "Nope."

It's quiet again for a moment. Neither of us having much to say or, maybe more accurately, neither of us knowing *what* to say.

"So we broke each other's heart," I say at last. I start walking forward again.

He joins me and smiles. "Agree to disagree," he says.

We continue walking down the street, stopping at a red light, waiting for a cross signal.

"I never had sex with Chris," I tell him as we walk farther and farther into the residential section.

"No?" Ethan says.

"No," I say, shaking my head.

"Any reason why not?" Ethan asks.

I sway my head from side to side, trying to find the words to explain what I felt back then. "I . . . I couldn't stand the thought of sharing that with someone other than you," I finally say. "Didn't seem right to do it with just anybody."

I was twenty-one by the time I had sex with someone else. It was Dave, my college boyfriend. The reason I slept with him wasn't that I thought he might mean something to me the way Ethan did. I did it because *not* doing it was getting weird. If I'm being honest, somewhere along the way, I lost that feeling that the person had to be special, that it was something sacred. "I bet you didn't turn down Alicia's advances," I say, teasing him. For a moment, I think I see him blush.

He guides me toward an ivy-covered building on a dark, quiet street. He opens the lobby door and lets me in first.

"You have me there," he says. "I'm embarrassed to admit that there have been times in my life when rejection from the woman I love has served only to encourage me sleeping with others. It's not my best trait. But it does numb the pain."

"I'm sure it does," I say.

He guides me to his apartment on the second floor.

"Doesn't mean anything, though," he says. "Sleeping with

Alicia didn't mean that I didn't love you. That I wouldn't have dropped everything to be with you. If I thought . . . well, you know what I'm getting at."

I look at him. "Yeah, I do."

He opens the door and gestures for me to walk in. I look at him and walk in front of him into his place. It's a studio apartment but big, making it cozy without seeming cramped. It's neat but not necessarily clean, which is to say that everything is in its place, but there are dust bunnies in the corners, a water ring on the dark wood coffee table. He has painted the walls a deep but unobtrusive blue. A flat-screen TV is mounted on the wall opposite the couch, and shelves overloaded with books cover every available space. His bed linens are a dark, forgiving gray. Did I know, back then, that this was the kind of adult he'd grow up to be? I don't know.

"It was very hard to get over you," he says.

"Oh, yeah?" I say. There is a lump in my throat, but I try to cover it up by being flirtatious and light. "What was so hard to get over?"

He throws his keys onto a side table. "Three things," he says.

I smile, letting him know I'm ready to listen. "These should be good!"

"I'm serious. Are you ready to hear them? Because I'm not messing around."

"I'm ready," I say.

Ethan puts up his thumb to start the count. "One," he says. "You always had your hair up, just like it is now, in that high bun thing. And very occasionally, you would take it down." He pauses and then starts again. "I just loved that moment. That moment between up and down, when it fell across your neck and around your face."

I find myself fiddling with the bun on the top of my head. I have to stop myself from adjusting it. "OK," I say.

"Two," he says. "You always tasted like cinnamon and sugar."

I laugh. If I wasn't sure before, I am now positive that he is being sincere. "From the cinnamon rolls."

He nods. "From the cinnamon rolls."

"And what's the third?" I ask. I almost don't want to know, as if it's the third thing he says that will undoubtably and irrevocably usher forth all those teenage feelings, a flood of blushing cheeks and quickening heartbeats. It is the teenage feelings that are the most intoxicating, the ones that have the power to render you helpless.

"You smelled like tangerines," he says.

I give him a look. "Orange Ginger."

"Yeah," he says. "You always smelled like Orange Ginger." He comes ever so close to my neck. "Still do."

He is close enough that I can smell him, too, the mixture of laundry detergent and sweat.

I can feel the skin of my cheeks start to burn, my pulse start to speed up.

"You smell good, too," I say. I don't move away.

"Thank you," he says.

"In high school, you smelled like Tide."

"I think that's what my mom used," he says.

"When you left, I smelled your old T-shirts," I say. "I used to sleep in them."

He listens to me. He takes my words, my feelings, and he spits them back out into facts. "You loved me," he says.

"Yeah," I say. "I did. I loved you so much it sometimes burned in my chest."

He leans forward ever so slightly. "I want to kiss you," he says.

I breathe in. "OK," I say.

"But I don't want to do this if . . . I don't want this to be a one-time thing."

"I don't know what it is," I say. "But it's not a one-time thing."

He smiles and leans in.

It's gentle at first, the touch of lip to lip, but I lean into it, and when I do, it overtakes us.

We back up to the closed front door behind us, my shoulders just grazing the door frame.

His lips move just like they used to, and his body feels just like it used to, and as much as two people can rewind the clock, as much as they can erase time, we do.

By the time we're in his bed, it feels as if we never left each other. It feels as if we never broke up, my parents never moved, I never started dating Chris Rodriguez, and Ethan never met Alicia Foster. It feels as if I never felt the chill of Boston in my hands or the wind of D.C. in my hair. As if I never felt the rain of Portland and Seattle on my shoulders or the heat of Austin on my skin. It's as if New York City, and all of its disappointments, never entered my heart.

It feels as if I finally made a good decision for once.

THREE DAYS LATER

I open my eyes.

My head feels heavy. The world feels hazy. My eyes adjust slowly.

I'm in a hospital bed. My legs are stretched out in front of me, a blanket covering them. My arms are by my sides. There is a blond woman in front of me with a stoic but kind look on her face. She's about forty. I can't be sure, but I don't think I've ever seen her in my life.

She is wearing a white coat and holding a folder.

"Hannah?" she says. "Nod if you can hear me, Hannah. Don't try to talk just yet. Just nod."

I nod. It hurts, just that little nod. I can feel it down my back. I can feel a dull ache all over my body, and it seems to be increasing exponentially.

"Hannah, my name is Dr. Winters. You're at Angeles Presbyterian. You've been in a car accident."

I nod again. I'm not sure if I'm supposed to. But I do.

"We can get into the details later, but I want to go over the big news now, OK?"

I nod. I don't know what else to do.

"First, on a scale of one to ten, how much pain are you in? Ten being so excruciating you don't think you can bear it for another second. One being you feel perfectly fine."

I start to try to talk, but she stops me.

"Show me on your fingers. Don't hold them up. Don't move your arms. Just show me with your hands at your sides."

I look down at my hands, and then I pull back the four fingers on my left hand.

"Six?" she says. "OK."

She writes something down in the folder and starts fiddling with one of the machines behind me.

"We're going to get you down to one." She smiles. It's a reassuring smile. She seems to think everything is going to be OK. "Soon you'll have an easier time moving your arms and torso, and speaking won't be too hard once you've been up for a little while. You have suffered blood loss and broken bones. That's an oversimplification, but it will work for now. You're going to be OK. Walking, at first, is going to be hard. You will need to practice a bit before it comes naturally to you again, but it will, one day, come naturally to you again. That's what I want you to take away from this conversation."

I nod. It hurts less this time. Whatever she did, it hurts less this time.

"Now, you've been unconscious for three days. Some of that time was because of the blow to the head you sustained during the accident, but the rest is because we put you under for surgery."

She's quiet for a moment, and I see her look off to the side. She turns back to me.

"It's perfectly normal if you don't remember the accident. It may take some time to come back. Do you remember the accident?"

I start to answer her.

"Just nod or shake your head for now," she says.

I shake my head slightly.

"That's fine. That is completely normal. Nothing to be concerned about."

I nod to let her know I understand.

"Now, as I said, we can go over the details of your injury and your surgery when you are feeling a bit stronger. But there is one last thing that I want to make sure you know as soon as possible."

I stare at her. Waiting to hear what she has to say.

"You were pregnant," she says. "At the time of the accident."

She picks up my chart and consults a piece of paper.

Wait, what did she just say?

"It looks like you were about ten weeks along. Did you know? Nod or shake your head if you feel up for it."

I can feel my heart start to beat faster. I shake my head.

She nods in understanding. "OK," she says. "That's more common than you think. If you're not trying to get pregnant and you don't always have regular periods, it's possible not to figure it out at this stage of the pregnancy."

I continue to stare, unsure what, exactly, is happening right now, stunned silent.

"The baby did not make it through," she says. "Which, unfortunately, is also common."

She waits for me to respond, but I have no response. My mind is blank. All I can feel is my eyes blinking rapidly.

"I am sorry," she says. "I imagine this is a lot for you to digest at once. We have a number of resources here at the hospital to help you deal with everything that has happened. The good news, and I really do hope you are able to see the good news, is that you are going to be physically back to normal soon."

She looks at me. I avert my eyes. And then I nod. It occurs to me that my hair is down around my face. I must have lost my hair tie. It feels sort of uncomfortable like this, down. I want it back up in a bun.

Did she just say I lost a baby?

I lost a baby?

"Here is what we are going to do," the doctor says. "You have a lot of people here who have missed you these past few days. A lot of people who have been excited for this moment, the moment when you wake up."

I close my eyes slowly.

A baby.

"But I find that some patients need some time alone right after they have woken up. They aren't ready to see Mom and Dad and their sister and friends."

"My mom and dad?" I start to say, but my voice comes out as an unintelligible whisper. It's scratchy and airy.

"You've had a tube in your throat for some time. Talking is going to be difficult but will come back the more you do it. Just take it slowly. One or two words at a time at first, OK? Nod and shake your head when you can."

I nod. But I can't resist. "They're here?" I say. It hurts to say it. It hurts on the edges of my throat.

"Yep. Mom, Dad, your sister, Gabby, right? Or . . . Sarah? Sorry. Your sister is Sarah, friend is Gabby?"

I smile and nod.

"So this is the question. Do you need some time on your own? Or are you ready for family? Lift your right arm for time alone. Left for family."

It hurts, but my left hand shoots up, higher than I thought it would go.

I open my eyes.

My head feels heavy. The world feels hazy. My eyes adjust slowly.

And then I smile wide, because right in front of me, staring back at me, is Ethan Hanover.

I stretch slowly and push my head further into the pillow. His bed is so soft. It's the kind of bed you never want to leave. I suppose, for the past few days, I really haven't.

"Hi," he says gently. "Good morning."

"Good morning," I say back. I am groggy. My voice is scratchy. I clear my throat. "Hi," I say. That's better.

"You haven't had a cinnamon roll since you've been here," he says. "That's at least three entire cinnamon-roll-less days." He is shirtless and under the covers. His hair is scattered and unkempt. His five o'clock shadow is way past five o'clock. I can smell his breath as it travels the short distance from his pillow to mine. It leaves something to be desired.

"Your breath stinks," I say, teasing him. I have no doubt that mine smells much the same. After I say it, I put my hand over my mouth. I talk through the spaces between my fingers. "Maybe we should brush our teeth," I say.

He tries to pull my hand away, and I won't let him. Instead, I dive under the covers. I am wearing one of his T-shirts and the underwear that I picked up from my suitcase at Gabby's yesterday. Other than the trip to her place to grab some stuff, Ethan and I haven't left his apartment since we got here Saturday night.

He dives under the covers to find me and grabs my hands, holding them away from my own face.

"I'm going to kiss you," he says.

"Nope," I say. "No, my breath is too terrible. Free me from your superhuman grip, and let me brush my teeth."

"Why are you making such a big deal out of this?" he says, laughing, not letting go of me. "You stink. I stink. Let's stink together."

I pop my head out of the covers to inhale fresh air, and then I go back under.

"Fine," I say, and I breathe onto his face.

"Ugh," he says. "Absolutely revolting."

"What if my breath smelled this bad every morning? Would you still want to be with me?" I say, teasing him.

"Yep!" he says, and then he kisses me deeply. "You're not very good at this game."

That's the joke we came up with Sunday night. What would it take to derail this thing between us? What could ruin this great thing we have going?

So far, we've established that if I became an Elvis impersonator and insisted that he come to all of my shows, he'd still want to be with me. If I decided to get a pet snake and name it Bartholomew, he'd still want to be with me. Perpetual halitosis, it looks like, isn't a deterrent, either.

"What if everything I put in the washing machine shrinks?" This one isn't hypothetical. This one is very real.

"Doesn't matter," he says as he moves off me and gets out of bed. "I do my own laundry."

I lie back down, my head on the pillow. "What if I mispronounce the word *coupon* all the time?"

"Clearly, that's fine, because you just mispronounced it." He picks his jeans up off the floor and pulls them on.

"No, I didn't!" I say. "'Cue-pawn.'"

"It's 'coo-pawn.'" He slips on his shirt.

"Oh, my God!" I say, sitting upright and outraged. "Please tell me you are joking. Please tell me you don't say 'coo-pawn.'"

"I can't tell you that," he says. "Because it would be a lie."

"So this is it, then. This is the thing that stands in our way."

He throws my pants at me. "Sorry, but no. You'll just have to get over it. If it makes you feel better, we will never use coupons for the rest of our lives, OK?"

I stand up and put my pants on. I leave his shirt on but grab my bra from the floor and slip it on underneath. It's such a bizarre and uncoordinated thing to do, to put on a bra while you still have a shirt on, that about halfway through, I wonder why I didn't just take the shirt off to begin with.

"OK," I say. "If you promise we will never talk about coupons, then fine, we can be together."

"Thank you," he says, grabbing his wallet. "Get your shoes on." I pull my hair down briefly so that I can redo my bun. He stares at me for a moment as it falls. He smiles when I put it back up. "Where are we going?" I ask him. "Why are we leaving the bed?"

"I told you," he says as he puts on his shoes. "You haven't had a cinnamon roll in three days."

I start laughing.

"Hop to it, champ," he says. He is now fully dressed and ready to go. "I don't have all day."

I put on my shoes. "Yes, you do."

He shrugs. I grab my purse and head out the front door so quickly he has to catch up. By the time we get down to the garage, he's narrowly in front of me and opens my door.

"You're quite the gentleman these days," I say as he gets into the front seat and turns on the car. "I don't remember all of this chivalry when we were in high school."

He shrugs again. "I was a teenager," he says. "I hope I've grown since then. Shall we?"

"To the cinnamon rolls!" I say. "Preferably ones with extra icing."

He smiles and pulls out of the driveway. "Your wish is my command."

My dad is sitting to my right, holding my hand. My mom is at the foot of the bed, staring at my legs. Sarah is standing by the morphine drip.

Gabby came in with them an hour ago. She's the only one who looked me in the eye at first. After giving me a hug and telling me she loved me, she said she'd leave us all alone to talk. She promised she'd be back soon. She left so that my family would have some privacy, but I also think she needed some time to pull herself together. I could see as she turned to leave that she was wiping her eyes and sniffling.

I think I am hard to look at.

I can tell that my mom, my dad, and Sarah have been crying on and off today. Their eyes are glassy. They look tired and pale.

I haven't seen them since Christmas the year before last, and it is jarring to see them in front of me now. They are in the United States. Los Angeles. The four of us, the Martin family, haven't been together in Los Angeles since I was a junior in high school. Our yearly family reunions have since taken place in their London apartment, a space that Sarah very casually and unironically refers to as a "flat."

But now they are here in my world, in my country, in a city that once was ours.

"The doctor said you're going to be able to walk again pretty soon," Sarah says as she fiddles with the arm of the bed. "Which

I guess is good news? I don't know." She stops and looks down at the floor. "I don't know what to say."

I smile at her.

She's wearing black jeans and a cream luxe sweater. Her long blond hair is blown dry and straightened. She and I have the same hair color naturally, a deep brown. But I see why she went blond. She looks good blond. I tried it once, but Jesus, did you know you have to go to the salon to get your roots done like every six weeks? Who has that kind of time and money?

Sarah's twenty-six now. I suppose she might look a bit more like me, have some curves to her, if she wasn't dancing all day. Instead, she's muscular and yet somehow willowy. Her posture is so rigid that if you didn't know her better, you might suspect she was a robot.

She's the type to do things by the book, the proper way. She likes fancy clothes and fine dining and high art.

For Christmas a few years ago, she got me a Burberry purse. I said thank you and tried really hard not to scuff it up, not to ruin it. But I lost it by March. I felt bad, but I also sort of felt like, *Well, what was she thinking giving* me *a Burberry purse?*

"We brought you magazines," she says now. "The good British ones. I figured if I was in a hospital bed, I'd want the good stuff."

"I'm . . . we're just so glad you're OK," my mom says. She's about to start crying again. "You gave us quite a scare," she adds. My mom's hair is naturally a dirty blond. Her coloring is lighter than the rest of us.

My dad has jet-black hair, so thick and shiny that I used to say his picture should be on boxes of Just For Men. It wasn't until I was in college that it occurred to me he was probably *using* Just For Men. He's been squeezing my hand since he sat down. He now squeezes it harder for a moment, to second my mom's statement.

I nod and smile. It's weird. I feel awkward. I don't have anything to say to them, and even though I couldn't really say anything anyway, it seems odd for us all to be sitting here, not speaking to one another.

They are my family, and I love them. But I wouldn't say we are particularly close. And sometimes, seeing the three of them together, with their similar non-American affectations and their British magazines, I feel like the odd man out.

"I'm sleepy," I say.

The sound of my voice causes them all to snap to attention.

"Oh, OK," my mom says. "We will let you sleep."

My dad gets up and kisses my temple.

"Right? We should leave? And let you sleep? We shouldn't stay, right? While you're sleeping?" my mom says as Sarah and my dad start laughing at her.

"Maureen, she's OK. She can sleep on her own, and we will be in the waiting room whenever she needs us." My dad winks at me.

I nod.

"I'll just leave these here," Sarah says, pulling a stack of magazines out of her bag. She drops them onto the tray by my bed. "Just, you know, if you wake up and you want to look at pictures of Kate Middleton. I mean, that's what I'd do all day if I could."

I smile at her.

And they leave.

And I am finally alone.

I was pregnant.

And now I'm not.

I lost a baby I didn't know existed. I lost a baby I was not planning for and did not want.

How do you mourn something like that? How do you mourn something you never knew you had? Something you never wanted but something real, something important. A life.

My mind rolls back to thinking about *when* I got pregnant. Rolls back to the times I took a pill later than I meant to or the time one accidentally rolled underneath the bed and I couldn't find it. I think about when I told Michael we should use a condom as backup for a few days and Michael said he didn't care. And for some reason, I thought that was OK. I wonder which exact time it was. Which time we made a mistake that made a baby.

A baby that is now gone.

For the first time since waking up, I start crying.

I lost a baby.

I close my eyes and let the emotion wash over me. I listen to what my heart and mind are trying to tell me.

I am relieved and devastated. I am scared. I am angry. I am not sure if any of this is going to be OK.

The tears fall down my face with such force that I cannot possibly catch them all. They make their way to my hospital gown. My nose starts to run. I don't have the physical capacity to wipe it on my sleeve.

My head hurts from the pressure. I roll toward my pillow and bury my face in the sheets. I can feel them getting wet.

I hear the door open, and I don't bother to look and see who it is. I know who it is.

She sighs and gets into bed next to me. I don't turn to see her face. I don't need to hear her voice. Gabby.

I let it erupt. The fear and the anger and the confusion. The grief and the relief and the disgust.

Someone hit me with their car. Someone ran me over. They

broke my bones, and they severed my arteries, and they killed the baby I didn't love yet.

Gabby is the only person on the planet I trust to hear my pain. I howl into the pillow. She holds me tighter.

"Let it out," she says. "Let it out."

I breathe so hard that I exhaust myself. I am dizzy with oxygen and anguish.

And then I turn my head toward her. I can see she's been crying, too.

It makes me feel better somehow. As if she will bear some of the pain for me, as if she can take some of it off my hands.

"Breathe," she says. She looks me in the eyes and she breathes in slowly and then breathes out slowly. "Breathe," she says again. "Like me. Come on."

I don't understand why she's saying this to me until I realize that I am not breathing at all. The air is trapped in my chest. I'm holding it in my lungs. And once I realize that's what I'm doing, I let it go. It spills out of me, as if the dam has broken.

Air comes back in as a gasp. An audible, painful gasp.

And I feel, for maybe the first time since I woke up, alive. I am alive.

I am alive today.

"I was pregnant," I say, starting to cry again. "Ten weeks." It is the first real thing I've said since I woke up, and I can feel now how much it was tearing up my insides, like a bullet ricocheting in my gut.

Talking isn't as hard as I thought it would be. I think I can talk just fine. But I don't need to say anything else.

I don't need to tell Gabby that I didn't know. I don't need to tell Gabby that I wouldn't have been ready for the baby I don't have.

She already knows. Gabby always knows. And maybe more to the point, she knows there is nothing to say.

So she holds me and listens as I cry. And every couple of minutes, she reminds me to breathe.

And I do. Because I am alive. I may be broken and scared. But I am alive.

Ethan and I are circling the block around the café he wants to go to. Despite the fact that it is Tuesday morning and you'd think most people would be working, the street is packed with cars.

"When are you going back to work, by the way?" I ask him. He's called in sick twice now.

"I'll go back tomorrow," he says. "I have some vacation days saved up, so it's not a problem."

I don't want him to go back to work tomorrow, even though, you know, clearly, he should. But . . . I've been enjoying this reprieve from the real world. I quite like hiding out in his apartment, living in a cocoon of warm bodies and takeout.

"What if I eat so many cinnamon rolls that I gain four hundred pounds? Then?"

"Then what?" he says. He's only half listening to me. He's focused on trying to find a place to park.

"Then would this be over? Would that be a deal breaker?"

He laughs at me. "Try all you want, Hannah," he says. "But there are no deal breakers here."

I turn and look out the window. "Oh, I'll find your weak spot, Mr. Hanover. I will find it if it's the last thing I do."

He laughs as we slow to a red light. He looks at me. "I know what it means to miss you," he says. The light turns green, and he speeds down the boulevard. "So you'll have to find a pretty insurmountable problem if I'm going to let you go again."

I smile at him, even though I'm not sure he can see me. I've been doing a lot of that lately, smiling.

We finally find a spot relatively close to the café.

"This is why people leave this city, you know," I say as he squeezes into the spot.

He turns the key and pulls it out of the ignition. He gets out of the car. "You don't have to tell me that," he says. "I hate this city every time I circle a block like a vulture."

"Well, I'm just saying, in New York, there's the subway. And in Austin, you can park anywhere you want. The Metro in D.C. is so clean that you could eat off the floor."

"Nowhere is perfect. But, you know, don't go racking up reasons to leave already."

"I'm not," I say. I'm slightly defensive. I don't want to be the person no one thinks is going to stick around.

"OK," he says. "Good."

He turns and opens the door to the café, letting me in first. We get in line, and it so happens that the line snakes around the bakery case. I see the cinnamon rolls on the top shelf. They are half the size of my head. Covered in icing.

"Wow," I say.

"I know," he says. "I've wanted to take you here ever since I first found this place."

"How long ago was that?" I ask, teasing him.

He smiles. For a moment, I wonder if he's embarrassed. "A long time. Don't feel like you need to trick me into admitting I've been hung up on you for years. I'm confident enough to say it outright." I smile at him as he laughs and steps forward. "A cinnamon roll, please," he says to the cashier.

"Wait, aren't you having one?"

"They are huge!" Ethan says. "I thought we'd split one."

I give him a look.

He laughs. "Excuse me," he says to the cashier. "Make that two cinnamon rolls. My apologies."

I try to pay, but Ethan won't let me.

We grab some waters, sit down by the window, and wait for a server to warm up the rolls. I fiddle with the napkin dispenser.

"If I hadn't stayed out with you on Saturday, would you have tried to sleep with Katherine?" I ask him. It's been in the back of my mind since that night. I'm trying to be better at actually asking the questions I have instead of avoiding them.

He starts sipping his water. I can tell he is put off by the question. "What are you talking about?"

"You were flirting with her. And it bothered me. And I just want to make sure this is . . . that this is just me and you, and we aren't . . . that there is no one else."

"As far as I'm concerned, there's not another woman on the planet. I'm into you. I'm only into you."

"But if I hadn't stayed out . . ."

Ethan puts his water down and looks me right in the eye. "Listen, I went to that bar hoping to get you alone, hoping to talk to you, to gauge how you felt. I tried on ten different shirts to find the right one. I bought gum and kept it in my back pocket in case I had bad breath. I stood in front of the mirror and tried to get my hair to look like I didn't do my hair. For you. You are the only one. I danced with Katherine because I was nervous talking to you. And because I want to be honest with you, I'll admit that I don't know what I would have done if you had turned me down on Saturday, but no matter what I would have done, it would have been because I thought you weren't interested. If you're interested, I'm interested. And only in you."

"I'm interested," I say. "I'm very interested."

He smiles.

The cinnamon rolls arrive at the table. The smell of the spice and the sugar is . . . relaxing. I feel as if I am at home.

"Maybe all of this time," I say to Ethan, "I've been looking for home and not realizing that home is where the cinnamon roll is."

Ethan laughs. "I mean, if you're going to go all over the country looking for where you belong, I could have told you years ago you belong in front of a cinnamon roll."

I grab a knife and fork and make my incision, right into the deep heart of the swirl. I put the fork to my mouth. "This better be good," I say before I finally taste it.

It is absolutely delicious. Wonderfully, indulgently, blissfully delicious. I put down my utensils and look up at the ceiling, savoring the moment.

He laughs at me.

"Would it surprise you if I finished this entire roll myself?" I ask.

"Not since you insisted on having your own," he says. He takes a bite of his. I watch as he chews it casually, as if it's a ham sandwich or something. He'll indulge my sweet tooth, but he doesn't share it.

"How about if I finish yours, too?" I ask.

"Yes, I would actually go so far as to say that would shock me."

"Challenge accepted," I say, except that none of the syllables comes out clearly. There is too much dough in my mouth. I accidentally spit cinnamon on him.

Ethan moves his hand to his cheek to wipe it away. On a scale of one to ten, I'm about a six for embarrassment. I think my cheeks turn red. I swallow.

"Sorry," I say. "Not very ladylike."

"Kinda gross," he says, teasing me.

I shake my head. "How about that? If I make a habit of spitting cinnamon roll chunks on you, is that a deal breaker?"

Ethan looks down at the table and shakes his head. "Just get over it, OK? You and me. It's happening. Stop trying to find cracks in it." He puts down his knife and fork. "Maybe there are no cracks in this. Can you handle that?"

"Yeah," I say, "I can handle that."

I can, right? I can handle that.

I've noticed that in TV shows, visiting hours are only certain set times. "Sorry, sir, visiting hours are over" and that sort of thing. Maybe this is true in the rest of the hospital, but here on whatever floor I'm on, no one seems to care. My parents and Sarah were here until nine. They only left because I insisted they go back to their hotel. My nurse, Deanna, was in and out of here all day and never said anything to them about leaving.

Gabby showed up about two hours ago. She insisted on setting up camp on the poor excuse for a sofa in here. I told her that she didn't have to stay the night with me, that I'd be OK on my own, but she refused. She said she'd already told Mark she was sleeping here. Then she handed me the bouquet he sent with her. She put it on the counter and gave me the card. And then she made a bed for herself and talked to me as she closed her eyes.

She fell asleep about a half hour ago. She's been snoring for at least twenty minutes. I, myself, would love to fall asleep, but I'm too wired, too restless. I haven't moved or stood up since I was standing in front of LACMA four days ago. I want to get up and move around. I want to move my legs.

But I can't. I can barely lift my arms above my head. I turn on a small light by my bed and open up one of Sarah's magazines. I flip through the pages. Bright photos of women in absurd outfits in weird places. One of the photo shoots looks as if it took place in Siberia with women wearing polka-dot bikinis. Apparently, polka dots are in. At least in Europe.

I throw the magazine to the side and turn the TV back on, the volume low. No surprise to find that *Law & Order* is on. I have yet to find a time when it isn't.

I hear the show's familiar *buh-bump* just as a male nurse walks into my room.

He's tall and strong. Dark hair, dark eyes, clean-shaven. His scrubs are deep blue, his skin a deep tan. He has on a white T-shirt underneath.

It only now occurs to me that Deanna probably isn't working twenty-four hours a day. This guy must be the night nurse.

"Oh," he says, whispering. "I didn't realize you had company."

I notice that he has a large tattoo on his left forearm. It appears to be some sort of formal script, large cursive letters, but I can't make out exactly what it says. "She won't wake up," I whisper back.

He looks at Gabby and winces. "Geez," he says softly. "She sounds like a bulldozer."

I smile at him. He's right.

"I won't be too long," he says. He moves toward my machines. I've been hooked up to these things all day, to the point where they are starting to feel like a part of me.

He starts checking things off his list just as Deanna did earlier today. I can hear the sound of the pen on the clipboard. *Check. Check. Check. Scribble.* He puts my chart back into the pocket. I wonder if it says in that file that I lost a baby. I push the thought out of my head.

"Would you mind?" he asks me, gesturing to the stethoscope in his hand.

"Oh," I say. "Sure. Whatever you gotta do."

He pushes the neck of my gown down and slips his hand between my skin and the cloth, resting the stethoscope over my heart. He asks me to breathe normally.

Deanna did this earlier, and I didn't even notice. But now, with him, it feels intimate, almost inappropriate. But of course, it's not. Obviously, it's not. Still, I find myself slightly embarrassed. He's handsome, and he's my age, and his hand is on my bare chest. I am now acutely aware of the fact that I am not wearing a bra. I turn my head so I'm not looking at him. He smells like men's body wash, something that would be called Alpine Rush or Clean Arctic.

He pulls the stethoscope off me when he's satisfied with his findings. He scribbles something on the chart. I find myself desperate to change the mood. A mood he's probably not even aware of.

"How long have you worked here?" I ask, whispering so as not to wake up Gabby. I like that I have to whisper. At a whisper, you can't tell my voice is shot.

"Oh, I've been here since I moved to L.A. about two years ago," he whispers as he stares at my chart. "Originally from Texas."

"Whereabouts?" I ask.

"Lockhart," he says. "You wouldn't have heard of it. Small town just outside of Austin."

"I lived in Austin," I say. "For a little while."

He looks up at me and smiles. "Oh, yeah? When did you move here?"

It's hard to answer succinctly, and I don't have the voice to give him the whole story, so I simplify it. "I grew up here, but I moved back last week."

He tries to hide it, but I can see his eyes go wide. "Last week?"

I nod. "Last Friday night," I say.

He shakes his head. "Wow."

"Seems sort of unfair, doesn't it?"

He shakes his head and looks back down at the chart. He clicks his pen. "Nope, you can't think about that," he says, looking back up at me. "From experience, I can tell you that if you go around trying to figure out what's fair in life or whether you deserve something or not, that's a rabbit hole that is hard to climb out of."

I smile at him. "You might be right," I say, and then I close my eyes. Conversation takes more energy than I thought.

"Anything I can get you?" he whispers before he leaves.

I shake my head slightly. "Er, actually . . . maybe a hair tie?" I point to my head. My hair is down around my shoulders. I am lying on it. I hate lying on my hair.

"That's an easy one," he says. He pulls one out of his shirt pocket. I look at him, surprised.

"I find them all over the hospital. Someday maybe I'll tell you about the elaborate reminder system I use them for." He comes close and puts one in my hand. I only get a slightly better look at his tattoo. I still can't make it out.

"Thanks," I say. I lean forward, trying to get a good angle, trying to gather all of my hair. But it's hard. My entire body aches. Moving my arms high enough seems impossible.

"Hold on," he whispers. "Let me."

"Well," I say, "I don't want a ponytail."

"OK . . ." he says. "I don't have to braid it, do I? That seems complicated."

"Just a bun. High up." I point toward the crown of my head.

I don't care if the bun looks good. I just want it out from under my head and neck. I want it contained and out of the way.

"All right, lean forward if you can." He starts to gather my hair. "I think this is the beginning of a complete disaster."

I laugh and push my body forward. I wince.

"Let's get you a bit higher dosage on the pain meds. Does that sound OK?" he says. "You shouldn't be in that much pain."

I nod. "OK, but I think they've turned it as high as it will go."

"Oh, I don't know about that. We might be able to go higher." He drops my hair momentarily and moves toward my IV. I can't see what he's doing; he's behind me. And then he's in front of me again, picking up my hair. "I mean, you might start saying weird things and having hallucinations," he jokes, "but better that you're not in pain."

I smile at him.

"All right, so I'm just gathering all of this hair and putting it on the top of your head and then wrapping a rubber band around it?"

"Yeah."

He leans into me, our faces close together. I can smell the coffee on his breath. I feel slight tugging and pressure. He's got some of my hair caught, pulling tightly against my scalp.

"Looser? Maybe?" I say.

"Looser? OK." His arms are in my face, but the tattoo is facing the other direction. I bet it's a woman's name. He seems like the kind of guy who met a woman on some exotic island and married her and they have four beautiful children and live in a house with a gourmet kitchen. She probably makes beautiful dinners that incorporate all the food groups, and I bet they have fruit trees in their backyard. Not just oranges, either. Lemons, limes, avocados. I think the medication is up too high.

"OK," he says. "Voilá, I guess." He backs away from me ever so subtly to check his work.

By the look on his face, I can tell that my bun looks ridiculous. But it *feels* right. It feels like a high bun. I feel like myself for the first time today. Which . . . feels great. I feel great. Also, I'm definitely high.

"Do I look silly?" I ask.

"It's probably not my best work," he says. "You pull it off, though."

"Thanks."

"You're welcome," he says. "Well, if you need any other hairstyles, just press that button. I'm here for the next eight hours."

"Will do," I say. "I'm Hannah."

"I know," he says, smiling. "I'm Henry."

When he turns and leaves, I finally get a good glimpse of his tattoo. *Isabelle.*

Man, all the good ones are taken by Isabelles.

I lay my head down, relishing the free space behind my neck.

Henry's head pops back in.

"What's your favorite flavor of pudding?" he asks me.

"Probably chocolate," I say. "Or tapioca? And vanilla is good."

"So all of them? You like all flavors of pudding?" he says, teasing me.

I laugh. "Chocolate," I say. "Chocolate is good."

"I take my break at two a.m.," he tells me. He looks at his watch. "If you're still up, which I hope for your sake you aren't, but if you are still up, maybe I'll bring you some chocolate pudding."

I smile and nod. "That'd be nice," I whisper.

It's quiet on the floor, and it's dark. Gabby is snoring so

loudly I think for sure that I will not be able to fall asleep, that I will be wide awake when Henry comes back.

I turn on the TV. I flip through the channels.

And then I wake up in the morning to the sound of Gabby's voice. "Where did this chocolate pudding come from?"

I lie on Ethan's couch and stare up at the ceiling. He went to work today. I spent the morning cleaning up his apartment. Not *his* messes, mind you. But my own. My clothes were strewn across all of his furniture. His kitchen sink was full of dirty dishes that were mostly, if not all, mine. My stray hairs were pasted in a tangled-rope fashion across his shower walls. But now everything is spotless, and I'm forced to admit I have nothing to do. With Ethan back to work and life returning to normal, I realize I have no normal.

Gabby is picking me up when she leaves her office around six. We are heading to her parents' house for dinner. But until then, I've got nothing.

I turn on Ethan's TV and flip through the channels. I check his DVR for anything that piques my interest. I come up empty and turn it off. The silence proves to amplify the voice in my head, telling me I need to get a life.

Flirting and spending your days in bed and eating cinnamon rolls with your old high school boyfriend is a wonderful way to pass the time. But what is going on between Ethan and me doesn't solve the challenges that lie ahead.

I grab a pen and a piece of paper from Ethan's desk and start scribbling down a plan.

I am a fly-by-the-seat-of-my-pants type of person. I am a

see-where-life-takes-you sort of person. But that sort of approach to life isn't yielding results for me. It gets me paying the bills waiting tables and sleeping with married men. I don't want that anymore. I want to try order instead of chaos.

I can do that. I can be an organized person. Right? I mean, I did clean this entire apartment today. It's orderly and contained now. There's no sign that Hurricane Hannah hit. And maybe that's because I don't have to be a hurricane.

I want to build a life here. In Los Angeles. So I'm starting with a list.

Suddenly, I start to feel queasy. My stomach turns sour. But then the phone rings, and my mind is elsewhere.

It's Gabby.

"Hi. Are you ready to be shocked? I'm making a list. An actual, organized life-plan list."

"Who is this, and what have you done with Hannah?" she says, laughing.

"If you want her back, you'll listen to me," I say. "I need a million dollars in unmarked, nonconsecutive bills."

"I'll need time to get together that kind of money."

"You have twelve hours."

"Oh," she says. "I definitely can't do that in twelve hours. Just kill her. It's fine. She'll like heaven." Why did it take me this long to realize I should be in the same city as her?

"Hey!" I say, laughing.

She starts laughing with me. "Ohhhh," she says. "Hannah, it's you! I had no idea."

"Yeah, yeah, yeah," I say. "But don't come crying to me when *you* get kidnapped."

She laughs again. "I called to tell you I'm coming by earlier than I thought. Probably around five, if that works for you. I'll bring you back to my place, and then we can head out to Pasadena to see my parents around seven or so."

"Awesome. I'll hurry up and finish this list," I say, and then we get off the phone.

I look at the piece of paper in front of me. It says "Buy a car." That's the first thing I wrote down. The only thing I wrote down.

I quickly scribble "Get a job," and I waver about whether or not to put down "Find an apartment." The truth is, between Ethan and Gabby, I have plenty of options for where to stay. It seems fair to assume I'll figure something out. But then I decide no, I'm putting it down. I'm not going to see what happens. I'm going to make a plan. I'm going to be proactive.

Car.

Job.

Apartment.

It seems so simple, written out in order. For a moment, as I look at it, I think, *Is that all?* And then I realize that simple and easy aren't the same thing.

By the time Gabby comes to pick me up, I'm standing on the sidewalk waiting for her.

I get into the car, and Gabby starts driving.

She looks at me and shakes her head, smiling. I am grinning from ear to ear.

"Did I call this, or did I call this?" she says.

"Call what?" I ask, laughing.

"You and Ethan."

I shake my head. "It just happened!" I say. "I didn't *know* it was going to happen."

"But didn't I say that it would?"

"Neither here nor there," I say. "The point is, we're together now."

"Together?" Gabby says, laughing. "Like, you're *together*?"

I laugh. "Yes, we're *together*."

"So I can assume that aside from the occasional ride here and there and a few meals, I have lost you to your newfound boyfriend?"

I shake my head. "No, not this time. I'm not seventeen anymore. I have a life to create here. Romance is great. But it's only one part of a well-rounded life. You know?"

Gabby puts her hands to her heart and smiles to herself. I start laughing. I wasn't trying to placate her. I just don't think that having a good boyfriend solves all my problems.

I've still got plenty of problems to solve.

Deanna comes in to bring me my breakfast and check up on me. Shortly after she leaves, Dr. Winters comes in and sits down with Gabby and me to discuss the details of my injury now that I'm a bit more stable. My parents are on their way, and I know they'd want to be here for this, but I can't wait. I have to know.

Dr. Winters explains that the crash severed my femoral artery and broke my right leg and pelvis. I was unconscious and rushed into surgery to stop the bleeding and repair the break. I lost a considerable amount of blood and sustained a pretty significant blow to the head when I fell. As she tells me all of this, she continues to stress the fact that all of my injuries are fairly common in a car accident of this magnitude and that I will be fine. Knowing just how bad it was makes it harder to believe that I will be OK. But I suppose just because something is hard to understand, that doesn't make it any less true.

When Dr. Winters is done going through some memory questions, she tells me that I will be sent home in a wheelchair. I won't be able to walk for a few weeks as my pelvis heals. And even then, I will have to start off very slowly and very gently. I will need physical therapy in order to exercise the muscles that have been damaged, and I'll be in pain . . . well, almost all the time.

"It's a long road ahead," Dr. Winters says. "But it is a steady one. I have no doubt that someday, sooner rather than later, you will be able to go for a run around the block."

I laugh at her. "Well, I've never gone for a run around the block in the past, so now that my legs are immobile, it seems like a good time to start."

"You joke," she says, getting up. "But I've had patients who were complete couch potatoes start training for marathons when they get the use of their legs back. Something about that temporary and jarring loss of mobility can really encourage people to see what they are capable of."

She pats my hand and moves toward the door.

"Make sure you tell the nurses if you need anything. And if you have any other questions, I'm here," she says.

"Thanks," I say, and then I turn to Gabby. "Great. So not only am I unable even to walk myself to the bathroom right now, but if I don't start dreaming of marathons and Nikes, I'm a slacker."

"I believe that is what she said, yes. She said if you don't start training for the L.A. Marathon this very second, your life is a waste, and you might as well pack it in."

"Man, Dr. Winters can be such a bitch," I say, and instantly, there is a knock at the door. For a moment, I'm terrified it's Dr. Winters. I didn't mean it. I was just joking. She's really nice. I like her.

It's Ethan.

"OK for me to sneak in?" Ethan says. "Is now a good time?"

He pulls a large bouquet of lilies from behind his back.

"Hi," I say. I love lilies. I wonder if he remembered that or if it's a coincidence.

"Hey," he says. His voice is gentle, as if speaking too loudly could hurt me. He hasn't moved from the door. "Is this . . . ? Am I . . . ?"

"It's OK," Gabby says. "Come on in. Have a seat." She moves to the other side of me.

He comes closer and hands me the flowers. I take them and smell them. He smiles at me as if I'm the only person in the world.

As I look at him, it comes back to me, almost like a dream at first, and then the more I remember, the more it grabs hold.

I remember Gabby handing me her phone. I remember looking down at it. Seeing Katherine's message.

Going home with Ethan. Is this a terrible idea?

I bury my face in the flowers instead of looking directly at him. In a hospital, where everything is so clinical and un-scented, where the air itself is stale, the smell of lilies almost feels as if it could make you high. I breathe in again, stronger, trying to inhale as much of their life and freshness as I can. The irony of the situation isn't lost on me. These are cut flowers. They are, by their very definition, dying.

"Mmm," I say. *He's not serious about us. He's not interested in an "us" if he went home with her. This is Michael all over again. This is me needing to learn that you have to face the truth of a situ-ation head-on. He almost kissed me, and then he went home with another girl.* "They smell great."

"How are you?" he says. He sits down in the chair next to the bed.

"I'm OK," I say. "Really."

He stares at me for a moment.

"Can you take these back?" I say, handing the flowers to Gabby. "I don't have anywhere to really . . ."

"Oh," Gabby says. "Let me go find some water and some-thing to put them in. Sound good?" She's trying to find a reason to leave us alone, and a perfect one just fell into her lap. She slips out the door and smiles at me.

"So," he says, breathing in hard.

"So," I say.

We are both quiet, looking at each other. I can tell he's worried about me. I can tell it's hard for him to look at me and see me in this hospital bed. I also know that it's not his fault I'm upset at the memory of him taking Katherine home. We had no claim on each other, made no promises.

And besides, this memory may be fresh for me because I just remembered it, because it was temporarily lost in the haziness of my brain, but it happened days ago. It's old news to him.

We both speak up at the same time.

"How are you, really?" he asks me.

"How've you been?" I ask him.

He laughs. "Did you just ask me how I've been? How have *you* been? That's the question. I've been worried sick about you."

"I'm OK," I say.

"You scared me half to death," he says. "Do you know that? Do you know how heartbroken I'd be to live in a world you weren't in?"

I know that I should believe him. I know that he's telling the truth. But the fact of the matter is that I worry that I'll believe him too much, that I'll become too easily swayed into believing what I want to believe about him. I don't want to do what I would have done before. I don't want to believe what a person says and ignore what he does. I don't want to see only what I want to see.

I want to be realistic, for once. I want to be grounded. I want to make smart decisions.

So when Ethan smiles at me and makes me feel as if I

invented the world, when he comes close to me and I can feel the warmth of his body and the smell of his laundry detergent just like in high school, I have to ignore it. For my own good.

"I really am OK," I tell him. "Don't worry. It's just some broken bones. But I'm OK."

He grabs my hand. I flinch. He sees me do it and takes his hand back.

"Have they been treating you well?" he says. "I hear hospital food leaves something to be desired."

"Yeah," I tell him. "I could use a good meal. Although the pudding isn't so bad."

"Did they say how long you'll be in here?" he asks. "I want to know when I can take you out on the town again."

I laugh politely. It's this sort of stuff. This sort of flirty, charming stuff. That's the stuff that gets me.

"It's gonna be a while," I say. "You might want to find another girl to paint the town red with."

"No," he says, smiling. "I think I'd rather wait for you."

No, you wouldn't.

I keep hoping Gabby will come back in with the flowers, but she's nowhere to be seen.

"Well," I say, "don't." My tone is polite but not particularly warm. Given the fact that it wasn't a very nice thing to say in the first place, I think I've shown my hand.

"OK," he says. "I should probably get going. You probably need your rest, and I should get to work . . ."

"Yeah," I say. "Sure."

He heads toward the door and turns around. "You know I would do anything for you, right? If you need anything at all . . . ?"

I nod. "Thanks."

He nods and looks down at the floor and then back up at me. He looks as if he's going to say something, but he doesn't. He just taps his hand on the door frame one time and then walks through it.

Gabby comes right back in. "Sorry," she says. "I didn't mean to eavesdrop, but I got back with the flowers a while ago, and I could hear you guys were having a conversation. I didn't want to . . ."

"It's cool," I say as she puts the flowers down on the counter by the door. I wonder where she found the vase. It's nice. The flowers are beautiful. Most men would have brought carnations.

She looks at me. "You're upset about the Katherine thing."

"So you did eavesdrop."

"I never said that I didn't. I just said I didn't mean to."

I laugh. "I'm not *upset* about the Katherine thing," I say, defending myself. "It just confirmed for me that trying something with him again . . . it's maybe not the best idea."

She grabs my hand for a moment. "OK," she says.

I pick up the remote and turn on the TV. Gabby grabs her purse.

"You're leaving?"

"Yeah, I have to get back to the office for a meeting. But your family's almost here. They texted me a few minutes ago saying they were parking. You'll have some time with them, and then I'll leave work, get a change of clothes for tomorrow, and be back here for our nightly slumber party."

"You don't need to stay here tonight," I say.

She frowns at me, as if I'm telling a lie.

"I'm serious," I say, laughing. "My parents can stay. Sarah can stay. No one has to stay. I'm serious. Go home. Spend time with Mark. I'm OK."

My mom pokes her head in. "Hi, sweetheart!" she says. "Hi, Gabrielle!" she adds when she sees her.

"Hi, Maureen," Gabby says, giving her a hug. "I was just taking off." She calls to me from the door. "I'll call you later. We'll discuss it."

I laugh. "OK."

My mom comes in farther. My dad joins her.

"Hi, guys," I say. "How are you?"

"How are we?" my dad says. "How are *we*?" He turns to my mom. "Would you listen to this kid? She gets in a car accident, and when she can talk, the first thing she asks us is how *we* are." He comes to me and gives me a gentle hug. I'm getting called out on this by everyone lately, but *How are you?* is a perfectly reasonable question to ask another human being as a greeting.

"Incredible," my mom says. She comes around my other side.

"Sarah will be up in a minute," my dad says.

"She gets frustrated trying to parallel park," my mom whispers. "She learned how to drive where you park on the left side of the road."

"You can't park in the garage here?" I ask.

My dad laughs. "Clearly, you have never visited someone in the hospital. The rates are maddening."

Good old Mom and Dad. Sarah comes in the door.

"You got it?" my mom asks.

"It's fine," Sarah says. She breathes. "Hi," she says to me. "How are you?"

"I'm OK," I say.

"You look like you feel better than yesterday," my dad says. "You've got some color in your face."

"And your voice sounds good," my mom adds.

Sarah steps closer to me. "I cannot tell you how good it feels to look at you and know you're OK. To hear your voice." She can see that my mom is getting teary. "But the bad news is that your bun is really screwed up," she says. "Here." She takes my head in her hands and pulls my hair out of the elastic.

"Easy now," I say to her. "There's a person attached to that hair."

"You're fine," she says. "Wait." She stops herself. "You are fine, right? Gabby said the damage is all on your lower half."

"Yeah, yeah," I say. "Go ahead."

She drops my hair and walks toward her purse. "You need your hair brushed. Is no one brushing your hair around here?"

She pulls a brush from her purse and starts running it through my hair. It feels nice, except for the moments when she finds deep-rooted tangles at the base of my scalp. I wince as she picks at them, trying to work them free.

"Do you remember when you were little," my mom says as she sits down, "and you used to get those huge knots in your hair from when you would try to braid it yourself?"

"Not really," I say. "But if it felt anything like Sarah yanking at my scalp, I can understand why I blocked it out."

It's not audible, and her face is behind me, but I know for a fact that Sarah is rolling her eyes at me.

"Yeah, you hated it then, too, and I told you to stop playing with your hair if you didn't want me to sit there and detangle it. You told me you wanted to cut it all off. And I told you no.

"Obviously," Sarah says as she puts the brush down and pulls my hair into a high bun.

"Can you do it higher?" I ask. "I don't like it when I can feel it hit the bed." She lets my hair down and tries again.

"OK, well, long story short," my mom says.

"It's a little late for that," my dad jokes. She gives him a look. The look wives and mothers have been giving to husbands and fathers for centuries.

"Anyway," she says pointedly, "you went into the kitchen when I wasn't looking and chopped off your own hair."

"Oh, right," I say, vaguely remembering seeing pictures of my hair cropped. "I think you told me this story before."

"It was so short. Above your ears!" she says. "And I ran into the kitchen and saw what you did, and I said, 'Why did you do that?' and you said, 'I don't know, I felt like it.'"

"A Hannah Savannah sentiment if there ever was one," my dad says proudly. "If that doesn't describe you, I honestly don't know what does. 'I don't know, I felt like it.'" He laughs to himself.

This is exactly the kind of stuff I'm trying to change about myself.

"Yeah, OK, Doug, but that's not the moral of the story," my mom says.

My dad puts his hands up in mock regret. "My apologies," he says. "I'd hate to guess the wrong moral to a story. Call the police!"

"Must you interrupt every story I try to tell?" my mom asks, and then she waves him off. "What I was getting at is that we had to take you to the hairdresser, and they cut your hair into a little pixie cut, which I'd never seen for a little girl. I mean, you were no more than six years old."

That's what I remember, seeing pictures of myself with hair cropped tight to my head.

"Get to the point, Mom," Sarah says. "By the time this story is over, I'll be ninety-four years old."

It's jarring to hear Sarah tease my mom. I would never say something like that to her.

"Fine," my mom says. "Hannah, your hair was gorgeous. Really stunning. Women kept stopping me at Gelson's to ask me where I had the idea to cut your hair like that. I gave them the number of the lady who did it. She ended up moving her business out of the Valley and into Beverly Hills. Last I heard, she cut that *Jerry Maguire* kid's hair once. The end."

"That story was even worse than I thought it was going to be," Sarah says. "There! I'm done."

"How's it look?" I ask my dad and mom.

They smile at me.

"You are one gorgeous girl," my dad says.

"Maybe people will see Hannah's bun and one day I can do Angelina Jolie's bun," Sarah says, teasing my mom.

"The hairdresser wasn't the point!" my mom says. "The point of the story is that you should always have faith in Hannah. Because even when it looks like she's made a terrible mistake, she's actually one step ahead of you. That's the moral. Things will always work out for Hannah. You know? She was born under a lucky star or something."

Sometimes I think my mom's anecdotes should come with Cliffs Notes. Because they're quite good once someone explains them to you.

"I really liked that story," I tell her. "Thank you for telling it. I didn't remember any of that."

"I have pictures of it somewhere," she says. "I'll find them when we get home and send one to you. You really looked great. That's why I'm always telling you to cut your hair off."

"But what would she do without *the bun*?" Sarah asks.

"Yeah," I say. "I am nothing without this bun."

"So fill us in, Hannah Savannah," my dad says. "The doctors said you will recover nicely, but, as is my fatherly duty, I'm worried about how you're feeling now."

"Physically and mentally," my mom says.

"I'm OK," I say. "They have me on a steady amount of pain-killers. I'm not comfortable, by any means. But I'm OK." No good would come from telling them about the baby. I put the thought right out of my head. I don't even feel as if I'm keeping anything from them.

"Are you really OK?" my mom asks. Her voice starts to break. My dad puts his arm around her.

I wonder how many times I'll have to say it before anyone believes it. Ugh, maybe it will have to be true first.

"You must have been so scared," my mom says. Her eyes start to water. My dad holds her tighter, but I can see that his eyes are starting to water, too. Sarah looks away. She looks out the window.

All of this joking-around, let-me-do-your-hair, old-family-memories thing is just a song and dance. They are heartbroken and worried. They are stunned and uncomfortable and miserable and sick to their stomachs. And if I'm being honest, something about that soothes me.

I can't remember the last time I felt like a permanent fixture of this group. I have, for well over a decade, felt like a guest in my own family. I barely even remember how we all were when we lived in the same place, in the same house, in the same country. But with the three of them in front of me now, letting the cracks in their armor show, I feel like a person who belongs in this family. A person who is needed to complete the pack.

"I wish you guys lived here," I say as I start to get emotional.

I've never said that before. I'm not sure why. "I feel like I'm on my own so much, and I just . . . I miss you a lot."

My dad comes closer and takes my hand. "We miss you every single day," he says. "Every day. Do you know that?"

I nod. Although I'm not sure yes is the most honest answer.

"Just because you're here and we're there, that doesn't mean we ever stop thinking about you," my mom says.

Sarah nods and looks away and wipes her eyes. And then she puts her hand on my knee. She looks me in the eye and smiles. "I don't know about these guys, but I love you like crazy," she says.

Carl and Tina moved to Pasadena a few years ago. They sold the place they had while we were in high school and downsized to a Craftsman-style house on a quiet street with lots of trees.

It's almost eight by the time Gabby, Mark, and I get to their place. Mark ran late at the office. He seems to run late at the office a lot or works late into the night. I would have thought that being a dentist was kind of predictable. But he always has last-minute stuff come up.

We pull into the driveway and head into the house. Gabby doesn't bother to knock. She goes right in.

Tina looks up from the kitchen and walks toward us with a big, bright smile and open arms.

She hugs Gabby and Mark and then turns to me. "Hannah Marie!" she says, enveloping me in a hug. She holds me tight and rocks me from side to side, like only a mother does.

"Hi, Tina," I say to her. "I've missed you!"

She lets go of me and gives me a good look. "Me, too, sweetheart. Me, too. Go on in and say hello to Carl. He can't wait to get a good look at you."

I walk on, leaving Gabby and Mark with Tina. Carl is in the backyard, pulling a steak off the grill. That's certainly a point for Los Angeles: you can grill twelve months out of the year.

"Do my eyes deceive me?" he asks as he's putting the steak down on a plate and closing the grill. "Could it be *the* Hannah Martin in front of me?"

Carl is wearing a green polo shirt and khakis. He almost always looks as if he's dressed for golf. I don't know if he actually has ever golfed, but he's got the look down pat.

"The one and only," I say, putting my arms out to present myself. He gives me a hug. He's a big man with a tight grip. I almost can't breathe. For a moment, it makes me miss my dad.

I hand Carl the flowers I brought.

"Oh, why, thank you so much! I've always wanted . . . chrysanthemums?" he asks me. He knows he's wrong.

"Lilies," I say.

"I was close," he says, and takes them out of my hand. "I don't know anything about flowers. I just buy them when I've done something wrong." I laugh.

He gestures for me to pick up the plate with the steak on it. I do, and we head inside.

We enter the house through the kitchen. Tina is pouring wine for Gabby and Mark. Carl steps right in.

"Tina, I bought you these lilies just now. You're welcome," he says, and winks at me.

"Wow, honey, so romantic," she says. "It's nice to know that you got them yourself. That you didn't rudely take the flowers that Hannah brought us."

"Yeah," Carl says as he hugs Gabby. He shakes Mark's hand and pats him on the back. "That'd be terrible."

Gabby takes her purse off her shoulder and takes my bag from me. She puts them both down in the hallway. "You can take off your shoes, too," Gabby says. "But just hide them."

I give her a confused look. Tina clears it up. "Barker," she says.

"Barker?"

"Barker!" Carl yells, and down the steps and into the kitchen comes a massive Saint Bernard.

"Oh, my God!" I say. "Barker!"

Gabby starts laughing. Barker runs right to Mark, and Mark backs away.

"I forgot my allergy pills," he says. "Sorry. I should hang back."

"You're allergic to dogs?" I ask.

He nods as Gabby gives me a look. I can't tell what the look is, because in one swift motion, she's down on the floor, rubbing Barker's back. Barker is only too happy to turn over and let her rub his belly.

"So!" Tina announces. "It's a steak-and-potatoes kind of night. Except that Carl has decided to pull out the big guns because you kids are here, so it's steak with *chimichurri* sauce, garlic-and-chive mashed potatoes, and brussels sprouts, because . . . I'm still a mom, and I can't stop myself from making sure you eat your vegetables."

My parents made me eat vegetables until I was about fourteen, and then they gave up. I always liked that about them. When I lived with Carl and Tina, I felt as if I was being force-fed riboflavin on a nightly basis.

Then again, their daughter is a nonprofit executive who married a dentist, so clearly, they were doing something right.

We all sit down at the table, and Carl immediately starts in with dad-like questions.

"Hannah, catch us up on what you've been doing," he says as he cuts the steak.

"Well." I open my eyes wide and sigh. I'm not sure where

to start. "I'm back!" I say, throwing my arms up and flashing my hands for effect. For a moment, I'm hoping this is enough. Clearly, it is not.

"Uh-huh," he says. "And?" He starts serving and passing plates around the table. When I get mine, it's got a lot of brussels sprouts on it. If I don't eat them all, Tina will say something. I just know it.

"And . . . I've mostly been floating from city to city as of late. The Pacific Northwest for a bit. New York, too."

"Gabby said you were living in New York," Tina says, starting to take a bite of her steak. "Was it fabulous? Did you see any Broadway shows?"

I laugh slightly, but I don't mean to. "No," I say. "Not much of that."

I don't want to get into anything about Michael. I don't want to admit to them the mess I got myself in. They may not be my parents, but Carl and Tina are incredibly parental. I care deeply what they think of me.

"New York wasn't for me," I say, sipping the wine they put in front of me and then immediately putting it back down on the table. It smells awful. I don't like it.

Gabby, seeing my discomfort, steps in. "Hannah is a West Coast girl, you know? She belongs back with us."

"Amen to that," Carl says, cutting his steak and taking a bite. He chews with his mouth open sometimes. "I've always said, go where the sunshine is. Anyone who heads for snowier climates is a moron." Tina rolls her eyes at him. He looks at Mark. "Mark, what are you doing drinking wine with a steak like this?"

Mark starts to stumble a little bit. I realize for the first time that Mark is slightly intimidated by Carl. It's not hard to see why. He's a formidable man to have as a father-in-law.

"It's what was in front of me," Mark says, laughing. "I'm not too discerning."

Carl gets up from the table and goes into the kitchen. He comes back and puts a beer in front of Mark.

Mark laughs. "All right!" he says. He seems genuinely much more interested in drinking the beer than the wine Tina gave him, but I don't know if that's just a show for Carl. He's also scratching his wrists and the back of his neck pretty aggressively. Must be Barker.

Carl sits back down. "Men drink beer," Carl says, sipping his own. "Simple as that."

"Dad," Gabby says, "gender has absolutely nothing to do with someone's preference for a drink. Some men like apple-tinis. Some women like bourbon. It's irrelevant."

"While I admit I have no idea what an appletini is, you're absolutely right," Carl says thoughtfully. "I was being reduc-tionist, and I'm sorry."

Now that I'm back in their home, I remember where it comes from. Where she gets the need to speak clearly and as accurately as possible about gender politics. It's Carl. He will have these antiquated ideas about men and women, but then he routinely corrects himself about them when Gabby brings it up.

"So, Hannah," Tina says, redirecting the conversation, "what's the plan? Are you staying in L.A. for a while?"

I swallow the piece of steak I'm chewing. "Yeah," I say. "I'm hoping to."

"Do you have a job lined up?" Carl asks.

Gabby steps in to defend me. "Dad, don't."

He looks defensive. "I'm just asking a question."

I shake my head. "No," I say, "I don't." I look at the wineglass in front of me. I can't bring myself to drink any more of it. I don't want to have to smell it again. I grab the water next to it and sip. "But I will!" I add. "That's on my list. Car. Job. Apartment. You know, the basic tenets of a functioning life."

"Do you have money for a car?" Carl asks.

"Dad!" Gabby says. "C'mon."

Mark stays out of it. He's too busy scratching his arms. Also, I get the impression that Mark usually stays out of a lot of things.

"Gabby! The girl lived with us for almost two years. She's practically my long-lost daughter. I can ask her if she needs money for a car." Carl turns to me. "Can't I?"

It's a weird relationship I have with the Hudsons. On the one hand, they are not my parents. They didn't really raise me, and they don't check in on me regularly. On the other hand, if I needed anything, I've always known they would step in. They took care of me during one of the most formative times in my life. And the truth is, my parents aren't here. My parents haven't been here for a while.

"It's fine," I say. "I have some money saved. I have enough for a down payment on a car or first, last, and security on an apartment. If I can find a cheap option for each, then I could maybe swing both."

"You're saying you have about five thousand dollars, give or take," Carl says.

Gabby shakes her head. Mark is smiling. Maybe he's just glad the heat is off him for now.

Tina pipes up before I can. "Carl, why don't we save the hard stuff for after dinner?"

"Hannah," he says directly to me, "am I making you uncomfortable? Is this bothering you?"

C'mon! What am I supposed to say to that? Yes, talking about how broke and unprepared for life I am makes me a little uncomfortable. But who on this planet, when asked directly if they are uncomfortable, admits they are? It's an impossible question. It forces you to make the other person feel better about invading your personal space.

"It's fine," I say. "Really."

Carl turns to Gabby and Tina. "She says it's fine."

"OK, OK," Tina says. "Who wants more wine?"

Gabby raises her glass. Mine is untouched. "I'm good," I say.

Tina looks at my plate. "Are you done?" she asks. Everyone else's plate is fairly clean except for a bite here or there. Mine is empty except for all of the brussels sprouts. "I have a fabulous dessert to bring out."

I know it's childish, but I'm honestly worried she will judge me for eating dessert without finishing my vegetables. I start casually eating them quickly. "Sounds great," I say between bites. "I'm almost done."

Tina leaves and heads into the kitchen. Carl has started to ask Mark how the dental practice is going when Tina calls for Carl to help her get another bottle of wine open.

"I'm sorry my dad is hounding you," Gabby says once both Carl and Tina are out of earshot.

I take the last of the brussels sprouts on my fork and cram them into my mouth. I chew quickly and swallow them down. "It's fine," I say. "I'm much less worried about your dad's questions than I am about your mom's judgment if I don't finish my vegetables."

Gabby laughs. "You're right to be worried."

Mark joins in. "One time, I didn't put any of her cooked carrots on my plate, and she pulled me aside later and asked if I was at all concerned about a vitamin A deficiency."

I take another sip of my water. I may have overshot it with the brussels sprouts. My stomach is starting to feel bloated and nauseated.

"I shouldn't have eaten them so quickly," I say, rubbing my stomach. "I suddenly feel . . . ugh."

"Oh, I've learned that one before," Gabby says, laughing.

"No, this is . . . I really don't feel well all of a sudden."

"Queasy or what?" Mark says.

"Yeah," I say. I burp. I actually burp. "Very queasy."

Tina and Carl come out, Tina with wine, Carl with a very large, very gooey, very aromatic batch of cinnamon rolls.

I smile wide as Tina winks at me.

"Do we know Hannah, or do we know Hannah?" Carl says.

He puts it down in front of me. "You get first dibs. I would expect nothing less of you than to pick the one with the most icing."

I inhale deeply, getting the smell of the cinnamon and the sugar. And then, suddenly, I have to get out of here.

I slam my chair out from under me and run toward the hallway bathroom, shutting the door behind me. I'm just in front of the toilet when it all comes back up. I feel faint and a little dizzy. I'm exhausted.

I sit down in front of the toilet. The cool bathroom tile feels good against my skin. I don't know how long I sit there. I'm startled back to reality by Gabby knocking on the door. She doesn't wait for me to answer before she comes in.

"Are you OK?" she says.

"Yeah." I stand up. I feel so much better now. "I'm good." I shake my head in an attempt to snap out of it. "Maybe I'm allergic to brussels sprouts?"

"Oof," she says, smiling. "Wouldn't that be nice?"

In a few minutes, after gathering myself and finding the mouthwash, I make my way back to the table.

"I'm so sorry about that," I say. "I think my body was shocked that I fed it vegetables."

Tina laughs. "You're sure you're OK?"

"Yeah," I assure her. "I'm feeling completely normal."

Gabby grabs her purse and my jacket. "But I'm thinking we should take her home," she announces.

I really do feel as if I could stay, but it's probably smart to head back. Get some sleep.

"Yeah," Mark says, scratching again. "I'm feeling a bit overwhelmed by the dog, too, if I'm being honest."

I don't know if anyone notices it except me, but Gabby rolls her eyes, ever so subtly. She's annoyed with him. For being allergic to dogs. I guess it's the small things in a marriage that grate on you the most.

"Oh, we're so sorry," Tina says. "We'll keep medication for you here from now on. In case you forget another time."

"Oh, thanks," Mark says. "Admittedly, the pills don't help that much." He then proceeds to talk for a full five minutes about all of his symptoms and which ones are and are not helped by allergy pills. The way he talks about it, you'd think being allergic to dogs was like being diagnosed with an incurable disease. Christ, even I'm annoyed with his allergy now.

"Well," Carl says as we move toward the door, "we love having you all here."

"Oh!" Tina says. "Hannah, let me pack up some cinnamon buns for you. Is that OK?"

"I'd love that," I say. "Thank you so much."

"OK, one second." She runs into the kitchen, and Gabby goes with her. Carl and I are standing by the front door. Mark is standing by the steps. He excuses himself to use the restroom. "My eyes are starting to tear," he says by way of explanation.

Carl watches him go and then pulls me over to the side.

"Buy a car," Carl says.

"Hm?"

"Buy a car. Live with Gabby and Mark until you earn some money for a deposit."

"Yeah," I say. "That sounds like the smart way to play it."

"And when you have the car, call my office." He pulls a business card out of his wallet and hands it to me. *Dr. Carl Hudson, Pediatrics.*

"Oh," I say. "I'm not sure I—"

"We have a receptionist," he says. "She's terrible. Absolutely terrible. I have to fire her."

"Oh, I'm sorry," I say.

"She makes forty thousand a year plus benefits."

I look at him.

"When we fire her, we're going to be looking for someone who can answer phones, schedule appointments, and be the face of the office."

"Oh," I say. He's offering me a job.

"If you tell me when you think you could take over, I'll keep her around for a few weeks. Make sure the job is available for you."

"Really?" I ask him.

He nods. "Wouldn't think twice about it. You deserve somebody looking out for you."

I am touched. "Wow," I say. "Thank you."

"When they ask how much you want to be paid, say forty-five. You'll probably get forty-two or forty-three. Full benefits. Vacation time. The whole kit and kaboodle."

"I'm not really trained for working in a doctor's office," I say.

He shakes his head. "You're bright. You'll get it quickly."

Tina and Gabby come out of the kitchen with tinfoil-wrapped cinnamon rolls and Tupperware full of leftovers. Mark comes out of the bathroom.

"Shall we?" Gabby says, heading for the door. She gives me some of the leftovers to carry and opens the front door.

Barker comes running toward us and paws me. I push him down. Mark jumps away from him as if he's on fire.

"You can heat those up in the microwave," Tina says. "Or in the oven at three-fifty."

"And let me know," Carl says, "about what we talked about."

The *thank you* that comes out of my mouth is directed at both of them, but it cannot possibly carry all the emotion I have behind it.

I say it again. "Thank you. Really."

"Anytime," Tina says as she gives me a hug good-bye.

I hug Carl as Tina hugs Gabby and Mark. A few more seconds of good-byes, including a heartfelt one from Gabby to Barker, and we are out the door.

Mark gets into the driver's seat. Gabby takes the passenger seat. I lie down in the back.

"How are you feeling?" Gabby asks.

"I'm fine," Mark says before he realizes she means me. He lets the moment pass.

"I'm good," I say. I mean it. Truly.

When I left the Hudsons' to go to college, it never occurred to me that I could come back.

I kept telling people, "My family is in London, my family is in London," but I should have said, "I also have family in Los Angeles. They live on a quiet, tree-lined street in a Craftsman-style house in Pasadena."

My family left at around nine tonight only after I insisted that they sleep at their hotel. They wanted to stay the night, but the truth is, there isn't anything for anyone to do but sit beside me and stare. And sometimes I need my own space. I need to not have to put on a brave face for a little while. Now I am alone in the peace and quiet. I can hear the hum of electricity, the faint beeping of other patients' machines.

People have been bringing me books left and right. They offer them up as a way to pass the time. Books and flowers. Flowers and books.

I pick up a book from the stack Gabby has made, and I start to read. The book is slow to start, very descriptive. Slow and descriptive would be fine on a normal day, on a day when I'm not trying to quiet my own voice, but that won't work for me right now. So I put it down and pick up another one. I go down the stack until I find a voice quick and thrilling enough to quiet my own.

By the time Henry comes in to check on me, I'm so engrossed that I've temporarily forgotten where I am and who I am. A gift if I've ever been given one.

"Still up?" Henry says. I nod. He comes closer.

I look at his tattoo again. I was wrong before. It isn't *Isabelle*. It's *Isabella*. The image in my head instantly changes from a glamorous blond waif to a voluptuous olive-skinned brunette. Good Lord, I need to get a life.

"Do you ever sleep?" he asks me as he puts a blood-pressure cuff around my arm. "Are you a vampire? What's going on here?"

I laugh and glance at the clock. It's just after midnight. Time means nothing in the hospital. Truly. When I was out in the real world, functioning in everyday society, and someone would say "Time is just a construct," I would roll my eyes and continue to check errands off my To Do list. But I was wrong, and they were right. Time means nothing. Never is that more clear than in a hospital bed.

"No, I'm OK," I say. "Last night, after I saw you, I fell asleep for at least nine hours."

"OK," he says. "Well, keep me posted if that changes. Sleep is an important part of healing."

"Totally," I say. "I hear you."

Henry looks even more handsome today than he did yesterday. He's not the kind of handsome that all women would be attracted to, I guess. His face isn't symmetrical. I suppose his nose is a bit big for his face. His eyes are small. But something about it just . . . works for him.

He puts my chart back into the pocket on my bed.

"Well, I'll see ya—" he says, but I interrupt him.

"Isabella," I say. "Is that your wife?"

I'm slightly embarrassed that I have said this just as he was clearly saying good-bye. But what are you going to do? It happened.

He steps back toward me. Only then do I think to look and see if he has a wedding ring. You'd think I'd have learned this shit by now. No ring. But actually, you know, what I *have* learned is that no ring doesn't mean no wife. So my question still stands.

"No," he says, shaking his head. "No, I'm not married."

"Oh," I say.

Henry doesn't offer who Isabella is, and I figure if he wanted to tell me, he would. So . . . this is awkward.

"Sorry to pry," I say. "You know how it is around here. You get bored. You lose your sense of what's appropriate to ask a stranger."

Henry laughs. "No, no, totally fine. Someone has a huge name tattooed on his forearm, I think it warrants a question. To be honest, I'm surprised people don't ask about it more often."

I laugh. "Well, thank you for checking in on—" I start to say, but this time, it's Henry who talks over me.

"She was my sister," he says.

"Oh," I say.

"Yeah," he says. "She passed away about fifteen years ago."

I find myself looking down at my hands. I consciously look back up at him. "I'm sorry to hear that."

Henry looks at me thoughtfully. "Thank you," he says. "Thanks."

I don't know what to say, because I don't want to pry, but I also want him to know that I'm happy to listen. What do I say, though? My first instinct is to ask how she died, but that seems like bad form. I can't think of anything, so I end up just staring at him.

"You want to ask how she died," Henry says.

I am instantly mortified that I am so transparent and also so tacky. "Yeah," I say. "You caught me. How terrible is that? So morbid and unnecessary. But it was the first thing I thought.

How did she die? I'm terrible." I shake my head at myself. "You can spit in my breakfast if you want. I'll totally understand."

Henry sits down in the chair and laughs. "No, it's OK," he says. "It's such a weird thing, right? Because it's the first thing the brain thinks to ask. *She died? How did she die?* But at the same time, it's, like, sort of an insensitive question to ask."

"Right!" I say, shaking my head again. "I'm really sorry."

He laughs at me. "You didn't do anything wrong. She was sixteen. She hit her head in a pool."

"That's terrible," I say. "I'm so sorry."

"Yeah," he says. "She wasn't supposed to be diving. But she was sixteen, you know? Sixteen-year-olds do things they aren't supposed to do. She was rushed to the hospital. The doctors did everything they could. We actually thought she might survive it, but . . . you know, some stuff you just don't come back from. We kept waiting for her to wake up, and she never did."

"Wow," I say. My heart breaks for him and his family. For his sister.

You spend so much time being upset about being in the hospital in the first place that it is almost jarring to realize how many people don't ever leave. I could have been just like his sister. I could have never woken up.

But I did. I'm one of the ones who did.

I consider for a moment what would have happened if I'd been standing just a little bit farther in the road or a little bit off to the side. What if I'd been thrown to the left instead of to the right? Or if the car had been going five miles per hour faster? I might not have ever woken up. Today could have been my funeral. How weird is that? How absolutely insane is that? The difference between life and death could be as simple and as uncomfortably slight as a step you take in either direction.

Which means that I am here today, alive today, because I made the right choices, however brief and insignificant they felt at the time. I made the right choices.

"I'm so sorry you and your family have had to go through that," I tell him. "I can't imagine what that must feel like."

He nods at me, accepting my sympathy. "It's why I became a nurse, actually. When I was in the hospital, with my parents, waiting and waiting for news, I just felt like I wanted to be in the room, helping, doing something, being involved, instead of waiting for someone else to do something or say something. I wanted to be making sure I was doing my best to help other people in the same position as my family was in back then."

"That makes a lot of sense," I say. I wonder if he knows how honorable it sounds. My guess is he doesn't, that it's genuine.

"It was a few years ago, the tenth anniversary of her death. I was in a daze, really. There was so much I hadn't dealt with that just sort of came out around then. By that point, my parents had divorced, and both had moved back to Mexico, where they are originally from. So I was just sort of dealing with the anniversary myself. Anyway, getting the tattoo made me feel better. So I did it. Didn't think too much past that."

I laugh. "That's my life story!" I tell him. "Made me feel better. So I did it."

"Maybe you should get that tattooed," he says.

I laugh again. "I don't know if I'm a tattoo sort of person. I'm way too indecisive. Although, I admit, yours is striking. It was the first thing I noticed when you walked in here."

Henry laughs. "And not my stunning good looks?"

"My apologies. It was the *second* thing I noticed."

Henry pats his hand on my bed and stands up to leave. "Now I'm running late," he says. "Look what you've done."

"I'm sorry," I say. "I mean, you should be apologizing to me, though. Distracting me from my much-needed rest." I smile.

He shakes his head. "You're right. What was I thinking? A pretty girl asks me a question, and suddenly, I can't keep track of the time. I'll be back to check on you later," he says, and slips out the door.

I find myself unable to hold back the smile that insists on shining through my face. I shake my head at myself, laughing at how ridiculous I'm being. But also, for a moment, I consider staying awake all night. I consider waiting around to see when he comes back.

But that's crazy. He's probably nice to all of his patients. Probably tells all the women they're pretty. I'm just bored and lonely in this place. Desperate for something interesting, something good.

I turn off the light by my bed and slide down a bit until my head rests comfortably on the pillow.

It's not hard to fall asleep once I decide to. That's one thing I've always liked about myself. It's never hard to fall asleep.

By the time we get back to Gabby and Mark's place, I have resolved to take the job. Gabby and Mark talked to me about it the entire way home, and Gabby told me she thought it was without a doubt a great idea. "I know for a fact that he is great to his employees, that their entire practice has a huge emphasis on nurse and staff morale," she said. "And my dad loves you, so you'll be the favorite."

By the time we say good night and retire to our rooms, it's starting to hit me that I have a job offer. I have a shot at a real job. Sometimes I don't realize how weighed down I am by my own worries until they are gone. But I feel much freer tonight than I did this morning.

I call Ethan from my bed to tell him the good news. He's through-the-roof excited for me. And then I tell him about the rest of the evening.

"I must be allergic to brussels sprouts," I tell him. "I barely made it from the table to the toilet before puking up my entire dinner."

"What? Are you still feeling sick? Hold on. I'm going to come get you," he says.

"No," I tell him. "I'm OK here. You don't have to."

"I want to. It's a good excuse to see you. I'm coming. You can't stop me."

I laugh and then realize that I never really thought I was

sleeping here tonight. I think I knew I was just going through the motions until he came to get me. "OK, yeah, yeah, yeah, come get me!" I say. "I'm excited to see you."

"I'll leave now," he says.

So within thirty minutes of us getting home, I am on my way out the door to meet Ethan's car.

When I walk into the living room to grab my bag, I see Gabby in the kitchen in her pajamas, getting a glass of water.

"Headed somewhere?" she asks, teasing me.

"Caught me," I say.

"I called it," she says. "Although I figured you'd have us drop you off at his place, so you lasted longer than I thought."

"At least I'm a little unpredictable."

"I wouldn't go that far," she says as I turn to the door. "Wait."

She pulls the cinnamon rolls off the counter and brings them to me. "Please take these with you. Leave them at Ethan's. I can't look at them without wanting to eat them all."

I laugh. "And you think I can?"

"Yeah, well," she says, "you attract cinnamon rolls everywhere you go. I can't live like that."

I take the cinnamon rolls. "I should send your parents a thank-you note," I say. I hear Ethan's car pull up.

Gabby looks at me as if that's the dumbest idea she's ever heard. "They would be insulted," she says. "It would be like if I sent them one for raising me. Stop."

I laugh.

"But also, go," she says. "Pretty sure he's right outside."

I give her a hug and tell her I'll see her tomorrow.

I walk out the door, and Ethan's car is parked right in front. I watch him for a moment before he knows he's being seen. He's turning the key out of the ignition. He's opening his door.

"You look gorgeous," he says.

I smile and then quickly find myself laughing at the idea that Gabby could have heard him. I can just imagine her opening up a window and calling down to the street, "OK, but that's not where a woman's worth lies!"

I smile at him and walk toward the car as he opens the passenger door for me. I hug him and get in. He gets in on his side and pulls away from the curb.

"Is that an entire batch of cinnamon rolls?" he asks. The smell has filled up the car.

"Yep," I say. "And if you're nice to me, I'll let you have one or five."

"Never a dull, cinnamon-roll-less moment with you."

"Never," I say.

Ethan grabs my hand at a stop sign. He kisses my cheek at a red light.

I feel like myself around him. And I like myself around him. So far, I like who I am in this city. I feel like a long-forgotten version of myself, a version I'm much more comfortable being than the New York me.

Suddenly, a small, wily dog runs out into the middle of the street.

Ethan quickly veers the car to the side of the road to avoid hitting it. The dog continues to make its way across to the other sidewalk. It's late enough that there are no cars coming up behind us yet. Ethan pulls over.

"We gotta get that dog," he says, just as I have my hand on the door handle, about to jump out and chase it down. We both get out of the car and run toward the dog, watching out for any possible oncoming traffic.

I can see it, just up ahead.

"On the right side of the street by the Dumpster," I say. "Can you see it?"

Ethan comes toward me, looking. He starts walking slowly after the dog.

"Hey, buddy," he says when he gets close. The dog prances on down the street, not a care in the world. Ethan creeps up, trying to grab hold, but the moment the dog sees him coming, it runs in the other direction. I run a bit faster and try to cut the dog off on the other side, but I just miss it. The dog is brown and a dingy white, bigger than I thought from far away but still on the smaller side, a terrier of some kind. Shaggy but short-haired, small but feisty.

There's a car coming. Ethan once again gets close and tries to grab the dog but fails. The dog thinks we are playing a game.

The car is now barreling down the road. I start to fill with panic that the dog will run into the street again. I'm a few feet away. The dog is playfully prancing off in the other direction.

I growl at it, loudly. I give it the best animal-like roar I can muster.

It stops in its tracks. I turn away from it and start running, hoping it will chase me. It does. Just as quickly as it was running away from me, it's now running toward me. When it reaches my feet, it jumps up onto me. I quickly bend down and pick it up. The car flies past us. Relief washes over me.

It's a female. No collar. No tags.

Ethan comes running up to meet me. I am holding the dog in my arms.

"Christ," he says. "I honestly thought she was a goner."

"I know," I say. "But she's OK. We got her."

She has curled right into my chest. She is licking my hand.

"Well, clearly, this dog is a trained killer," Ethan says.

I laugh. "Yeah, I have no doubt she's just biding her time until she can attack."

"So no tags," Ethan says. "No leash, no nothing."

"Nope," I say, shaking my head. "My guess is we will have to take her to a vet tomorrow and see if she's chipped. Put some fliers up."

"OK," he says. "In the meantime . . ."

"We can't leave her out on the street," I say. "Do you have room for *two* women to join you this evening?"

Ethan nods. "I'm sure we can find a spot for her."

We both start walking back to the car. When we get there, Ethan opens the door for both of us.

"We should probably name her," I say. "You know, temporarily."

"You don't think we can just call her the Dog?" Ethan says as he goes around to his side.

"No, I think she deserves a noble name. Something epic. Grandiose."

"A big name for a small dog," Ethan offers.

I nod. "Exactly."

Ethan starts driving. We think for a minute, and then I'm convinced I've got it. "Charlemagne," I say. "She's little Charlemagne."

"Charlemagne was a man," Ethan says. "Does that matter?"

"But doesn't it sort of sound more like a woman's name?"

Ethan laughs. "Now that you mention it, yes. All right, well, there you go, Charlemagne it is. Tomorrow, Charlemagne, we're going to find your owner and make someone very happy. But tonight you belong with us."

When we get through the front door of Ethan's apartment, I finally let her go. She immediately starts running around, zipping through the rooms. We watch her, stunned by her energy, until she finally gets a running start and jumps onto the bed. She curls up in the corner.

"I can't keep her," he says to me. "Not that you're saying you think I should, I just . . . want to be clear about that. I can't have pets in my building."

I shake my head. "No, I know. We'll find her real owners tomorrow. Maybe I'll take a bus to a vet first thing."

"I can give you my car," he says. "I could get a ride from someone."

"It's OK," I say. "Since I'm going to take this job with Carl, I have to get a car anyway. I'll turn her in at the vet in the morning and then maybe take a cab or a bus to a few dealerships, see about buying a car."

"You're taking a job," he says. "You're buying a car."

"Yeah," I say.

"You're putting down roots."

"I guess I am."

He smiles at me, holding my gaze much longer than necessary. "With a dog in the bed, I'm guessing we're not gonna get busy," he jokes.

"Probably not."

He shrugs. "Well," he says, his eyes focused on me, "I guess this relationship will have to be about more than just sex. Are you OK with that?"

I smile. I can't help myself. "I suppose I could focus on your mind for once."

He laughs and takes off his shirt. He unzips his pants and flings them onto a chair. "This is as unsexy as I get," he says. "Now, I know it's still really sexy, but . . ."

"I'll try to control myself," I say.

"That'd be best."

Ethan pulls back the covers and gets into bed wearing just his boxers. I undress and pick up his T-shirt from the floor. I slip it over my shoulders and get in next to him.

"You're not sexy at all," Ethan says. "Not one bit."

"No?" I ask doubtfully.

"Pssh, if you think I'm thinking about how great your breasts look in my T-shirt, you are dead wrong. Not having sex with you is the easiest thing I've ever done."

I laugh and curl up into him. Charlemagne is nestled somewhat in the middle. We can barely fit, the three of us. But we make it work.

"Oh, wait," I say just as Ethan turns out the light. "Turn the light back on."

"OK?" he says, and he does.

I hop out of bed and find the list I made earlier this afternoon. I grab a pen and cross out "Get a job."

I hold it up for him. "Only two more to go."

"Ugh," he says, looking at me. "Please get your legs underneath the covers where I can't see them. They're even nicer than your boobs."

I wake up at around two in the afternoon to an unexpected treat.

"Surprise!" Tina says as she and Carl walk into the room. Gabby trails in behind them with an apologetic look on her face. Tina has brought a vase full of some of the nicest flowers I've ever seen.

Flowers, flowers, flowers. Would it kill someone to bring me chocolates?

"They made me promise not to warn you," Gabby says.

Carl rolls his eyes and comes closer to me. "Surprises are better," he says. He leans down and hugs me lightly. Tina is right behind him. As he moves out of the way, she takes position. She smells like vanilla.

"Thank you both for coming."

"Are you kidding?" Tina says. "Gabby has had to hold us back from visiting sooner. If I had my druthers, I'd have been here days ago and not left the room."

She puts the vase of flowers on the table, next to the others.

Carl sits himself right down in the chair next to me. "How are you?" he says. He looks at me intently, with compassion, sympathy, and expertise. I'm not sure if he's asking as a friend, a father figure, or a physician.

"I'm OK," I say.

"Try to move your toes for me," he says, looking intently at the foot of the bed.

"Dad!" Gabby says. "You're not her doctor. Dr. Winters has been doing a fabulous job."

"You can't have too many doctors looking at a patient," Carl says. "Hannah, try to move your toes."

I don't want to try to move my toes.

"Later, Dad," Gabby says. "OK? You're making Hannah uncomfortable."

"Hannah, am I making you uncomfortable?"

What am I supposed to say to that? *Yes, you're making me uncomfortable?* Actually, screw it, yes, life is too short to go around lying.

"Yeah," I say. "A little. It's hell being in this bed, dealing with this body right now. I'd love to just forget about my toes for a few minutes."

Carl looks me in the eye and then nods and looks at Gabby. He puts his hands up. "My apologies! We'll put it on the back burner." I think he's done, but then he speaks up again. "Just make sure you're giving that doctor a challenge now and again. Make sure she's working hard for you, has you as a priority."

"Will do," I say. When he winks at me, I wink back.

"So," Tina says, "has Gabby told you about our dog, Barker? I'm completely in love with this guy. Anywhere I go, I insist that people look at pictures."

She moves toward me with her cell phone and gives Gabby a smile. She doesn't care about me looking at Barker. She is trying to change the subject so Carl doesn't keep going.

"I keep trying to persuade Gabby to get a Saint Bernard just like him," Tina says as she swipes through picture after picture of Barker in various rooms of their house.

"I know," Gabby says, "but Mark's allergic to dogs. It's a whole thing."

We talk for a while, catching up on what I've been up to, what they've been up to, the three of us making fun of Gabby. And then they start to head out. I appreciate that they came but aren't staying long. They seem to understand perfectly the toll that being around other people can take on someone in the hospital.

"When you get out of here," Tina says, "and you're feeling up for it, I want to talk to you about a lawsuit."

"A lawsuit?"

Tina looks to Gabby for permission to continue talking, and Gabby subtly grants it.

"Gabby has filled me in on the situation with the person who hit you, and I talked to a friend of mine who is an ADA."

I don't know whether to be ashamed or proud of the fact that I know that an ADA is an assistant district attorney because of all the *Law & Order* I've been watching.

"OK," I say.

"They have the woman who hit you. She's being charged with a hit-and-run."

"Well, that's good, right?"

"Yeah," Carl says, nodding. "Very good."

"But we wanted to put something in your head. Your medical bills are going to be significant," Tina says. "I'm sure you've spoken to your parents about this, and we don't want to step on anyone's toes, but we want you to know that we will help you, if you need help paying for them."

"What?" I say.

"Only if you need it," Carl says. "We just want you to know that we're here, as a resource, if you need us."

"And," Tina says, "we will help you file a lawsuit against this woman if that's what you decide to do."

I'm overwhelmed by the generosity and thoughtfulness of the Hudsons. "Wow," I say. "I'm . . . I don't know what to say."

Tina grabs my hand. "Don't say anything. It was just important to us that you knew. We will always have your back."

"As far as we're concerned, you're an honorary Hudson," Carl says. "But you already know that, right?"

I look at him and nod, with full honesty.

Carl and Tina go to the door, and Gabby walks them out. When she gets back into the room, I'm staring at the ceiling, trying to process all of it. I hadn't thought about medical bills. I hadn't thought about the person who did this to me.

Someone *did this* to me.

Someone is to blame.

Someone made me lose the baby I didn't know I had.

"You OK?" Gabby asks.

I look at her. I shake it off. "Yeah," I say. "I am. Your parents are . . . I mean, they're . . . they're incredible."

"They love you," Gabby says, sitting down in the chair.

"Do you really think I should sue?"

Gabby nods. "Yeah," she says. "No doubt about it."

"I'm not the suing type," I say, although what do I think that means, exactly?

"I saw it happen, Hannah. That lady hit you while you were in the crosswalk with a walk signal. There was no mistaking what happened. She knew she hit someone. And even then, she did not stop. She kept driving. So knowing that this woman drove away from the scene of a crime that could have been deadly, knowing that she made no attempt to help you or call an ambulance, I think she deserves not just to go to jail but also to make personal amends for what she has done." Gabby's angry. "If you ask me, she can go fuck herself."

"Jesus, Gabby."

She shrugs. "I don't care how it sounds. I hate her."

For a moment, I try to put myself in Gabby's shoes. She watched me get hit by a car. She watched me fall to the ground. She watched me pass out. And she probably thought I might die right there in front of her. And suddenly, I hate that woman, too. For putting her through that. For putting me through this. For all of it.

"OK," I say. "Will you look into it? Or, I mean, tell your mom that I said it was OK?"

"Sure," she says.

"It's a shame *Law & Order* doesn't cover civil suits. Then I'd probably be so well versed in it I could represent myself."

Gabby laughs and then gets up as she sees my parents and Sarah come in. Sarah is dressed in black linen pants with a cotton T-shirt and a gauzy sweater. Even if she didn't have a suitcase with her, you'd know she was headed to the airport.

"All right," Gabby says, kissing me on the cheek. "You're in good company. I'll be back tomorrow." She hugs my family and takes off.

My family didn't tell me they were flying back to London today, so it's a bit of a surprise. But if I'm being completely honest, it's also an immense relief. I love my family. It's just that having them around takes energy I simply don't have right now. And the idea of spending tomorrow without having to entertain company, just Gabby and myself, feels as close to a good day as I'm going to get.

"You guys are off?" I ask. My tone is appropriately sorrow-ful. I make an effort not to allow my inflection to go up at the end of the question, weighing it down so the words stay even.

My mom sits down next to me. "Just Sarah is, honey," she says. "Your father and I aren't going anywhere."

I can feel my smile turn to a frown, and I catch myself. I smile wider. I am a terrible daughter, wanting them to go. "Oh, cool," I say.

Sarah leaves her suitcase by the door and comes around to the other side of me. My father is looking up at the TV. *Jeopardy!* is on.

"I'm so sorry I have to leave," Sarah says. "I've already taken so much time off, and I can't miss any more. I'll lose my part."

"Oh, it's totally fine," I tell her. "I'm going to be fine. There's no need for anyone to stay."

Hint.

"Well, your mother and I certainly aren't leaving anytime soon," my dad says as he finally pulls his attention away from the TV. "We're not leaving our little Hannah Savannah while she's still healing."

I smile, unsure what to say. I wonder if he still calls me Hannah Savannah, as if I were a child, because he really only knows me as a child. He doesn't know me very well as an adult. Maybe it's his way of convincing himself I haven't changed much since they left for London, as if time stood still and he didn't miss anything.

"My flight leaves in a few hours, but I still have time to hang out for a little bit," Sarah says.

Jeopardy! begins Double Jeopardy, and my dad takes a seat, enraptured.

We all listen as one of the contestants chooses the topic "Postal Abbreviations."

"Ugh, so boring," Sarah says.

I wish they would change the channel. I don't want to watch *Jeopardy!* I want to watch *Law & Order.*

Alex Trebek's voice is unmistakable. "This Midwestern state is the only one whose two-letter postal abbreviation is a preposition."

At this, my father throws his hand up and says, "Oregon!"

My mother shakes her head. "Doug, they said Midwestern. Oregon is in the Pacific Northwest."

I'm tempted to mention that *or* is not a preposition, but I don't.

"What is Indiana?" the contestant answers.

"That is correct."

My father slaps his knee. "I was close, though."

He wasn't close. He wasn't close at all. He's so clueless sometimes. He's so absolutely clueless.

"Yeah, OK, Dad," Sarah says.

And the way she says it, the effortlessness of their interactions, as if they are all comfortable saying whatever comes into their own heads, highlights how out of place I feel in my own hospital room when they are here.

I just . . . can't do this. I don't want my family to stay here with me. I want to be left in peace, to heal.

I'm supposed to take it easy in the hospital. I'm supposed to rest. But being with them is not easy, and this is not rest.

Sarah's car is ready to take her to the airport shortly after *Jeopardy!* ends. She grabs her bag and comes over to me, hugging me gently. It's a halfhearted hug, not because she doesn't mean it but because I can't really hug anyone at the moment.

Then she turns to my parents. She hugs them each goodbye.

"You have your passport accessible?" my mom asks her.

"Yeah, I'm good."

"And George is picking you up at Heathrow?" my dad asks.

"Yeah."

There's a stream of questions about logistics and *Did you remember* type things, followed by *I'll miss yous* and *I love yous* all around.

Then she's gone. And it's just my parents and me.

It's never just my parents and me.

And right this second, looking at them as they look back at me, I realize I have nothing to say to them. I have nothing to talk about, nothing I want to do, nothing I need from them, nothing to give them.

I love my parents. I really, really do. But I love them the way you love the grandmother you aren't as close to, the way you love your uncle who lives across the country.

They are not my support system.

And they need to go.

"You guys should feel free to go home, too," I say, as kindly as my voice will allow.

"Nonsense," my mother says, sitting down. "We're here for you. We're going to be with you every step of the way."

"Yeah," I say. "But I don't need you to be." As much as I try to make it sound casual, it comes out raw and heavy.

The two of them look at me, unsure how to respond, and then my mom starts crying.

"Mom, please don't cry," I say. "I didn't mean—"

"No," she says. "It's fine." She wipes her tears. "Would you excuse me for a moment? I just . . . need to get some water."

And then she's gone. Out into the hallway.

I should have kept my mouth shut. I should have just pretended for a little while longer.

"I'm sorry," I say to my dad. He's not looking at me. He's looking down at the floor. "I really am. I'm sorry I said that."

He shakes his head, still not looking at me. "No, don't be."

He looks up and meets my eye. "We know you don't need us. We know you have a whole life you've managed to create for yourself without us."

Some life.

"I—"

"You don't have to say anything. Your mom has a harder time facing all of this than I do, but I'm glad you said something, honestly. We should talk about it freely, be honest with each other more." He comes closer to me and grabs my hand.

"We screwed up, your mother and I. We screwed up." My dad has strikingly gorgeous green eyes. He's my dad, so I don't often notice, but when he looks at you with the intensity he's looking at me with now, it's hard to ignore. They are green the way blades of grass are green, the way dark emeralds are green. "When we got to London and moved in, both your mother and I realized we had made a huge mistake not bringing you with us. We never should have let you stay in Los Angeles. Never should have left you."

I look away. His green eyes are now starting to glass over. His voice is starting to quiver. I can't handle it. I look at my hands.

"Every time we called you," he continues, "the two of us would get off the phone and cry. But you always seemed fine. So we kept thinking that you were fine. I think that was our biggest mistake. Taking you at your word and not wanting to tell you what to do. I mean, you seemed happy with the Hud-sons. Your grades were good. You got into a good school."

"Right," I say.

"But looking back on it now, I can see that doesn't mean you were fine."

I wait, trying to see if he will elaborate.

"It's a hard thing," he says. "To admit you have failed your child. You know, so many of my friends nowadays are empty-nesters, and they say that the day you realize your kids don't need you anymore is like a punch to the gut. And I never say it, but I always think to myself that knowing your kid doesn't need you may hurt, but knowing your kid did, and you weren't there . . . it's absolutely unbearable."

"It was only a couple of years," I say. "I would have gone to college anyway and left home then."

"And it would have been on your own terms, your own choice. And you would have known that no matter what happened, you could come home. I don't think we ever made that clear to you. That we were your home."

I can't help but cry. I want to hold the tears in. I'm trying so hard to keep them to myself, not to let them bubble over. I do OK for a moment. But, as with a well-matched arm wrestle, one of us eventually goes down. And it's me. The tears win.

I grab my father's hand and squeeze it. It is, I think, the first time in a long time that I don't feel self-conscious around him. I feel like myself.

He pats my hand and looks up at me. He wipes a tear from my eye and smiles. "There's something that your mother and I have been discussing, and we were going to broach it with you when you were feeling better," he says. "But I want to talk to you about it now."

"OK . . ."

"We think you should move to London."

"Me?"

He nods. "I have no doubt that almost losing your life in a car accident makes you assess your life, and let me tell you, almost losing your daughter in a car accident puts things in perspective real quick. We should be a proper family again. I'm lucky to be your father, lucky to have you in my life. I want *more* of you in my life. Your mother thinks the same. We should have asked you years ago, and we just assumed you knew we'd want you there. But I'm no longer assuming anything. I'm asking you to come. Please. We're asking you to move to London."

It's all too much. London. And my dad. And my mom crying out in the hall. And the hospital bed. And . . . everything.

I look down, away from his eyes, and I hope that when I look back up, I'll know how to respond. I just have to look away long enough to figure out what to say.

But nothing comes to me.

So I do what I always do when I'm lost. I deflect. "I don't know, Dad, the weather is better here."

He laughs and smiles wide at me. "You don't like constant clouds and rain?"

I shake my head.

"Promise me you'll think about it?"

"I promise," I say.

"Who knows, maybe London's the city you were meant for all along."

He's joking. He has no idea the significance something like that might have for me.

And then I realize just how odd it is that I've never come up with that idea myself. In all of my traveling, all of my city hopping, I never once set my sights on the city my family lived in. Does that mean it's not the right place for me? Or is it a sign that this is exactly what I needed to finally see, that London is where I should be? I want to follow my fate, but I also sort of don't want to go to London.

"I'm going to ask you a question," he says. "And I need you to be completely honest with me. Don't worry about how you're going to make your mother and me feel. I want you to worry only about you and what you need."

"OK," I say.

"I'm serious, Hannah."

"OK."

He speaks with a gravity that takes me by surprise. "Would it be easier on you if we left?"

There it is. What I want. In my lap. But I'm not sure I'm capable of reaching out and grabbing it. I don't know if I can bear to say it out loud, to tell my father that I need him to leave, especially after the conversation we've just had.

My dad interjects before I can formulate a response. "I'm not worried about my feelings or your mom's feelings. I'm worried about you. You are my only concern. You are all I care about. And all I need from you is enough information to make the right decision for my daughter. What do you need? Do you need some peace and quiet for now?"

I look at him. I can feel my lip quiver. I can't say it. I can't bring myself to say it.

My dad smiles, and with that smile, I know that he's not going to make me say it. He nods, taking my nonresponse as an answer. "So, it's good-bye for now," he says. "I know it doesn't mean you don't love us."

"I do love you," I say.

"And we love you."

We've said it many times to each other, but this time, this particular time, I can feel it in my chest.

"All right, let me go break the news to your mother."

"Oh, I'm so sorry," I say, putting my hands to my face. I feel terrible.

"Don't be. She's tougher than she realizes sometimes. And she just wants what's best for you."

He slips out into the hallway. Momentarily alone, I find myself tense and tearful.

Soon the door opens, and my parents come in. My mom can't say anything. She just looks at me and runs to me, wrapping her arms around my shoulders.

"We're gonna go," she says.

"OK," I say.

"I love you," she says. "I love you so much. The day you were born, I cried for six hours straight, because I had never loved anyone that much in my life. And I never stopped. OK? I never stopped."

"I know, Mom. I love you, too."

She wipes her tears, squeezes my hand, and lets my father hug me.

"I'm proud of you," he says. "Proud of the person you are."

"Thanks, Dad."

And then that's it. They walk to the door.

My dad turns back to me. "Oh," he says, "I almost forgot."

He picks up a box he left on the counter when he walked in. He hands it over to me.

I open it. It's a cinnamon roll from Primo's. The glaze is stuck to the box, and the dough has started to unravel.

"You remembered," I say. It's such a thoughtful gift, such a tender gesture, that I know I'm going to start crying again if he doesn't leave this minute.

He winks at me. "I'd never forget a thing like that."

And then he's gone out the door, to join my mother and sister. They'll take a cab to LAX and then fly across the country, over the Atlantic, and land at Heathrow.

And I'll stay here.

And I can honestly say that until this moment, I never realized how much my parents have always, always loved me.

Since Ethan left for work, I've been sitting here with Charlemagne trying to figure out what vet to take her to and what bus route to use.

I puked again this morning, shortly after he left. I was feeling sort of queasy when I woke up, and then I thought I felt better, so I opened his fridge to see if there was anything for breakfast. I picked up a package of bacon, and the smell made me sick to my stomach. I threw up and ended up feeling much better. Suddenly, I was starving, which was when I remembered the cinnamon rolls.

I grabbed one for me and one for Charlemagne, but I thought better of it. She's a little thing, after all. So I ripped hers in half, giving one half to her on the floor and adding the other to my plate. I wolfed all of it down in three big bites. Then I ate another one.

In college, during the few times I got so drunk I puked, I always immediately felt hungry afterward. It was as if my body had gotten rid of everything bad and wanted to replace it with something delicious. I'd get up in the morning, go to Dunkin' Donuts, and inhale a cinnamon cake doughnut, the closest thing they had to what I wanted. Some things don't change, I guess.

Now Charlemagne and I are on the couch. She's cuddled up in my lap as I'm leaning over her, trying to figure out if dogs are allowed on public buses. I don't see anything definitive on the Web site, so I close my computer and decide just to take on the day and see where it leads me. If they won't let her on the bus, I'll figure something out.

I lock Ethan's apartment door and head outside. First things first. Charlemagne needs a collar and a leash if I'm going to get her across town. I walk to Target, which isn't all that far from Ethan's place. I have Charlemagne bundled in my arms. I expect someone to stop me here in the store, but no one even bats an eyelash. I had this whole plan to claim she was a service animal, but it isn't necessary. I grab a collar and a leash and head to the register. The cashier looks at me sideways but doesn't say anything. I act as if it's perfectly normal to be holding a dog in a store. In general, I find that when you are doing something you are not supposed to be doing, the best course of action is to act as if you are absolutely supposed to be doing it.

Once I put a collar on her and attach the leash, I decide to go with the same tactic on the bus. I act confident as I wait for the bus to arrive. When it does, I get on during a rush of people, hoping this will distract the bus driver.

No such luck.

"You can't have that dog on here," the bus driver says.

"She's a service dog," I say.

"Doesn't have a service tag," the driver says.

I start to answer, but he cuts me off.

"Wouldn't matter anyway. No dogs."

"OK," I say. I want to debate this a bit and see if I can per-suade him to let us on, but my mind is blank, and I'm holding up the line. "Thanks," I say as I get off.

I'm getting this dog to the animal hospital if it's the last thing I do.

I walk back to Target. I go in, again with my head tall, holding Charlemagne in my arms. I head right for the school supplies and buy a backpack. I go back to the same cashier, the one I know won't say anything, and I have her ring me up.

"You're not supposed to have dogs in here," she says. "That'll be fourteen eighty-nine."

"Thanks," I say, pretending I didn't hear that first part. I quickly head out, walk around the corner, and put the bag down on the sidewalk. I lift Charlemagne and put her into the bag, and then I zip it up, leaving a hole at the top for her to breathe.

I walk around to the bus station and wait for another bus. When it comes, I walk on as if I have a backpack full of books, not filled with a tiny terrier. Between my attitude and the fact that Charlemagne doesn't bark, we're golden. I take a seat in the far back. I gently put the bag down at my feet and unzip it a bit more. She waits quietly at the bottom of the backpack. She doesn't make a sound.

I keep her at my feet. She sleeps for most of the ride, and when she's not sleeping, she's just looking up at me sweetly, with her kind face and her huge eyes. Her face is shaggier than the rest of her. She needs a bath. I'm glad she's not begging to be let out of the backpack, glad she's not trying to sit in my lap or play. She has the sort of face that makes you want to jump through hoops to please her, and I don't want us to get kicked off the bus.

We pass street after street, and we've been on the bus for quite a while. Just when I think I've gotten on the wrong bus, that this all has been for nothing, I see the animal hospital up ahead.

I hit the button to request the stop, and soon the bus is

starting to pull over. I stand up, picking up the backpack gently and heading for the double doors in the back of the bus. I'm standing there, waiting for them to open, when Charlemagne starts barking.

I stare at the doors, willing them to open. They don't. Everyone is staring. I can feel their eyes on me, but I refuse to look at anyone to confirm.

I see the driver start to turn around to find the source of the noise, but the doors open up, and I run off the bus. Once we are on the sidewalk, I grab Charlemagne out of the bag. Some of the people on the bus watch us through the window. The bus driver glares at me. But then the bus is off again, crawling down the streets of Los Angeles at a snail's pace, while Charlemagne and I are standing free as birds, just a block from the animal hospital.

"We did it!" I say to her. "We fooled them all!"

She puts her head down on my shoulder and then reaches up and licks my cheek.

I put her down, her leash firmly in my hand, and we make our way toward the building and into the lobby.

There are dogs everywhere. It smells like a kennel in here. Why do cats and dogs have that same musky odor? Individually, they aren't so bad, but the minute you get a group together, it's . . . pungent.

"Hi," I say to the receptionist.

"How can I help you?" she asks.

"I found a dog on the street last night, and I wanted to find out if she's chipped."

"OK," she says. "We are a bit tied up at the moment, but sign in here, and I'll see if we can get that done sooner rather than later." She points me toward a clipboard. Under *Dog's Name*, I put "Charlemagne," and under *Pet Owner* I put my own name, even though her name's probably not really Charlemagne and I'm not really her owner.

"Ma'am?" the receptionist calls to me.

"Yes?"

"No one will be able to help you until six," she says.

"Six?"

"Yeah," she says. "I'm sorry. We've had a few unexpected procedures. We're backed up all afternoon. You're welcome to take the dog home and come back."

I think about putting Charlemagne back into the bag, getting onto the bus, and then doing it all over again this evening. I have no doubt that Charlemagne and I would put up a good fight, but eventually, the bus drivers of Los Angeles are going to be on to us.

"Can I leave her here? And meet the doctor here at six?" It makes me sad to think that she'd be here without me. But that's sort of the point, right? I'm trying to find out who Charlemagne belongs to. Because she *doesn't* belong to me.

The receptionist is already shaking her head. "I'm sorry. We can't do that. People in your position often come and leave the dog, and then they don't come back, and we end up having to put the dog in a shelter."

"OK," I say. "I get it."

She whispers softly to me, "If you leave a large deposit, even a credit card, I can often persuade the vet techs to make room in the kennels. I mean, since we know you'll be coming back."

"You're saying you want collateral?" I ask her, a joking tone to my voice.

She nods, very politely, demurely.

I pull out my wallet and take out my credit card. The receptionist stands up and puts her hands out, ready to take Charlemagne, but I find her much harder to part with than my MasterCard.

"It's OK," the receptionist says to Charlemagne. "We're gonna take good care of you for a few hours while Mommy runs some errands."

"Oh," I say. "Sorry. I'm not her . . . mommy." The word is almost laughable, the thought that I am anyone's, anything's, *mommy*.

"Oh, I know," she says. "But you're her person at the moment, so . . ."

"Still," I say, "I don't want to confuse her."

And then I pick up my wallet and walk out the front door without looking anyone in the eye, because that is the dumbest thing I've ever said. The problem is not that I don't want to confuse the *dog*. The problem is that I don't want to confuse *myself*.

I walk outside and grab my phone. I look for car dealerships in the area. No sense in wasting time. There is a cluster of three dealerships just a mile and a half down the road. I start walking.

I'm going to cross one more thing off my list today.

Soon I might just be a functioning human being.

I called Gabby right after my family left. I told her my dad said I should move to London.

She asked me how I felt about it, and I told her I wasn't sure.

Even though I haven't lived in the same place as Gabby for very long, I somehow can't imagine living that far away from her again.

"You have a lot going on right now," Gabby said. "Just try to get some sleep, and we can go over the pros and cons when you're ready."

When I put down the phone, I did exactly what she said. I fell asleep.

I woke up a little bit ago and looked at the clock: two a.m.

"You're up," Henry says as he walks into my room. "You were asleep earlier."

"Snoring better or worse than Gabby was the other night?"

"Oh, worse," he says. "Definitely worse."

I laugh. "Well, can't you people do something about that? Some sort of surgery?"

"I wouldn't worry too much about it," he says, coming toward me. "You've been through enough, don't you think?" He marks things down on my chart.

"How am I doing?" I ask.

He pops the chart back down and clicks his pen. "You're

good. I think tomorrow they'll put you in the wheelchair and get you mobile."

"Wow!" I say. "Really?" How quickly in life you can go from taking walking for granted to one day being amazed that someone might let you sit in a wheelchair.

"Yeah," he says. "So that's exciting, right?"

"You bet your ass it is," I say.

"Somebody bring you a pastry?" Henry says. His deep blue scrubs are a flattering color. I don't mean that they specifically flatter him. I just mean I've noticed most of the nurses wear a sort of rose pink or light blue. But the navy blue he has is just much more attractive. If I were a nurse, I'd wear dark blue scrubs, sunup to sundown.

"Yeah," I say. I can't believe I forgot. I immediately grab the box. "My dad brought me a cinnamon roll."

"Oh, man, my weak spot," Henry says. "I don't have much of a sweet tooth, but I love a good cinnamon roll."

I am so eager to express my own love for cinnamon rolls that I stumble over my words. "That's what . . . I am . . . you love? . . . Me, too."

He laughs at me.

"I mean, I love cinnamon rolls. I have a cinnamon roll problem," I say.

"No such thing," he says.

Now that we are talking about it, I'm finding it impossible not to eat some of it right now. I open the box and pull off a piece. "You want some?" I ask.

"Oh, that's OK," Henry says.

"You sure? My dad got this from Primo's. I'd argue it's one of the best cinnamon rolls in all of Los Angeles."

He puts his pen into his shirt pocket. "You know what? OK. I'd actually love a bite."

I hand him the box. He picks off a small piece.

"Oh, come on," I say. "Take a real piece."

Henry laughs and takes a bigger piece. "I'm pretty sure this is How to Interact with Patients 101: Do Not Take Their Food."

I laugh. "Nobody's perfect."

"No," he says, chewing. "I suppose not." And then he adds, "Damn, that's good."

"Right? I don't want to brag, but I consider myself a cinnamon roll connoisseur."

"I'm starting to believe it," he says.

"Maybe I should start dropping hints to my visitors that I want more cinnamon rolls. I can probably get us a pretty good stash."

"Tempting," he says. "You feeling OK?"

The minute he says it, I remember who we really are, why we are really here, and I fall back down to earth just the littlest bit.

"Yeah," I say. "I am. Each day feels a little bit better."

"Think you'll feel ready to get into the wheelchair tomorrow? It can be painful, moving around for the first time, being lifted, all of that. You up for it?"

"Are you kidding me? I'm up for anything."

"Yeah," he says. "That's what I thought."

He heads toward the door and then stops. "If you love cinnamon rolls as much as I do, then I'll bet you also love churros. Have you had a churro?"

I give him an indignant look. "Are you kidding me? Have *I* had a churro? I'm from Los Angeles. I've had a churro."

"Oh, well, excuse me . . . Sassypants."

I start laughing. "Sassypants?"

He laughs, too. "I don't know where that came from. It just popped out of my mouth. I'm as stunned as you are."

I start laughing so hard that my eyes water. My whole body is convulsing. You realize when your body is broken just how much of it you use to laugh. But I can't stop laughing. I don't want to stop laughing.

"I guess it was a little weird of me to say," he says.

"A little?" I say between breaths.

He laughs at himself with me.

And then, suddenly, there's a shooting pain down my leg. It is sharp, and it is deep, and it is gut-wrenching. My laughter stops immediately. I cry out.

Henry rushes toward me.

The pain doesn't stop. It hurts so badly I can't breathe. I can't talk. I look down at my feet and see that the toes on my right foot are clenched. I can't unclench them.

"It's OK, you're OK," he says. He moves toward my IV. "You're gonna be OK in a second, I promise." He comes back to me. He grabs my hand. He looks into my eyes. "Look at me," he says. "C'mon, look at me. The pain is gonna go away in a second. You're having a spasm. You just have to bear through it. It's gonna be OK."

I move my gaze to his face. I focus on him through the pain. I look into his eyes, and he stares into mine.

"You got this," he says. "You got this."

And then the pain begins to fade away.

My toes straighten.

My body relaxes.

I can breathe easily.

Henry moves his hands out of mine. He slides them up my arms to my shoulders. "You OK?" he says. "That had to hurt."

"Yeah," I say. "Yeah, I'm OK."

"It's good we are going to get you up and moving soon. Your body needs to be up and about."

"Yeah," I say.

"You did great."

"Thanks."

"You gonna be OK? On your own?"

"Yeah," I say. "I think so."

"If it happens again, just hit the button, and I'll be here." He takes his hands off me. With one swift motion, so subtle I'm almost not sure it happened, he moves a fallen hair out of my face. "Get some rest. Tomorrow is going to be a big day."

"OK," I say.

He smiles and heads out the door. At the very last second, he pops his head back in. "You're badass, you know that?"

I say, "You probably say that to all your patients," and then when he leaves, I think, *What if he doesn't? What if he only says that kind of stuff to me?*

M a'am," the dealer says to me. We are sitting at his desk. I've already made my decision. "Are you sure you don't want a *new* car? Something fun? Something a bit more . . . your style?"

I'm considering a used Toyota Camry. The dealer keeps trying to get me to look at this bright red Prius. Admittedly, I'd rather have the bright red Prius. There might have been a time in my life when I would have said "Screw it" and used all my money on the down payment for the Prius, forcing myself to figure out the rest when it came time. Because I love that red Prius.

But I'm trying to make new decisions so that they lead me to better places.

"The Camry's fine," I say. I already test-drove it. I've asked all the right questions. They want ninety-five hundred dollars for it. I tell him I'll give him seventy-five hundred. We go back and forth. He gets me up to eight. He keeps going to his manager to get new negotiating numbers. Eventually, the manager comes over and whines about how little I am willing to pay for the car.

"If I sell it to you for less than eighty-five hundred, I won't make any money off the deal," he says. "You know, we need to make money. We can't just be giving cars away."

"OK," I say. "I guess we can't make this work." I get up out of the chair and grab my purse.

"Sweetheart," the manager says, "don't be crazy."

This is why Gabby has to keep talking about women's rights and gender equality. It's because of dipshits like this.

"Look, I told you I'd pay eight thousand even. Take it or leave it."

Carl is an excellent negotiator. Really cutthroat. When I was a senior, Carl would take either Gabby or me to do all of his negotiating so we learned how to haggle. Mechanics, salesmen, plumbers, you name 'em, Carl made us negotiate prices with them directly. When Carl's Jeep needed a new set of wheels, he stood out around the corner from the shop as I went in and tried to talk the guy down on his behalf. When I'd go back out to him to report the new price, Carl would shake his head and tell me I could do better. And I always did. I was especially proud when the tire guy threw in a free car detailing after my prodding. Gabby once got the guy repairing the hot-water heater to come down five hundred bucks. Carl and Tina took us out to Benihana that night to celebrate the victory.

Carl has always said that people who don't haggle are suckers. And we aren't suckers.

"I'm buying a car today. Doesn't have to be from you," I say to the manager.

The manager rolls his eyes. "All right, all right," he says. "Eighty-one hundred, and it's a deal."

I shake his hand, and they start drawing up the paperwork. I put three thousand down and drive off the lot with a car. There goes most of my money. But it's OK. Because I have a plan.

When I get far enough from the dealership, I pull over to the side of the road and start hitting my hands against the steering wheel, yelling into the air, trying to get out all the nervous energy that's in me.

I'm doing this. I'm making a life for myself. I am *doing* this.
I call Carl at his office.

"Hello!" he says, his voice buttery and pleased to hear from
me. "Tell me you're taking the job."

"I'm taking the job."

"Outstanding. I'm going to put you on the phone with
Joyce, our HR person here. She will talk to you about a start
date, salary, benefits, all of that good stuff. If you don't talk
her up to at least forty-two, I'm going to be disappointed in
you."

I laugh. "I just paid eighty-one hundred for a ninety-five-
hundred-dollar car. I got this. I promise."

"That's what I want to hear!" he says.

"Carl, seriously, thank you for this."

"Thank *you*," he says. "Honestly. This worked out perfectly.
Rosalie showed up an hour and a half late this morning and
didn't even bother with an excuse. She denies it, but a patient
told me last week that she swore at them. So I'm eager to let
her go, and I'm just glad we don't have to go through résumés
to replace her."

I laugh. "All right," I say. "I'm excited to start working with
you . . . *boss*."

He laughs and puts me through to Joyce. She and I talk
for about thirty minutes. She says she's going to give Rosalie
notice. So my start date will be in two weeks. But if Rosalie
decides not to stay the two weeks, the job could start sooner. I
tell her I'm OK with that.

"That's why sometimes it really is best to hire someone you
know," Joyce says. "I know I'm in HR and I'm supposed to say
that you should vet all the applicants, but the truth is, when

you have a personal connection, it just makes it easier to be flexible."

She offers me forty thousand, and, hot off the trail of my car purchase, I talk her up to forty-four. I get full health benefits. "And the good news," she says, "is that we cover the rest of your family at a very low cost."

"Oh," I say. "Well, it's just me."

"Oh, OK," she says. "And you'll have two weeks' paid vacation a year and, of course, maternity leave if necessary."

I laugh. "Won't be necessary," I say.

She laughs back. "I hear you."

We finish discussing odds and ends, and soon everything is settled.

"Welcome to Hudson, Stokes, and Johnson Pediatrics," she says.

"Thank you," I say. "Glad to join."

I know he's still working, but I find it impossible not to call Ethan.

"What's up, buttercup?" he says. I'm surprised he answered.

"Do you have a minute?"

"Sure," he says. "Let me just step outside."

I can hear him walk through a door, and the background quiets down.

"What's up?"

"You'd better not ever try to negotiate with me," I tell him. "Because I just talked the car salesman *down* fourteen hundred dollars, and I talked the human resources lady *up* four thousand. So basically, I'm a force to be reckoned with."

Ethan laughs. "A car owner and a job . . . haver."

"You're damn right."

"And did you find Charlemagne's home?"

"They can't see her until six," I say. "So I bought the car, and now I'm headed back. I'm thinking I'll just kill some time in the waiting room, see if the doctor doesn't free up early."

"Six?"

"Yeah. She's there now. I had to leave a credit card so they'd keep her there until I get back."

Ethan laughs again. "What, like collateral?"

"That's exactly what I said!"

He laughs. "Listen, I'm leaving here in a half hour. What part of town are you in? I'll come meet you."

"Oh, that would be awesome!" I say. "I'm in West L.A. The vet is off of Sepulveda."

"Jesus, that's far from my house," he says. "You took a bus there?"

"Yeah," I say.

"With Charlemagne?"

"I may or may not have hidden her in a backpack."

Ethan laughs. "Why don't I come meet you and we can grab an early dinner? Find a happy hour somewhere. I know of a Mexican place close to the animal hospital. I could buy you a celebratory burrito!"

"I'm in!"

I get lost more than once on my way there. Then I try to take an alley, only to realize there is a big truck coming at me from the opposite direction. I have to reverse out slowly and blindly back onto the street and find another way. But I get there eventually. That's me in a nutshell. I'll get there eventually.

I pull into the parking lot of the restaurant, and Ethan is waiting for me by the entrance.

"Is this the new car?" he says dramatically. "I like it. Unexpected. I thought for sure you'd pull up in something cherry red."

I laugh at him. "I'm way more into practical decisions nowadays," I say. "Stable guys, full-time jobs . . ."

"Stray dogs," he adds.

I laugh and correct him. "I am merely helping Charlemagne find her true family," I say as we head into the restaurant. "But the stable guy and the full-time job, those are . . ." I find myself intending to finish the sentence by saying "for keeps," but I quickly realize I don't want to do that.

It's too early to be talking about how serious Ethan and I are or may be in the future. We have a history together, and we have potential to be something very real, but we just started dating again. I think the best thing to do is allow myself to imagine the future in my head but not put it into words just yet.

Which is to say that I think it's very possible that Ethan is the one for me. But I'd rather be dead than say it out loud.

Luckily, Ethan appears to be on the exact same page, because he looks at me, grabs my hand, squeezes it, and says, "I hear you."

The hostess asks if we want to be seated in the dining room or at the bar, and we go for the bar. As we sit down, Ethan orders guacamole.

"I'm very proud of you," he says when the waitress leaves.

"Thank you," I say. "I'm proud of me, too. I mean, I didn't like where my old habits got me, you know? And I feel really motivated to turn over a new leaf."

I think things have been working out for me so far partly because I have people believing in me. Gabby and the Hudsons and Ethan are so encouraging that it makes me feel I can do all the things I set out to do. In other cities, I never had a true support system. I had plenty of friends and, at times, caring boyfriends. But I don't know that I ever had someone truly believing in me even when I didn't. Now I do. And I think maybe I need someone in my corner in order to thrive. I think I am one of those people who need people. Because my family left and I was OK with it, I always thought that I was more of a lone wolf. I guess I thought I didn't need anyone.

"Well, I admire it," Ethan says.

The waiter sets the guacamole down in front of us. I grab a chip and dip in. But before I can even bring it to my lips, it smells awful. I put the chip down.

"Oh, God," I say. "Is it rancid or something?"

"Uh," Ethan says, genuinely confused. "The guacamole?"

"Smell it," I say. "It smells funky."

"It does?" He dips a chip in, brings it to his nose, and eats it. "It's fine. It tastes great."

I smell it again and can't stand it. I hold my stomach.

"Are you OK?" Ethan asks.

"Yeah," I say. "I just need to get away from that."

"You look really pale. And you're sweating. On your forehead a bit."

Just like last night, a wave of nausea runs through me. My throat constricts and turns sour. I'm not sure I'll be able to hold this in very long. I run at full speed to the bathroom, but I don't make it to the toilet. I puke in the sink. Luckily, it's a private bathroom.

Ethan comes in and closes the door behind us.

"This is the ladies' room," I tell him.

"I'm worried about you," he says.

"I'm fine," I say, although I am seriously starting to doubt that.

"You said you puked last night, too," he says.

"Yeah," I tell him. "And this morning."

"Do you think maybe you have the flu? Should you see a doctor? I mean, why else would you be puking all the time?"

The minute he asks the question, I know I don't have the flu.

I understand perfectly now why everything in my life has been going so well. The universe is just lining everything up in perfect order so that I can roll through and ruin it the way I always do.

Classic Hurricane Hannah.

I'm pregnant.

I wake up to the sound of someone fumbling around in the dark. But I don't see anyone. I only hear them.

"Henry?" I ask.

A figure pops up from the floor.

"Sorry," he says. "I can't find my cell phone. I thought I might have dropped it in here."

"It's weird to think that you're here, hovering over me when I'm sleeping," I tell him.

"I wasn't *hovering*," he says. "I was crawling."

I laugh. "Much worse."

"You didn't see it, right? My phone?" he asks me.

I shake my head.

"Dammit," he says, and I watch as he absentmindedly pulls at a few hair ties around his wrist.

"You told me you'd explain the hair ties," I say. I point to my own head. The one he gave me is the one I'm still using to keep my bun together. Luckily, I can now do it myself with little fanfare. But I still don't have a mirror, so I can't be sure it looks good.

He laughs. "Good memory. A lot of car accident patients struggle to remember basic details."

I shrug. "What can I say? I've always been ahead of the rest."

"I started finding hair ties all over the hospital where I worked back in Texas," he says. I find myself smiling as he sits down. I like that he sits down. I like that he is staying. "And I didn't want to throw them away, because they seemed like they would be useful to somebody, so I started collecting them. But then no one ever asked for one, so they just kept piling up. And then, one day, my boss asked me to do something, and I didn't have a piece of paper to write on, so I put a hair tie around my wrist to remind me, sort of like someone might do with a rubber band. Then I started to do it all the time. And then I started to do it for more than one thing at a time. So if there were four things I needed to remember, four hair ties. If I had two things to do and someone gave me a third task, another hair tie."

"How many times have you stood staring at your wrist trying to remember what one of the hair ties was for?"

He laughs. "Listen, it's not a perfect system." He bends down for a moment. I assume he thinks he sees his cell phone.

He stands back up. He must have been wrong. "Anyway," he says, "that's my hair tie organizational system."

"And the plus is, you have a hair tie for any woman who needs one."

"Right," he says. "But no one has ever asked for one but you."

I smile at him.

"How are you feeling?" he asks me. "OK? No more spasms?"

"No more spasms."

"Good," he says as he looks around the room some more for his phone.

"We could call it," I offer. "Your phone, I mean." There is a hospital phone next to me, on the bed table. I pull it toward me and pick up the receiver. "What's the number?"

I can't quite interpret the look on his face.

"What did I do?" I ask him.

"I can't give you any personal contact information," he says. "It's against the rules."

I am feeling ever so slightly embarrassed. I put the receiver back in the cradle to save face. "Oh, OK. Well, you can dial yourself," I say. "I'll close my eyes."

He laughs and shakes his head. "It won't do much good anyway," he tells me. "The ringer's off."

I can tell that both of us want to change the subject. We just aren't sure how.

"I tried that Find My Phone app," Henry offers.

"Oh, that's great!" I say.

"It said the phone is located at Angeles Presbyterian."

I laugh. "How helpful," I say.

"Well," he says, "if you see it . . ."

"If I see it, I'll ring my little nurse bell."

"And I'll come running," he says.

Neither of us has anything left to say, and yet he doesn't leave. He looks at me. We hold each other's gaze for just a second longer than normal. I look away first. I'm distracted by a dull blueish light that starts flashing in a slow rhythm.

"Eureka!" he says.

I start laughing as he ducks down. When he pops back up with his phone, he's not at the foot of the bed, where he was before. He's by my side. "I knew I'd find it," he says.

Instinctually, I find myself reaching out toward him, to touch him the way I might a friend. But I quickly remember that he's not my friend, that to touch his arm or hand tenderly might be weird. So I pretend I'm going for a high-five. He smiles and enthusiastically claps my hand.

"Nice work," I say.

For a moment, I wonder how things would be different if

I could walk. And we weren't in a hospital but in a bar some-where. If I'd worn my favorite black shirt and tight jeans. I wonder how this all might be different if there was a beer in my hand, and the lights were low because people were danc-ing, not because people were sleeping.

Is it crazy to think he would say hello and introduce him-self? Is it crazy to think he would ask me to dance?

"Anyway, I should be going," he says. "But I'll come check on you soon. I don't like to go too many hours without mak-ing sure you're still breathing." And he leaves before I can say good-bye.

I don't know. Maybe, just maybe, if Henry and I met at a dinner party, we'd spend the entire night talking, and when the night wound down, he'd offer to walk me to my car.

W hat is it?" Ethan asks me. "What's the matter? Are you going to vomit again? What can I do?"

"No," I say, slowly shaking my head. "I'm totally fine now."

I got my period before I left for L.A. I remember getting it. I remember thinking that I was glad it ended a day sooner than normal. I remember that. *I remember that.*

"Totally good," I tell him. "I think maybe those brussels sprouts are still messing with me."

"OK," he says. "Well, maybe we should head home."

I shake my head. "Nope," I tell him. "Let's hang out until we can go talk to the vet about Charlemagne."

"You're sure?"

I look at my phone. I want to run out of here and buy a pregnancy test, but there is no way I could just up and ditch Ethan without him asking what is going on. And I can't share this with him. I can't even bring up the possibility until it's no longer simply a possibility.

"All right," he says. "If you really are feeling OK."

"I am." The lying begins.

"I'll head out first," he says. "Just so no one thinks we were doin' it in here."

His joke catches me off guard, and I find myself laughing out loud. "OK," I say, smiling.

He ducks out, and I stay in the bathroom for a minute.

I breathe in and out, trying to control my brain and my body. And then I pick up my phone and Google the one thing that could convince me I'm wrong about this. The one piece of evidence I have that maybe I'm not pregnant.

can i be pregnant if i got my period

"You cannot have a menstrual period while you are pregnant . . ." My heartbeat slows. I start to calm. This might all just be OK. "But some women do have vaginal bleeding during pregnancy."

I click on another one.

"My cousin didn't know she was pregnant for four months because she got her period all during her pregnancy."

I click again.

"You may still get your period at the beginning of your pregnancy due to what is called implantation bleeding when the egg implants in the uterus."

Crap.

"Typically, the bleeding will be lighter and shorter than a normal period."

I turn off my phone and slump down on the floor.

Despite every piece of common sense available to me, I got pregnant. And it isn't by the handsome, charming, perfect man I'm starting to believe is the one.

It's by the asshole with a wife and two kids in New York City.

I get hold of myself. No good comes from imploding or exploding right now. I breathe in. I open the door. I walk out of the bathroom and join Ethan at the table.

"How should we kill the time?" he asks. "Should we get away from this horrible guacamole and go find you a cinnamon roll?"

He's going to leave me. My perfect person. The man who

jumps at the chance to get me a cinnamon roll. He's going to leave me.

I shake my head. "You know what?" I say. "Let's just order some burritos and chow down."

"Sounds like heaven," he says as he flags down a waiter.

We order. We talk about his job. We make jokes. And we eat tortilla chips.

With every chip I eat and every joke I make, I push the news further into the recesses of my mind. I bury my problems and focus on what is in front of me.

I am great at pretending everything is fine. I am great at hiding the truth. I almost believe it myself for a minute. By the time our burritos have come and gone, you'd think I'd forgotten.

We head to our cars and plan to meet up at the vet.

"You're perfect," Ethan says as he shuts my car door for me. "You know that?" When he says it, it becomes clear just how much I *haven't* forgotten.

"Don't say that," I tell him. "It's not true."

"You're right," he says. "You're too pretty. I need a girl less pretty."

~

When we get back to the animal hospital, the vet is ready to talk to us.

He pulls us into an exam room, and one of the vet techs brings out Charlemagne. She runs right to me.

"There you are!" I say to her. I pick her up and hold her in my arms.

"So you are the ones who found her?" the vet asks us.

"Yeah," Ethan says. "Running through the street."

The vet looks dismayed. "Well, she's not chipped. She is also not spayed. And she's undernourished. She should be about two or three pounds heavier," he says. He is tall, with a thick gray beard and gray hair. "That may not sound like a lot, but on a dog this size . . ."

"Yeah," Ethan says. "It's a considerable deficit."

"Any idea how old she is?" I ask.

"Well, her teeth aren't fully in yet, so she's still a puppy."

"How young, do you think?"

"No more than four months, maybe five," he says. "My guess is that she lives with someone who isn't paying too much attention . . ."

"Right," I say.

"Or it's possible she's been on the street for a while."

I find it hard to believe she's been on the street for a while. Dogs that live out on the street wouldn't run into the middle of the road. That seems to defy the very concept of survival of the fittest. If you are a dog that runs into the middle of the road, especially in the dark of night, then you are probably not going to last long on the mean streets of . . . anywhere.

"A lot of times, people don't spay their dogs," the vet continues, "and are surprised when they end up pregnant."

Ha!

"Caring for a nursing dog and a litter of puppies, when you don't expect to, can be overwhelming."

I'll say.

"Sometimes people keep them until they can't deal with it anymore and put the puppies out on the street."

Good God.

I look at Ethan, who, not knowing how uncomfortably close

this man is hitting the nail on the head, seems disturbed by all of it. Which makes sense. I am, too. I know that people are awful and do terrible things, especially to things that are help-less, especially to animals that are helpless. But when I look at Charlemagne, it's hard to comprehend. I barely know her, and I'm starting to think I'd do anything for her.

"So we have no real recourse," Ethan says. "In terms of find-ing out who she belongs to."

The vet shrugs. "Well, not through this route, at least. You could put fliers up around where you found her or go door-to-door. But either way, if you are at all considering keeping her, I might recommend you do that instead of tracking down an original owner, if there is one."

"Oh," Ethan says, "we weren't—"

"And if we did," I say, interrupting him, "would we just schedule an appointment with you guys to get all of that stuff taken care of? Get her spayed and chipped?"

"Yeah," the vet says. "And she'll need a series of shots. We can help you with fattening her up, too. Although, assuming she has consistent access to food, she'll probably take care of that one on her own."

"All right," Ethan says. "Thank you very much for your help." He extends his hand for a handshake. The vet reciprocates. I do the same.

"My pleasure," he says. "She's a sweetheart. I hope you guys can help her find a good home. If not, contact the front desk, and we can help you try to get her into a no-kill shelter. It's not easy. There are already so many other dogs in the city taking up spots, but we try to help."

By the time we leave the animal hospital, the sun has set, and the air is crisp. I have Charlemagne in my arms, her leash wrapped around my hand. She's shaking a bit, maybe because of the cold. I can't help but wonder if it's because she knows her fate is uncertain.

"What are you thinking?" I ask him.

"I don't know," Ethan says. We are standing by our cars. For a moment, I'm stunned that I bought the car just this afternoon. Feels like a lifetime ago. "I can't really have a dog at my place."

"I know," I say.

"I mean, I want to help her, and I don't want her on the street, but I had no intention of adopting a dog," he says. "And I don't know how you can adopt her, you know? Because . . ."

"Because I don't have a place just yet."

"Right."

He looks at me. I look at Charlemagne. I'm not bringing her to a shelter. I'm not doing it. With everything that has happened today, my fate is uncertain, too. Charlemagne and I are kindred spirits. We are both directionless idiots, the kind of girls who run out into the street without thinking.

I may make a lot of mistakes, and I may act without thinking, and I may be the sort of woman who doesn't even realize she's pregnant when it should be blatantly obvious, but I also know that sometimes I get myself into messes and then get myself out of them. Maybe I can get Charlemagne and me out of this mess by throwing us into it.

Charlemagne and I rode a city bus today with just a backpack and a smile. We are a team. She is mine.

"I'm not letting her go back to people who mistreat her," I say. "Not that we could find them even if we wanted to. And I'm certainly not leaving her out on the street or headed to a kill shelter."

Ethan looks at me. I can tell he understands where I'm

coming from but doesn't necessarily get where I'm heading.
"OK . . ." he says. "So what do we do?"

"I'm going to keep her," I say. "That's what I'm going to do."

She's not his problem. She's my problem. I'm *choosing* to
take care of her.

The parallels do not escape me. And maybe that's part of
the reason I am doing this. Maybe it's a physical manifestation
of what I'm going through emotionally right now.

I have a baby that's not his. I'm taking on a dog he didn't ask
for. I'm not going to make these things his problem.

"OK," he says. "Well, she can stay at my place for tonight,
and then tomorrow we can figure out a long-term plan."

He says "we." *We can figure out a long-term plan.*

"That's all right," I tell him, moving toward my car. "I should
sleep at Gabby's tonight."

"You're not going to stay with me?"

I shake my head. "I should really sleep there. She won't
mind Charlemagne for the night." Yes, she will. Mark is allergic
to dogs. Taking Charlemagne back to their apartment is kind of
a crappy thing to do. But I need space away from Ethan. I need
to be on my own.

"She can be at my place," he says. "For tonight. Really."

I shake my head again, moving away from him. I open my
car door. I put Charlemagne on the passenger's seat and shut
her in.

"No," I tell him. "It's fine. This is the better plan."

"OK," he says. He is clearly dejected. "If that's what you
want."

"I'll call you tomorrow," I tell him.

All he says is "Cool." He says it looking at my feet instead
of my face. He's upset, but he doesn't want to show it. So he

nods and gets into his car. "I'll talk to you tomorrow, then," he says out his window. Then he turns on his lights and drives off.

I get into my car. I look at Charlemagne. Suddenly, the tears that have been waiting under the surface all night spring forth.

"I screwed it all up, Charlemagne," I tell her. "I ruined it all."

She doesn't respond. She doesn't look at me.

"It was all going to be perfect. And I ruined it."

Charlemagne licks her paw, as if I'm not even talking.

"What do I do?" I ask her. If you were watching us from the outside, you might think I expect her to answer. That's how sincere my voice is, how desperate it sounds. And maybe, on some level, it's true. Maybe if, all of a sudden, she started talking and told me what I need to do to fix this, I would be more relieved than shocked.

Alas, she remains a normal dog instead of a magical one. I put my head on the steering wheel of my brand-new used car, and I cry. And I cry. And I cry. And I cry.

And I wonder when I have to tell Michael.

And I wonder when I have to tell Ethan.

And I wonder how I'm going to afford a baby.

And I wonder how I could be so goddamn stupid.

And I wonder if maybe the world hates me, if maybe I am fated to always be screwing up my life and never getting ahead.

I wonder if I'll be a single mom forever. If Ethan will ever talk to me again. If my parents will come meet my kid or if I'll have to fly internationally with a baby on holidays.

And then I wonder what Gabby will say. I imagine her telling me it will all be OK. I imagine her telling me this baby was meant to be. I imagine her telling me that I'm going to be a great mother.

And then I wonder if that's true. If I will be.

And then . . . finally . . . I wonder about my baby.

And the realization hits me.

I'm going to have a baby.

I find myself smiling just the tiniest bit through my heavy, fearful tears.

"I'm going to have a baby," I say to Charlemagne. "I'm going to be a mom."

This time, she hears me. And while she doesn't start magically talking, she does stand up, walk over the center console, and sit in my lap.

"It's you and me," I say. "And a baby. We can do that, right?"

She curls into my lap and goes to sleep. But I think it speaks volumes that I believe if she could talk, she'd say yes.

It's early in the morning when I hear a knock on my door. I'm alone in my room. I've been up for only a few minutes. My bun is half undone around my shoulders.

Ethan peeks his head in. "Hey," he says, so quiet it's almost a whisper. "Can I come in?"

"Of course," I say. It's nice seeing him. I may have gotten a bit infatuated with the idea that he and I have something romantic left between us, but I can see now that we don't. I will probably always love him on some level, always hold a spot for him in my heart. But dating again, being together, that would be moving backward, wouldn't it? I moved to Los Angeles to put the past behind me, to move into the future. I moved to Los Angeles to change. And that's what I'm going to do.

But that doesn't mean that we can't still mean something to each other, that we can't be friends.

I pat the side of the bed, inviting him to sit right here next to me.

He does. "How are you feeling?" he asks. He has a bakery box in his hand. I'm hoping I know what it is.

"Is that a cinnamon roll?" I ask him, smiling.

He smiles back and hands it over.

"You remembered," I say.

"How could I forget?"

"Wow!" I say as I open the box. "This is a huge one."

"I know," he says. "I saw them a few years ago at this bakery on the Westside, and I thought of you. I knew you'd love them."

"This is so exciting! I mean, I'll have to eat this with a knife and fork." It's way too big for me to eat on my own. I resolve to wait and share it with Henry tonight. I hand it back to Ethan. "Can you put it on the table?"

"You don't want it now?"

I do sort of want it now, but I'd rather wait for Henry. I shake my head.

"You didn't answer my question," he says. "About how you are feeling."

I wave him off. "I'm OK. I'm feeling good. There are some ups and downs, but you've caught me at an up moment. Word on the street is I get to try out my wheelchair today." I watch as the look on Ethan's face changes. I get a glimpse, just for a moment, of how sad it must be to hear me excited about a wheelchair. But I refuse to be brought down about this. This is where I'm at in life. I need a wheelchair. *That's* OK. Onward and upward.

Ethan looks off to the side and then down at the floor. He's looking everywhere but at me.

"What's up?" I ask. "What's bothering you?"

"It just all seems so senseless," he says, looking up at me. "The idea of you being hit by a car. Almost losing you. When I heard what happened to you, I immediately thought . . . you know, she should have been with me instead. If I had been able to persuade you to stay out with me, you wouldn't have been standing in the middle of the road when . . . I mean, what if this all could have been prevented if I'd . . . done something different?"

It's sort of absurd, isn't it? How we grab on to facts and consequences looking to blame or exonerate ourselves? This has nothing to do with him. I chose to go home with Gabby and Mark because that's the choice I made. Nine billion choices I've made over the course of my life could have changed where I am right now and where I'm headed. There's no sense focusing on just one. Unless you want to punish yourself.

"I've looked at this problem up, down, and sideways," I tell him. "I've lain in this bed for days wondering if we were all supposed to do something different."

"And?"

"And . . . it doesn't matter."

"What do you mean, it doesn't matter?"

"I'm saying things happen for a reason. I'm saying there's a point to this. I didn't stick around with you that night because I wasn't supposed to. That wasn't what I was meant to do."

He looks at me. He doesn't say anything.

"You know," I continue, "maybe you and I would have gone out that night and stayed out partying and drinking until the early morning. And maybe we could have walked around the city all night, talking about our feelings and rehashing old times. Or maybe we would have left that bar and gone to another bar, where we ran into Matt Damon, and he would say that we seemed like really cool people and he wanted to give us a hundred million dollars to start a cinnamon roll factory."

Ethan laughs.

"We don't know what would have happened. But whatever would have happened wasn't *supposed* to happen."

"You really believe that?" Ethan says.

"I think I have to," I tell him. "Otherwise, my life is an absolute disaster."

Otherwise, my baby is gone for no reason.

"But yes," I say. "I really do believe that. I believe I'm destined for something. We are all destined for something. And I believe that the universe, or God, or whatever you want to call it, I believe it keeps us on the right path. And I believe I was supposed to choose Gabby. I wasn't supposed to stay with you."

Ethan is quiet. And then he looks up at me and says, "OK. It wasn't . . . I guess it wasn't meant to be."

"Besides," I say, trying to make a joke, "let's be honest. If I'd stuck around with you, we'd just have ended up making out and ruining everything. This way is better. This way, we can finally be friends. Good, real friends."

He looks at me, looks me right in the eye. We don't say anything to each other for a moment.

Ethan finally speaks up. "Hannah, I—"

He stops halfway through his sentence when Henry comes walking in the door.

"Oh, sorry," Henry says. "I didn't know you had visitors."

I feel myself perk up at the sight of him. He's wearing the same blue scrubs from last night.

"I thought you were night shift," I say. "Deanna is my day nurse."

"I'm covering," he says. "Just for this morning. I'll come back if I'm interrupting."

"Oh," Ethan says.

"You're not interrupting anything," I say over him.

Ethan gathers himself and looks at me. "You know what? I should be getting to work," he says.

"OK. You'll come visit me again soon?"

"Yeah," he says. "Or maybe you'll be out of here in a few days."

"Yeah," I say. "Maybe."

"Anyway," he says, "enjoy the cinnamon roll."

Henry laughs. "This is a girl who loves her cinnamon rolls," he says.

Ethan looks at him. "I know," he says. "That's why I brought her one."

I took three pregnancy tests in the bathroom of the CVS just down the street from Gabby's place. I could have left Charlemagne in the car, but I felt terrible doing that, even with the windows cracked, so I put her in the backpack and brought her with me. She yipped in the bathroom once or twice, but no one seemed to care.

All three sticks were positive. And there wasn't a single part of me that was surprised.

Now it's almost nine p.m., and I'm pulling up in front of Gabby's. She must hear my car, because she looks out the window. I see her and laugh. She looks like a crotchety old lady. I'm half expecting her to call out, "What's all that racket?"

By the time I open her front door, Charlemagne trailing behind me on the leash, Gabby is standing on the other side of the door. I feel bad about what I'm doing, by the way. I feel bad about bringing a dog into Mark's house. I know he's allergic, and I'm doing it anyway. But I couldn't stay with Ethan. And I couldn't abandon Charlemagne. So here we are.

"You bought a car?" Gabby says. She's in her pajamas.

"Where's Mark?" I ask her. Charlemagne is behind me. I don't think Gabby can see her.

"He's working late again," Gabby says.

"I have some news," I tell her.

"I know, you bought a car."

"Well, I have more news."

Charlemagne yips. Gabby looks at me askance.

I pull Charlemagne around to the front.

"You have a dog?"

"I am adopting her," I tell her. "I'm really sorry."

"You are adopting a dog?"

"Is it OK if she stays here just for tonight? I bought Mark a whole bunch of allergy pills." I take the five packages of medication that I got in the over-the-counter antihistamine aisle.

Gabby looks at me. "Uh . . . I guess?"

"Great. Thank you. I have news."

"You have more news?"

I nod, but Gabby continues to stare at me. I stare back, unsure if she's really prepared for this. Unsure if I'm really prepared for this.

"We should maybe sit down," I tell her.

"I need to sit down for this?"

"*I* need to," I tell her.

We move over to her couch. I pick up Charlemagne and put her in my lap. Quickly, Charlemagne moves off me and sits on the sofa. I see Gabby waver about whether she wants a dog on her sofa, so I pick up Charlemagne and put her on the floor.

"I'm pregnant."

Hearing it out loud, hearing the words come out of my mouth, brings forth a flood of emotions. I start to cry. I bury my head in my hands.

Gabby doesn't say much at first, but soon I feel her hands on my wrists. I feel her pull my hands away from my face. I feel her take her fingers and put them on my chin, forcing me to face her.

"You know it's going to be OK, right?" she says.

I look at her through my tears. I nod and do my best to say "Yes."

"Does Ethan know?" Gabby asks.

I shake my head. "No one does. Except you. And Charlemagne."

"Who is Charlemagne?" she asks me.

I look at the dog and point to her.

"Oh," Gabby says. "Right. Makes sense. I didn't think we were still naming people Charlemagne."

I start crying again.

"Hey," she says. "Come on. This is good news."

"I know," I say through my tears.

"It's Michael's," she says, as if it's just dawning on her.

"Yeah," I say. Charlemagne starts whining and jumping, trying to join us on the couch. Gabby looks at her and then picks her up and puts her in my lap. She curls up and closes her eyes. I do feel better, honestly, having her in my lap.

"OK, stop crying for a minute," Gabby says.

I sniffle and look at her.

"We are going to handle this, and we are going to be fine."

"We?"

"Well, I'm not going to let you go through this alone, you moron," she says. The way she says the word *moron* makes me feel more loved than I've felt in a long time. She says it as if I'd be a complete idiot to think I was ever alone. And to know that the idea is absolutely absurd to her, to know that it's so far-fetched as to make me a moron, it's a nice feeling. "You know, years from now, you're going to look back on this as the best thing that ever happened to you, right?"

I snort at her. "I'm having a baby with a married man, and

I'm pretty sure it's going to ruin my relationship with my new old boyfriend."

"First of all," she says, "let's not go assuming things. You never know what Ethan will say."

"You know what I'm pretty sure he's not going to say? 'Hey, Hannah, I'm super excited to take on the responsibilities of raising another man's baby.'"

I'm right, of course. Which is why Gabby changes the subject. "You are going to love this baby," she says. "You know that, right? You are such a loving person. You have so much love to give, and you are so loyal to the people you love. Do you have any idea what a great mom you are going to be? Do you have any idea how loved this kid is going to be? The love it will have from its Aunt Gabby will eclipse the sun."

I laugh, despite myself.

"Hannah, you can do this. And one day soon, you're not going to imagine how you ever found meaning in your life before you did." Maybe she's right.

"What if your dad fires me before I'm even hired? 'Hi. Hello. You gave me this job when you thought I wasn't pregnant, and now you're stuck with me.'"

"This is why you puked at dinner," Gabby says.

"Should have been your dad's first clue." To be honest, it probably should have been my first clue.

"Would you listen to yourself? We're talking about my dad. The man who picked up the boutonnieres for our dates to the prom. My dad once sat there with a pair of tweezers pulling tiny pieces of glass out of your foot when you dropped my mom's favorite crystal vase."

"Oh, don't remind me," I say.

"But that's my point. My dad loves you. Not like 'Oh, I'm

telling you my dad loves you.' I mean, he has love in his heart for you. My father loves you. Both my parents do. They like being there for you. My dad's not going to fire you when he finds out you're pregnant. He and my mom are going to jump for joy and tell everyone who will listen that the generation of grandchildren is finally arriving."

I laugh.

"Also, he can't fire you for being pregnant. It's illegal. That's Human Resources 101."

The minute she says "human resources," I remember talking to Joyce. I remember her telling me I have insurance and maternity leave. For a flash, I almost feel as if Gabby is right. That things will be OK.

"OK," I say. "So I still have a job."

"And you still have me, and my parents, and Mark, and . . ." She looks at the dog and smiles. "And Charlemagne."

"I have to call Michael and tell him, right?"

"Yes? No?" she says. "I have no idea. But I'll think about it with you. We'll weigh the pros and cons."

"Yeah?"

"Yeah. And we will come up with an answer. And then you'll do it."

She makes it sound so easy.

"And Ethan might not leave me?"

"He might not," she says, although I can tell by her voice that she has less confidence in this one. "But I can tell you, if he does, it's because it wasn't meant to be."

"You think things are meant to be?" I ask her. For some reason, I think I'll feel better if things are meant to be. It gets me off the hook, doesn't it? If things are meant to be, it means I don't have to worry so much about consequences and mistakes. I can take my hands off the wheel. Believing in fate is like living on cruise control.

"Are you kidding? I absolutely do. There is a force out there, call it what you will. I happen to believe that it's God," she says. "But it pushes us in the right direction, keeps us on the right path. If Ethan says he can't handle the fact that you're pregnant, he's not the one for you. You were meant for someone else. And we will handle *that* together, too. We will handle all of this together."

I close my eyes briefly, and when I open them, the world seems a little brighter. "So what do I do now?"

"Tomorrow morning, we're getting you prenatal vitamins and making an appointment to see an OB/GYN so we can figure out how far along you are."

"It would have to be at least eight weeks," I tell her. "I haven't slept with Michael in a while."

"OK," she says. "So we know that. Still, we'll make the appointment."

"Oh, no," I say out loud. "I had a beer. Last week at the bar."

"It's OK," I hear her say. "It's going to be fine. It happens. You weren't wasted. I saw you."

I am a terrible mother. Already. Already I am a terrible mother.

"You're not a terrible mother if that's what you're worried about," Gabby says, knowing how my brain works almost better than I do. She picks Charlemagne up off my lap and gestures for me to get up. She leads the two of us into my bedroom. "It happens. And it's OK. And starting tomorrow morning, you're going to learn all the things you have to stop doing and all of the things you have to start doing. And you're going to be phenomenal at all of it."

"You really think that?" I ask her.

"I really think that," she says.

I put on my pajamas. She gets in on one side of the bed. Charlemagne lies down with her.

"She's a cute one, this little Charlemagne," Gabby says. "How did she end up at my house?"

I laugh. "It's a long story," I say. "In which I make a snap decision that I now realize was probably hormone-driven."

Gabby laughs. "Well, she's precious," she says. "I like having her around."

I look at Charlemagne. "Me, too."

"I hate Mark's stupid dog allergy," she says. "Let's keep her in here all night and see if he itches. I bet you he won't. I bet you it's all in his head."

I laugh and get into bed next to Gabby. She holds my hand.

"Everything is going to be great, you know," she says.

I breathe in and out. "I hope so."

"No," she says. "Say it with me. Everything is going to be great."

"Everything is going to be great," I say.

"Everything is going to be great," she says again.

"Everything is going to be great."

You know, I almost believe it.

Gabby turns the light off.

"When you wake up in the middle of the night, terrified because you remember that you're pregnant," she says, "wake me. I'm here."

"OK," I say. "Thank you."

Charlemagne snuggles up between the two of us, and I wonder if maybe it's actually Gabby, Charlemagne, and me who were meant to be.

"Mark and I have started talking about when to have a baby," she says.

"Wow, really?" Even though I'm actually having a baby, I can't quite wrap my brain around people having babies.

"Yeah," she says. "Maybe soon. I could hurry up and get pregnant. We could have kids the same age."

"We'd force them to be best friends," I say.

"Naturally," she says. "Or maybe I'll just leave Mark. You and I could raise your baby together. That way, I don't even need to have one. Just me and you and the baby."

"With Charlemagne?" I ask.

"Yeah," she says. "The world's most adorable lesbian couple." I laugh.

"Only problem is, I'm not attracted to you," she says.

"Ditto," I tell her.

"But just think of it. This baby would be raised by an interracial lesbian couple. It would get into all the good schools."

"Think of the pedigree."

"I've always said God made a mistake making us straight women."

I laugh and then correct her. "I'm trying to believe that God doesn't make mistakes."

H enry checks some stuff and puts the clipboard down.

"Dr. Winters says we can try the wheelchair," he tells me. His voice is solicitous. As if we're doing something taboo.

"Now?" I say. "Me and you?"

"Well, the female nurses can't bench-press as much I can. So yeah, I'll be the one lifting you into the chair."

"You never know," I say. "Maybe every single one of those nurses can bench the same as you, and you don't know because you never asked."

"Well," he says, "regardless of who can bench-press what, it's my job to lift you. But before I do, we've got some stuff to cover."

"Oh," I say. "OK, go for it."

He tells me it may hurt. He tells me it's going to be an adjustment. We can't do much at first, just get into the wheelchair and learn to move around a bit. Simply moving into the chair initially might wear me out. Then Henry starts unhooking me from a few of the machines that have come to feel like my third and fourth arms. He leaves the IV in. He tells me that while I'm in the hospital, that's coming with us.

"Do you feel ready?" he asks me once everything is set up and I'm all that's left to deal with.

"As I ever will," I tell him.

I'm scared. What if this hurts? What if this doesn't work? What if I have to stay in this bed for the rest of my life, and I can never move, and this is it for me? What if my life is sugar-free Jell-O and dry chicken dinners? I'll just lie here in a hospital gown that doesn't close in the back for the rest of my waking days.

Oh, God. Oh, God. This gown doesn't close in the back.

Henry is going to see my ass.

"You're going to see my butt, aren't you?" I ask as he moves toward me.

To his credit, he doesn't laugh at me. "I won't look," he says.

I'm not sure that answer is good enough.

"I'm a professional nurse, Hannah. Give me a little credit. I'm not gonna sneak a peek at your tush for kicks."

I can't help but laugh as I consider my choices. Which is to say that I consider that I don't really have a choice at all if I want to get out of this bed.

"Cool?" he says.

"Cool," I say.

He takes my legs and spins me. I inch myself toward him.

He gets up close to me. He puts his arm around my back, his other arm under my legs.

"One," he says.

"Two," I say with him.

"Three!" we say as he lifts me, and then, within seconds, I'm in the wheelchair.

I'm in a wheelchair.

Someone just had to lift me into a wheelchair.

I was going to have a baby, and it died.

"OK?" Henry says.

"Yeah," I say, shaking my head and pushing the bad thoughts out of my mind. "Yes!" I add. "I'm excited about this! Where are we going?"

"Not much of anywhere this go-around," he says. "Right now, we just want to get you comfortable in the chair and familiar with it. Maybe just wheel around the room a bit."

I turn and look at him. "Oh, come on," I say. "I want out of this room. I've been peeing in a bedpan for days. I want to see something."

He looks at his watch. "I'm supposed to check on other patients."

I get it. He has a job. I'm a part of his job. "OK," I say. "Tell me how it works."

He starts showing me how to push the wheels and how to stop. We roam around the room. I push myself so hard that I crash into the wall, and Henry runs toward me and grabs me.

"Whoa, there," he says. "Take it slow."

"Sorry," I say. "Got away from me."

"I guess we know you probably won't ever be a race-car driver."

"Pretty sure I ruled that out when I got hit by a car."

Henry could, at this moment, feel bad for me. But he doesn't. I like that. I like that so much.

"Well, don't be a pilot, either," he says. "Or did you already cross that one off because you were hit by a plane?"

I look up at him, indignant. "Do you talk to all of your patients this way?" I ask him. There it is. The question I've been pondering for days. And I said it as if I didn't care about his answer in the slightest.

"Only the bad ones," he says. Then he leans down and grabs

the arms of my wheelchair. His face is in mine, so close that I can see the pores on his skin, the specks of gold in his eyes. If this were any other man in any other situation, I'd think he was going to kiss me. "If you happened to roll yourself out of this room," he says with a sly smile across his face, "I'm sure it would take a minute before I caught up with you and wheeled you back in here."

Henry slowly takes his arms off my chair, clearing the way.

I don't look at the door. I stare at him. "If I just happened to scoot my wheels this way," I say, "and push myself right out into the hallway . . ."

"I might not notice until you'd had a nice breath of air out there."

"So this is OK?" I say, looking at him but heading for the door.

He laughs. "Yeah, that's OK."

"And if I get to the threshold?"

He shrugs. "We'll see what happens."

I keep rolling myself forward. My arms are already tired from pushing myself. "If I just roll on right past it?"

He laughs. "You should probably take your eyes off me and watch where you're going," he says, just as I ram a wheel into the door frame.

"Oops," I say, backing up and then straightening. And then I roll myself right out into the hallway.

It's busier than I would have thought. There are more stations, more nurses, than I get a glimpse of in my room. And I'm sure it's the very same air I breathe from my hospital bed, but it seems fresher somehow out here. The hallway is even blander, more banal, than what I imagined from my bed. The floor underneath my wheels is squeaky clean. The walls on either side of me are an innocuous shade of oatmeal. But in some ways, I might as well have landed on the moon. That's how novel and foreign it feels for a split second.

"All right, Magellan," Henry says, grabbing the handles on the back of my chair. "Enough discovering for one day."

When we cross through the doorway back into my room, I thank him. He nods at me.

"Don't mention it."

He wheels me back to my bed.

"You ready?" he says.

I nod and brace myself. I know it's going to hurt when he picks me up, when he puts me down. "Go for it," I say.

He puts his arms underneath my legs. He tells me to put my arms around his neck, to hold on to him tightly. He leans over me, putting his other arm around my back. My forehead grazes his chin, and I can feel his stubble.

I land back on my bed with a thud. He helps me move my legs straight and puts my blanket back on me.

"How are you feeling?" he asks.

"I'm good," I say. "Good."

The truth is, I feel as if I am about to cry. I am about to break down into tears the size of marbles. I don't want to be back in this bed. I want to be up and moving and living and doing and seeing. I have tasted the glory of sitting in the hallway. I don't want to be back in this bed.

"Good," he says. "So I think Deanna is taking over for me in an hour or so. She'll be in to check on you and see how you're doing. I'll tell Dr. Winters that it went well today. I bet they will have you headed for physical therapy in no time. Keep it up."

I know that a nurse telling a patient to "keep it up" is normal. I know that. I think that is what bothers me about it.

Henry is by the door, heading out.

"Thanks," I call to him.

"My pleasure," he says. "See you tonight." And then he seems to suddenly feel nervous. "I just mean . . . if you're awake."

"I know what you mean," I say, smiling. I can't help but feel as if he's looking forward to seeing me. I suppose I could be wrong. But I don't think I am. "See you tonight."

He smiles at me, and then he's gone.

I'm so jittery that I can't sit still, and yet sitting still is all I'm capable of. So I turn on the TV. I sit and wait for something interesting to happen. It doesn't.

Deanna comes in a few times to check on me. Other than that, nothing happens.

The hospital is a boring, boring, boring, quiet, sterile, boring place. I turn the TV off and turn onto my side as best I can. I try to fall asleep.

I don't wake up until Gabby comes in around six thirty. She's got a pizza in her arms and a stack of American magazines.

"You snore so loud," Gabby says. "I swear I could hear you down the hall."

"Oh, shut up," I say. "The other night when you slept here, Henry compared you to a bulldozer."

She looks at me and puts the pizza and magazines down on the table. "Who is Henry?"

"The night nurse guy," I say. "Nobody."

The fact that I call him nobody makes it seem as if he's somebody. I realize that now. Gabby raises her eyebrow at me.

"Honestly," I say, my voice even. "He really is just the night nurse."

"OK . . ." she says.

And then I slump over and bury my red face in the palms of my hands. "Ugh," I say, looking back up at her. "I have a massive, embarrassing, soul-crushing crush on my night nurse."

I am eleven weeks pregnant. The baby is healthy. Everything looks good. The doctor, Dr. Theresa Winthrop, assured me that I am not the only woman who has gotten almost out of her first trimester before figuring out she was pregnant. I feel a little bit better about that.

On the way back to the car, Gabby stops me. "How are you feeling about all of this? You know that if you don't want to, you don't have to do this. Eleven weeks is early."

She's not telling me anything I don't know. I've been pro-choice my entire life. I believe, wholeheartedly, in the right to choose. And maybe, if I didn't believe I could give a child a home or a good life, maybe I'd avail myself of my other options. I don't know. We can't say what we would do in other circumstances. We can only know what we will do with the ones we face.

"I know I don't have to do this," I tell her. "I am choosing this."

She smiles. She can't help herself. "I have some time before I have to go back to the office," she says. "Can I buy you lunch?"

"That's OK," I tell her. "I want to get home before Charlemagne pees all over your house."

"It's fine," she says. "Mark didn't say anything this morning about feeling itchy, by the way. I'm convinced it's all in his head. I'm already planning to persuade him that we should keep both you and Charlemagne with us. We're near his office, actually. Should we go surprise him for lunch and begin our campaign? Plus, I want to see the look on his face when you tell him where we've been this morning."

"I'm honestly concerned that my dog is ruining your home."

"What's the point of owning your own place if you can't get a little pee on it?" Gabby says.

"OK. But don't come crying to me when she stains the hardwood."

We get into the car and drive only a few blocks before Gabby pulls into an underground lot and parks. I've never seen Mark's office before. It occurs to me that I also haven't been to the dentist in a while.

"You know, while we're here," I say, "I really should make an appointment to get my teeth cleaned."

Gabby laughs as we get into the elevator. She presses the button for the fifth floor, but it isn't responding. The doors close, and we somehow end up going down to the lowest level of the garage. The doors open, and an elderly woman gets in. It takes her about thirty years.

Gabby and I smile politely, and then Gabby hits the fifth-floor button again, which now lights up, a bright and inviting orange.

"Which floor?" she asks the elderly lady.

"Three, please."

We head up, and the door opens again on the floor we got in on. Gabby turns to me and rolls her eyes. "If I knew it was going to be ten stops on the elevator, I would have suggested we go eat first," she whispers to me. I laugh.

And there is Mark.

Kissing a blond woman in a pencil skirt.

Gabby left at around ten tonight to go home to Mark. I haven't seen Mark since I've been in the hospital. It's not weird necessarily, because Mark and I were never particularly close. But it seems strange that Gabby is so often here on nights and lunch breaks and Mark hasn't even stopped by. Gabby keeps saying that he's been working late a lot. Apparently, he had to attend a dental conference in Anaheim this week. I don't know much about the life of a dentist, but I always figured dentists were the kind of people who were home in time for dinner. I guess that's not the case with Mark. Either way, his working benefits me greatly, since Gabby spends her time with me instead, which is really all I want anyway.

Since she left, I've just been reading the magazines she brought. I like these magazines much better than the British ones. Which is good, because I slept through most of the day today, so I know I won't be tired for quite some time.

"I knew you'd be up," Henry says when he comes into the room. He's pushing a wheelchair.

"I thought you'd take the night off," I say.

He shakes his head. "I went home this morning. Slept my eight hours, had some dinner, watched some TV. I got in a little while ago."

"Oh," I say.

"And I checked on all my other patients, and they are all sleeping and not in need of my assistance."

"So . . . another lesson?" I ask.

"I'd call this more of an adventure." He has a wild look in his eye. As if we are doing something we shouldn't be doing. It's exciting, the idea of doing something I shouldn't be doing. All I've been doing is healing.

"All right!" I say. "Let's do it. What do I need to do?"

He pulls the rail down on my bed. He moves my legs. We move the same way we moved this morning, only faster, easier, more familiar. I'm in the chair within a few seconds.

I look down, my legs in front of me, in the chair. Henry grabs my blanket and puts it in my lap.

"In case you get cold," he says.

"And so I don't flash anyone," I say.

"Well, that, too, but I didn't want to say it." He stands behind me, attaches my morphine bag to my chair, and pushes me forward.

"Where are we going?" I ask.

"Anywhere we want," he says.

We get out into the hallway.

"So?" he says. "Where first?"

"Cafeteria?" I say.

"Do you really want more cafeteria food?" he asks.

"Good point. How about a vending machine?" I offer.

He nods, and away we go.

I'm outside of my room! I'm moving!

Some doctors and nurses stand outside a room or two, but for the most part, the halls are empty. It's also quiet except for the occasional regulatory beeping.

But I feel as if I'm flying down a California freeway with the top down.

"Favorite movie," I say as we make our way around one of the many corners of the hospital.

"*The Godfather*," he says with confidence.

"Boring answer," I tell him.

"What? Why?"

"Because it's obvious. Everyone loves *The Godfather*."

"Well, sorry," he says to me. "I can't love a different movie just because everyone loves the movie I love."

I turn back to look at him. He makes a face at me. "The heart wants what it wants, I guess," I say.

"I guess," he says. "You?"

"Don't have one," I say.

Henry laughs. "You can't make me pick one if you don't have one."

"Why not? It's a fair question. I just don't happen to have an answer."

"Just pick one at random. One you like."

"That's the problem. My answer is always changing. Sometimes I think my favorite movie is *The Princess Bride*. But then I think, no, *Toy Story* is obviously the best movie of all time. And then, other times, I'm convinced that no movie will ever be as good as *Lost in Translation*. I can never decide."

"You think too much," he says. "That's your problem. You're trying too hard to find the perfect answer when *an answer* will do."

"What do you mean?" I ask. We're stopped in front of a soda vending machine, but this isn't what I meant. "Wait, I meant a snack machine. Not a Coke machine."

"My apologies, Queen Hannah of the Hallway," he says, and pushes us forward. "If someone asks you your favorite movie, just say *The Princess Bride*."

"But sometimes I'm not sure it *is* my favorite movie."

"But it will do, is what I'm saying. It's like when I asked you what kind of pudding you liked, and you named all three flavors. Just pick a flavor. You don't need to find the perfect thing all the time. Just find one that works, and go with it. If you had, we'd be on to favorite colors by now."

"Your favorite color is navy blue," I say.

"Yep," he says. "But you can tell that from my scrubs, so you haven't convinced me you're telepathic."

"What's mine?" I ask him. I can see a vending machine at the end of the hall. I also really hope Henry has money, because I didn't bring any.

"I don't know," he says. "But I bet you it's between two colors."

I roll my eyes at him, but he can't see me. He's right. That's what's frustrating.

"Purple and yellow," I say.

"Let me guess," he says in a teasing voice. "Sometimes you like yellow, but then, when you see purple, you think maybe that's your favorite."

"Oh, shut up," I say. "They are both pretty colors."

"And," he says as we reach the machine, "either of them would suffice."

He pulls a dollar out of his pocket.

"I have one buck," he says. "We have to share."

"Some date you are," I joke, and immediately wish I could take it back.

He laughs and lets it go. "What will it be?"

I search the machine. Salty, sweet, chocolate, peanut butter, pretzels, peanuts. It's impossible. I look back at him.

"You're gonna be mad," I say.

He laughs. "You have to pick one. I only have a dollar."

I look at all of them. I bet Henry likes Oreos. Everyone likes Oreos. Literally every human.

"Oreos," I say.

"Oreos it is," he says. He puts the dollar into the slot and punches the buttons. The Oreos fall just in front of me, at my level. I pull them out of the drawer and open them. I give him one.

"Thank you," he says.

"Thank *you*," I say. "You paid for them."

He bites it. I eat it whole. "There's no wrong way to eat an Oreo," he says.

"That's Reese's. There's no wrong way to eat a Reese's," I correct him. "Oh, man! We should have gotten Reese's."

He pulls another dollar out of his scrubs and puts it into the machine.

"What? You said you only had a dollar! You lied!"

"Oh, calm down. I was always going to buy you two things," he says. "I'm just trying to help you be decisive."

He laughs at me as he says it, and I open my mouth wide, outraged. I hit him on the arm. "Jerk," I say.

"Hey," he says. "I bought you *two* desserts."

The Reese's fall. I grab them and give him one again. "You're right," I say. "And you took me on a journey into the hallway. Which you probably weren't supposed to do."

"It wasn't specifically sanctioned, no," he says, biting his peanut butter cup. Mine is already gone. I practically swallowed it whole.

I could ask him, right now, why he's being so nice to me. Why he's taking so much time with me. But I'm afraid if I call attention to it, it will stop happening. So I don't say anything. I just smile at him. "Will you take me the long way back?" I ask.

"Of course," he says. "Do you want to see how far you can wheel yourself before your arms get tired?"

"Yeah," I say. "That sounds great."

He's a great nurse. An attentive listener. Because that is truly all I want in this world. I want to try to do something myself, knowing that when I have nothing left, someone will take me the rest of the way.

He turns me around to face the right direction, and he stands behind me. "Go for it," he says. "I got you."

I push, and he follows me.

I push.

And I push.

And I push.

We get through two big hallways before I need a rest.

"I'll take it from here," he says, grabbing the back of my chair and pushing me forward. He leads us to an elevator and pushes the call button. "You sleepy? You want to head back?"

I turn as best I can to look at him. "Let's say I'm not sleepy, what would we do?"

He laughs. The elevator opens. He pushes me in. "I should have known you wouldn't choose sleep."

"You didn't answer my question. What would we do?"

He ignores me for the moment and pushes the button for

the second floor. We descend. When the door opens, he pushes me out and down a long hallway.

"You're really not going to tell me?"

Henry smiles and shakes his head. And then we turn a corner, and he opens a door.

The cold, fresh air rushes over me.

He pushes me through. We are on a smoking patio. A tiny, dirty, dingy, sooty, beautiful, refreshing, life-affirming smoking patio.

I breathe in deeply.

I can hear cars driving by. I can see city lights. I can smell tar and metal. Finally, there are no walls or windows between me and the spinning world.

Despite my best efforts, I feel myself tearing up.

The air funneling in and out of my lungs feels better, brighter, than all the air I've inhaled since I woke up. I close my eyes and listen to the sounds of traffic. When a few of my tears fall from my eyes, Henry crouches down next to me.

He is on my level. Once again, we are face-to-face.

He pulls a tissue out of his pocket and hands it to me. And right then, as his hand grazes mine and I catch his eye, I don't need to wonder what would happen if he and I met at a dinner party. I know what would happen.

He would walk me home.

"Ready?" he says. "To go back?"

"Yeah," I say, because I know it's time, because I know he has a job to do, because I know we aren't supposed to be out here. Not because I'm ready. I'm not ready. But as he pushes me through that door and it closes behind us, I am, for the first time, so full of joy to be alive that I'd be happy going just about anywhere.

"You're a great nurse," I tell him as we head back. "Do you know that?"

"I hope so," he says. "I love my job. It's the only thing I've ever really felt I was meant for."

We get back to my room. He puts my wheelchair by my bed.

He puts his arms underneath me. "Put your arms around my neck," he says. And I do.

He lifts me and holds me there for a moment, the full weight of my body in his arms. I am so close to him that I can smell his soap on his skin, the chocolate still faintly on his breath. His eyelashes are longer and darker than I noticed before, his lips fuller. He has a faint scar under his left eye.

He puts me down in my bed. I swear he holds on to me just a moment longer than he needs to.

It is perhaps the most romantic moment of my life, and I'm in a hospital gown.

Life is unpredictable beyond measure.

"Excuse me," comes a stern voice from the hallway. Both Henry and I look up to see a female nurse standing in the doorway to my room. She is older and a bit weathered. She has her light-colored hair pulled up in a butterfly clip. She is wearing pale pink scrubs and a patterned matching scrub jacket.

Henry pulls away from me abruptly.

"I thought Eleanor was covering for you the second half of the night," the nurse says.

He shakes his head. "You might be thinking of Patrick. Patrick needs his shift covered until seven."

"OK," she says. "Can I speak to you when you're done here?"

"Sure," Henry says. "I'll be right there."

The nurse nods and leaves.

Henry's demeanor changes. "Good night," he says as he moves to leave.

He's almost out the door when I call to him. "Thank you," I say. "I really—"

"Don't mention it," he says, not looking back at me, already out the door.

Gabby is throwing things around the house. Big things. Porcelain things. They are crashing and shattering. Charlemagne is by my feet. We are standing at the door to the guest room. I'm trying to stay out of it. But I'm pretty much in it.

Gabby never went back to work. I drove us home while she stared straight ahead, virtually oblivious to the world. She didn't say much all afternoon. I kept trying to ask her if she was all right. I kept trying to offer her food or some water, but she kept refusing. She's been as responsive as a statue all afternoon.

And then, the second Mark came through the door and said, "Let me explain," that's when she reanimated.

"I'm not interested in anything you have to say," Gabby said.

And he had the gall to say, "C'mon, Gabby, I deserve a chance to—"

That's when she threw a magazine at him. I couldn't blame her. Even I would have started throwing things at him then, when I heard those stupid words come out of his mouth. She started by throwing whatever was nearby. More magazines, a book that was on the coffee table. Then she threw the remote control. It cracked, and the batteries went flying. That's when Charlemagne and I hightailed it to safer ground.

"Why is there a dog here?" Mark asked. He started scratching his wrists slowly. I don't even think he knew he was doing it.

"Don't ask about the fucking dog!" Gabby said. "She was here all night, and you didn't even notice. So just shut the fuck up about the dog, OK?"

"Gabby, talk to me."

"Screw you."

"Why were you at my office today?" he asked her.

"Oh, you've got to be kidding me! You've got a lot worse problems than how you got caught!"

That's when she walked into the kitchen and started breaking big stuff. Porcelain stuff.

Which brings us to now.

"Who is she?" Gabby screams.

Mark doesn't answer. He can't look at her.

She pauses ever so briefly and looks around at the mess. Her shoulders slump. She can see me off to the side. She catches my eye. "What am I doing?" she says. She doesn't say it to me or Mark, really. She says it to the room, the house.

I take advantage of the moment and walk, through the shards, to put my arms around her. Mark moves toward us, too.

"No," I say abruptly and with force. "Don't you touch her."

He backs away.

"You're going to move out," Gabby says to him as I hold her. I start rubbing her back, trying to soothe her, but she pushes me away. She gathers her strength. "Get your shit and leave," she says.

"This is my place, too," Mark says. "And I'm just asking for a few minutes to talk this out."

"Get. Your. Shit. And leave," Gabby says. Her voice is strong and stoic. She is a force to be reckoned with.

Mark considers fighting back more; you can see it on his face. But he gives up and goes into the bedroom.

"You're doing the right thing," I tell her.

"I know that," she says.

She sits down at the dining-room table, catatonic once again.

Charlemagne starts walking toward us, but Gabby sees her before I do.

"No!" she shouts at the dog. "Be careful."

She stands up and gently walks over to Charlemagne and picks her up. She carries her in her arms over the broken plates. She sits back down at the table with Charlemagne in her lap.

Mark flies through various rooms in the house, getting his things. He slams doors. He sighs loudly. Now seems like the time to start realizing that I never liked him.

This goes on for at least forty-five minutes. The house is silent except for the sounds of a man moving out. Gabby is practically frozen still. The only time she moves is to reposition Charlemagne in her lap. I stand by, close, ready to move or to speak at a moment's notice.

Finally, Mark comes out into the living room. We stare at him from the dining-room table. "I'm leaving," he says.

Gabby doesn't say anything back.

He waits, hoping for something. He gets nothing from her.

He walks to the front door, and Charlemagne jumps down onto the floor.

"Charlemagne, no," I say. I have to say it twice before she stays put.

Mark looks at her, clearly still confused about why there is a dog named Charlemagne in the house, but he knows he won't get any answers.

He opens the front door. He's almost gone by the time Gabby speaks up.

"How long has this been going on?" she asks him. Her voice

is strong and clear. It does not waver. It does not break. She is not about to burst into tears. She is fully in control. At least for this moment.

He looks at her and shakes his head. He looks up at the ceiling. There are tears in his eyes. He rubs them away and sniffs them back up. "It doesn't matter," he says. His voice, too, is strong. But it is full of shame; that much is clear.

"I said, how long has this been going on?"

"Gabby, don't do this—"

"How long?"

Mark looks at his feet and then at her. "Almost a year," he says.

"You can go," she says.

He turns away and does just that. She goes to the window to watch him leave.

When he's finally gone, she turns to me.

"I'm so sorry, Gabby," I say to her. "I'm so sorry. He's an asshole."

Gabby looks at me. "You slept with somebody's husband," she says. She doesn't need to draw any direct conclusions from this. She doesn't need to say out loud what I know she's thinking in her head.

"Yep," I say, both owning my actions and feeling deep shame for them. "And it was wrong. Just like this was wrong."

"But I told you it didn't mean you were a bad person," she says. "I told you that you could still be a wonderful, beautiful person."

I nod. "Yeah, you did."

"And you did this to somebody."

I want to claim that the situation is different. I want to say that what I did with Michael isn't as bad as what this other woman has done with Mark. I want to, once again, hide behind the fact that I didn't *know*. But I did know. And what I did was no different from this.

I slept with someone's husband. I shouldn't have done that.

And now I'm having a baby by that man. And I'm going to raise that baby.

Pretending this child isn't the result of a mistake I made doesn't make it any less true.

And I know now that I have to face things. I have to admit things in order to move forward.

"Yes," I say. "I did a terrible thing. Just like Mark and that woman did a terrible thing to you."

Gabby looks at me. I pull her over to the sofa, and I sit us both down.

"I made a mistake. And when I did, you saw that I was still a good person, and you reserved your judgment, because you had faith in me. That was a wonderful gift. Your belief in me. It's made me believe in myself. It's made me start to change the things I've needed to change. But you don't have to do that for them. You can just hate them."

I swear, she almost smiles.

"We can both just hate them for as long as we need to, and then, one day, when we feel stronger, we'll probably forgive them for being imperfect, for doing a terrible thing. One day, sooner than you think, I bet we'll go so far as to wish them the best and not give them another thought, because we'll have moved on with our lives. But you don't have to believe that right now. You can just hate him. And I can hate him for what he did to you. And maybe one day, he'll change. He'll be a person who did something in the past that he would never, ever, ever do again."

She looks at me.

"Or he'll just be shitty forever, and you're better off being as far away from him as possible," I tell her. "There's that theory, too."

She smiles a smile so small and so quick that I start to question if I really saw it. "I'm sorry," she says finally. "I didn't mean to bring you into this. I'm just . . . I'm sorry."

"Don't give it another thought," I say.

Gabby cries into her hands and then collapses into my arms. "He's not even allergic to dogs," she says. "I've wanted a dog for years, and I couldn't because of him, but I swear, it's all in his head. I bet you he's not even allergic to them."

"Well, now you've got one," I say. "So there's a silver lining. Why don't we just sit here and think of silver linings for right now? What's another one? Did he always forget to take out the trash? Did he leave his wet towel on the bed?"

She looks up at me. "His penis is small," she says. "Seriously, like a golf pencil." And then she starts laughing. "Oh, it feels good to admit that. I don't have to keep pretending his penis isn't small."

I start laughing with her. "That wasn't exactly where I thought you were going to go with this, but OK! That's a good one."

Gabby laughs. It's a deep belly laugh. "Oh, God, Hannah," she says. "The first time I saw it, I thought, *Where's the rest of it?*"

I laugh so hard when she says this that I have to struggle to breathe. "You are making this up," I say.

"Nope," she says, her hands up in the air as if she's swearing to God. "He just has a terrible penis."

Both of us are laughing so hard that tears are coming out

of our eyes. And then, abruptly, it is time to stop. I can see the mood change much the same way you can feel summer turn to fall. One day, everything's sunny, and then, suddenly, it's not.

"Oh, Hannah," she says, burying herself into my chest. Charlemagne sits at our feet.

"Shhh," I say, rubbing her back. "It's OK. It's going to be OK."

"I'm not sure that's true," she says into my chest.

"It is," I say. "It is true."

She looks up at me, her eyes now bloodshot and glassy. Her face is splotchy. She looks desperate and sick. I've never seen her like this. She's seen me like this. But I've never seen her like this.

"I know it's going to be OK, because you are Gabrielle Jannette Hudson. You are unstoppable. You are the strongest woman I've ever known."

"Strongest person," she says.

"Hm?" I'm not sure I quite heard her.

"I'm the strongest *person* you know," she says, wiping her eyes. "Gender is irrelevant."

She's absolutely right. She is the strongest person I know. Her gender is irrelevant. "You're right," I say. "Just one more reason I know you are going to get through this."

She starts heaving tears. She's hyperventilating. "Maybe he had a good reason. Or there is something I misunderstood."

I want to tell her that she could be right, that maybe there is some piece of information that makes all of this better. I want to tell her that because I want her to be happy. But I also know it's not true. And part of loving someone, part of being the recipient of trust, is telling the truth even when it's awful.

"He was cheating on you for almost a year," I tell her. "He didn't make a one-time mistake or get confused."

She looks up at me and starts crying again. "So my marriage is over?"

"That's up to you," I say. "You have to decide what you will tolerate and what you can live with. Why don't you try to relax and I'll get you some dinner?"

"No," she says. "I can't eat."

"Well, what can I do for you?"

"Just sit here," she says. "Just sit next to me."

"You got it," I tell her.

"Charlemagne, too," she says. I get up and pick up Charlemagne. The three of us sit here on the couch.

"My husband is cheating on me, and you're pregnant by a married man," Gabby says.

I close my eyes, taking it in.

"Life sucks," she says.

"Sometimes, yeah," I tell her.

We are both quiet.

"It hurts," she says. She starts crying again. "It hurts so bad. Deep in my gut, it hurts."

"I know," I tell her. "You and I are a team, right? Whatever you face in life, I'll face it with you. Everything that you were prepared to do for me last night, I'm prepared to do for you today. So count on me, OK? Let's get through this together. Lean on me. Squeeze my hand."

She looks at me and smiles.

"When it hurts so bad you don't think you can stand it," I say, "squeeze my hand." I put my hand out for her, and she takes it.

She starts crying again, and she squeezes.

And I think to myself that if, by being here, I have taken away one one-hundredth of the pain that Gabby feels, then maybe I have more of a life's purpose than I ever thought.

"Divide the pain in two," I tell her. "And give half of it to me."

Gabby comes in on Saturday morning, and before she can even get into the room, I tell her to stop. Deanna is standing by my bed.

"Wait," I say to Gabby. "Wait right there."

Deanna smiles and puts out her hand. "You ready?" she says. I nod. Deanna helps me get my feet on the ground. I push my weight onto Deanna's hands, and she helps me put weight on my feet. I'm standing up. Actually standing up. Not without resting on another human being, but still. I'm standing up. She and I have been practicing all morning.

"OK," I say, "I gotta sit down." Deanna helps rest me back on the bed. The relief is immense.

"Oh, my God!" Gabby says, clapping for me as if I'm a child. "Look what you did! This is nuts!"

I smile and laugh. My energy and Gabby's excitement must be infectious, because Deanna is laughing and smiling with us.

"It's crazy, right?" I say. "I've been practicing as much as possible. This morning, Dr. Winters was giving me some tips on how to steady myself. I can't move just yet, really. But I can stand."

"Wow," Gabby says, putting down her purse.

She moves toward us. Deanna helps me get back into bed.

"I am so impressed," Gabby says. "You're ahead of schedule."

"I'll come by to check on you soon," Deanna says. "Good job today."

"Thank you," I tell her as she leaves.

When she's gone, I tell Gabby about last night.

"Henry took me outside," I say.

"You walked outside?"

"No," I say. "In a wheelchair. He took me out on the smoking patio."

"Oh," she says.

This is not sounding nearly as romantic as it felt.

"Oh, never mind," I say. "You had to be there."

She laughs. "Well, I'm proud of you that you stood up today."

"I know! Before you know it, I'll be crawling and eating solid foods."

"Well, don't do it when I'm not here!" she says. "You know I like to get that stuff on videotape."

I laugh. "Just be glad you don't have to change my diaper," I tell her. I'm just making a joke, but it hits a little too close to home. I still can't get to the bathroom on my own. "How are you?" I ask, inviting her to sit down. "How is Mark?"

"He's good," she says. "Yeah."

Something seems off. "What's on your mind?" I ask her.

"No, nothing," she says. "He seems very . . . I don't know. I think the accident, all of this craziness, maybe it jolted something in him. He's been very sweet, very attentive. Bringing me flowers. He bought me a necklace the other day." She starts playing with the one around her neck. It's a string of gold with a diamond at the center.

"That one?" I say, leaning forward. I take the diamond in my hand. "Wow, is that a real diamond?"

"I know," she says. "I made a joke when he gave it to me, like 'OK, what did you do wrong?' "

I laugh. "On TV, it's always that a man comes home with

flowers and jewelry when he invites his boss over for Thanksgiving dinner without asking you first or something."

"Right," she says, laughing. "Maybe he's cheating on me. I'll have to go home and look at all of his shirt collars for lipstick stains, right?"

"Yeah," I say. "If soap operas are any indication, you will find bright red lipstick stains on his collar if he's cheating."

Gabby laughs.

For a moment, I know we are both thinking of the fact that I was once the woman wives watch out for. That I lost a married man's baby. Sometimes I wonder if this accident wasn't a clean slate. If it wasn't permission to start again, to do better.

And then I wonder, if it is a clean slate, what am I going to do with it?

"Well, what are you doing here?" I ask her. "Don't hang out with your lame best friend. Go hang out with your thoughtful, romantic husband. I mean, he could be buying you cashmere and chocolate right now."

"No, right now, I'd rather be here. I'd rather be with you. Besides, Mark said he had to go into work today. Said he'd be unavailable until late tonight. There were billing problems at work, I guess."

"He doesn't have an office manager or someone to do that stuff?"

Gabby thinks it over. "Well, no, he does," she says. "But he says lately, he needs more time to look over their work. So what should we do today? Should I get us a book to read together? Are we watching *Law & Order*?"

I shake my head. "Nope. We're going on an adventure," I tell her.

"Where are we going?"

"Wherever we want," I tell her, and I point to the wheelchair in the corner.

She brings it over, and I skooch myself closer to the edge of the bed.

"Can you pull the railing down?" I ask her. "It's that button there, and then you just press down."

She's got it.

"Now, just move the wheelchair to the side, just to the . . . yeah."

I swing my legs down off the bed.

"Sorry, one last thing. Can you just grab me around my waist? I can do this. I just need a little bit of help."

She grabs me under my arms. "Ready?" she says.

"Yep!" I say, and at the same time Gabby lifts me, I push myself up.

It's not graceful. It's actually quite painful, very noisy, and I end up with my ass half hanging out of my gown, but I'm in the seat. I'm mobile.

"Can you . . ." I say, gesturing toward the half of my gown.

"Oh, right," Gabby says, and she moves it as I try to lift myself just a little to get situated.

"Thanks," I say. "Now, can you take my morphine bag and put it on my chair here?"

She does.

"Ready?" I ask her.

"Ready," she says.

"Oh!" I say, right before I start to push. "Do you have dollar bills?"

"Yeah," she says. "I think I have one or two. Why, are we going to a strip club?"

I laugh as she grabs her purse.

And then we are off.

I see Deanna in the hallway, and she tells me not to go too far. I lead us down the hallway and to the right, just as Henry led me the other day.

"Do you have a favorite movie?" I ask Gabby. If I had to guess, I'd say her favorite movie is *When Harry Met Sally* . . .

"*When Harry Met Sally* . . ." she says. "Why do you ask?"

"I don't know what my favorite movie is," I say.

"Why does that matter? Lots of people don't have a favorite movie."

"But, like, even for the purposes of the conversation, I can't just *pick* one. I can't just decide on a movie to say is my favorite."

"I hope it isn't news to you that you're indecisive."

I laugh. "Henry says that you don't need *the* answer. You just need *an* answer."

"Henry, Henry, Henry," Gabby says, laughing at me. We come to an intersection in the hallway, and I veer left. I'm pretty sure the vending machines are to the left.

"Hardy-har-har, but I'm asking an honest question," I tell her. I'm still pushing myself down the hall. I've still got the strength to keep going.

"What are you actually asking me?"

"Do you think it's true that you don't need the perfect answer but just, you know, *an* answer?"

"To your favorite movie, yes. But sometimes there is only one answer. So I don't think this is a universal philosophy."

"Like what?"

"Like who you marry, for one. That's the biggest example that comes to mind."

"You think there is only one person for everyone?"

"You don't?" The way she asks me this, it's as if it has never occurred to her that I might not. I might as well have said, "You think we're breathing oxygen?"

"I don't know," I say. "I know I did think that at one time. But . . . I'm not sure anymore."

"Oh," she says. "I guess I never considered the alternative. I just assumed, you know, God or fate or life or whatever you want to call it leads you to the person you were meant to be with."

"That's how you feel about Mark?"

"I think Mark is the person life led me to, yeah. He's the only one for me. If I thought there was someone else better suited for me, why would I have married him? You know? I married him because he's the one."

"So he's your soul mate?"

She thinks about it. "Yes? I mean, yeah. I guess you'd say that's a soul mate."

"What if you two end up getting divorced?"

"Why would you say a thing like that?"

"I'm just asking a hypothetical. If there is only one person for everyone, what happens when soul mates can't make it work?"

"If you can't make it work, you aren't soul mates," she tells me.

I hear her out. I get it. It makes sense. If you believe in fate, if you believe something is pushing you toward your destiny, that would include the person you're supposed to spend the rest of your life with. I get it.

"But not cities," I say.

"Huh?"

"You don't have to find the perfect city to live in. You just have to find one that will work."

"Right," she says.

"So I can just pick one and leave it at that," I say. "I don't have to test them all out until something clicks."

She laughs. "No."

"I think I've been jumping from place to place thinking that I'm supposed to find the perfect life for myself, that it's out there somewhere and I have to find it. And it has to be *just so*. You know?"

"I know that you've always been searching for something, yeah," Gabby says. "I always assumed you'd know it when you found it."

"I don't know, I'm starting to think maybe you just pick a place and stay there. You pick a career and do it. You pick a person and commit to him."

"I think as long as you're happy and you're doing something good with your life, it really doesn't matter whether you went out and found the perfect thing or you chose what you knew you could make work for you."

"Doesn't it scare you?" I ask her. "To think that you might have gone in the wrong direction? And missed the life you were destined for?"

Gabby thinks about it, taking my question seriously. "Not really," she says.

"Why not?"

"I don't know. I guess because life's short? And you just kind of have to get on with it."

"So should I move to London or not?" I ask her.

She smiles. "Oh, I see where this is going. If you want to go to London, you should. But that's as much as you'll get from me. I don't want you to go. I want you to stay here. It rains a lot there. You know, for what it's worth."

I laugh at her. "OK, fair enough. We have a bigger problem than London anyway."

"We do?"

"We're lost," I say.

Gabby looks left and then right. She can see what I see. All the hallways look the same. We're in no-man's-land.

"We're not near the vending machines?" she asks.

"Hell if I know," I say. "I have no idea where we are."

"OK," she says, taking hold of my chair. "Let's try to get ourselves out of this mess."

G abby insisted on going to work today. I tried to persuade her to stay home, not to put extra pressure on herself, but she said that the only way she could feel remotely normal was to go to work.

Ethan called me twice yesterday, and I didn't call him back. I texted him telling him that I couldn't talk. I fell asleep last night knowing I'd have to face him today. I mean, if I keep avoiding him, he'll know something is up.

So I woke up this morning, resolved to work this out. I called Ethan and asked if he was free tonight. He told me to come by his place at around seven.

Which means I have the rest of the day to call Michael. I want to have answers for Ethan's questions when he asks. I want to have all of my ducks in a row. And this is a big duck.

I take a shower. I take Charlemagne for a walk. I stare at my computer, reading the Internet for what feels like hours. When it's six o'clock in New York, when I know Michael will be leaving work, I pick up my phone. I sit down on my bed and dial.

It rings.

And rings.

And rings.

And then it goes to voice mail.

On some level, I'm relieved. Because I don't want to have to have this conversation at all.

"Hi, Michael. It's Hannah. Call me back when you have a minute. We have something we need to talk about. OK, 'bye."

I throw myself backward onto the bed. My pulse is racing. I start thinking of what I'll do if he never calls me back. I start imagining that maybe he will make this decision *for* me. Maybe I'll call him a few times, leave a few messages, and he will just never call back. And I will know that I tried to do the right thing but was unable to. I could live with that.

My phone rings.

"Hannah," he says, the moment I say hello. His voice is stern, almost angry. "We're done. You said so yourself. You can't call me. I finally have things back on track with my family. I'm not going to mess that up again."

"Michael," I say to him. "Just hold on one minute, OK?" Now I'm pissed.

"OK," he says.

"I'm pregnant," I tell him finally.

He's so quiet I think the line has gone dead. "I'll call you back in three minutes," he says, and then he hangs up.

I pace around the room. I feel a flutter in my stomach.

The phone rings again.

"Hi," I say.

"OK, so what do we do?" he asks. I can hear that he's in a closed space. His voice is echoing. He sounds as if he's in a bathroom.

"I don't know," I say.

"I can't leave my wife and children," he says adamantly.

"I'm not asking you to," I tell him. I hate this conversation. I have been working to put this behind me, and now I'm right back in the middle of it.

"So what are you saying?" he asks.

"I'm not saying anything except that I thought you should know. It seemed wrong not to tell you."

"I can't do this," he says. "I made a mistake, being with you. I can see that now. It was my fault. I shouldn't have done it. It was a mistake. Jill knows what I did. We're finally in a good place. I love my children. I cannot let anything ruin that."

"I'm not asking anything of you," I say to him. "That's the truth. I just thought you should know."

"OK," he says. He is quiet for a moment and then, timidly, asks me what he's probably wanted to ask me since I brought this up. "Have you considered . . . not having the baby?"

"If you're going to ask me to have an abortion, Michael, you should at least say the word." Such a coward.

"Have you considered having an abortion?" he asks.

"No," I tell him. "I'm not considering having an abortion."

"What about adoption?"

"Why do you care?" I ask him. "I'm having the baby. I'm not asking for your money or your attention or support, OK?"

"OK," he says. "But I don't know how I feel about having a baby out there."

These are the sorts of things that people should really be thinking about before they have sex, but I'm one to talk.

"Well, then, step up to the plate and deal with it or don't," I say. "That's your business."

"I suppose it's no different from donating sperm," he says. He's not talking to me. He's talking to himself. But you know what? I don't want him to help me raise this baby, and he doesn't want to help me. Clearly, he's just looking to absolve himself of any guilt or responsibility, and if that's what it takes to make this simple, then I will help him do just that.

"Think of it like that," I tell him. "You donated sperm."

"Right," he says. "That's all it is."

I want to tell him he's a complete ass. But I don't. I let him tell himself whatever he needs to. I know that this baby could ruin his family. I don't want that. That's the truth. I don't want to break up a family, regardless of who is right and wrong. And I don't need him. And I'm not sure that my child is better off having him around. He hasn't shown himself to be a very good man.

"OK," I say.

"OK," he says.

Just as I am about to get off the phone, I say one thing, for my unborn kid. "If you ever change your mind, you can call me. If you want to meet the baby. And I hope that if he or she wants to meet you one day, you'll be open to it."

"No," he says.

His answer jars me. "What?"

"No," he says again. "You are making the choice to have this baby. I do not want you to have it. If you have it, you have to deal with the child not having a father. I'm not going to live my life knowing that any day a kid could show up."

"Classy" is all I say.

"I have to protect what I already have," he says. "Are we done here?"

"Yeah," I tell him. "We're done."

We are lost in the maternity ward, and we can't seem to find our way out. First, we were stuck in the delivery department. Now we're outside the nursery.

The last thing I want to do right now is look at beautiful, precious babies. But I notice Gabby is no longer behind me. She's staring.

"We are going to start trying soon," she says. She's not even looking at me. She's looking at the babies.

"What are we going to start trying to do?"

She looks at me as if I'm so stupid I'm embarrassing her. "No, Mark and I. We're going to try to have a baby."

"You want to have a kid?"

"Yeah," she says. "I was going to ask what you thought when you got here, but I didn't get a chance before the accident, and . . . and then, when you woke up . . ."

"Right," I say. I don't want her to say it out loud. The inference is enough. "But you think you're ready? That's so exciting!" My own ambivalence about a baby doesn't, for a minute, take away from the joy of her having one. "A little half Gabby, half Mark," I add. "Wow!"

"I know. It's a really exciting thought. Super scary, too. But really exciting."

"So you'll be . . . doing the ol' . . . actually, is there even a popular euphemism for trying to have a baby?"

"I don't know," she says. "But yes, we'll be doing the ol' . . ."

"Wow," I say again. "I just can't believe that we are old enough to the point where you're going to actually *try* to get pregnant."

"I know," she says. "You spend your whole life learning how *not* to get pregnant, and then, one day, you suddenly have to reverse all of that training."

"Well, this is awesome," I say. "You and Mark are so good together. You're going to be great parents."

"Thank you," she says, and squeezes my shoulder.

A nurse comes up to us. "Which one are you visiting?" she asks.

"Oh, no," Gabby says. "Sorry. We are just lost. Can you point us back to general surgery?"

"Down the hall, take your first right, then your second left. You'll see a vending machine. Follow that hall to the end, take a left . . ." The directions go on and on. Clearly, I took us much farther away than I meant to.

"OK," Gabby says. "Thank you." She turns to me. "Let's go."

We go past what looks like a neonatal unit, maybe intensive care. And then we go through double doors and find ourselves in the children's ward.

"I don't think this is the right way," I say.

"She said there was a left up here somewhere . . ."

I look over at the nurses and then peek through the windows as we move farther down the hall. It's mostly toddlers and elementary-school-age kids. I see a few teenagers. Almost all of them are in hospital beds, hooked up to machines, as I have been. A lot of them wear stockings or caps. It occurs to me that they are covering their bald heads.

"OK," Gabby says. "You're right. We're lost."

I pull over to the side of the hallway.

"I'm just going to go ask a nurse for a map," Gabby says.

"OK," I say.

From my vantage point, I can see into one room with two kids in it. The kids are talking. Two preteen girls in separate beds. A doctor is standing to the side, talking to a set of parents. Both parents look confused and distraught. The doctor leaves. As he does, I can see there is a nurse standing with them. The nurse starts to leave, too, and the parents catch her at the door. They are close enough to me now that I can make out the conversation.

"What did all of that mean?" the mom says.

The nurse speaks gently. "As Dr. Mackenzie said, it's a bone cancer mostly found in adolescents. It can sometimes occur in families. It's rare, but possible, that multiple siblings may develop it. That's why he wants to see your younger daughter, too. Just to be sure."

The mom starts crying. The dad rubs her back. "OK, thank you," the dad says.

The nurse doesn't leave then, though. She stays. "Sophia is a fighter. I'm not telling you anything you don't know. And Dr. Mackenzie is an exceptional pediatric oncologist. I mean, exceptional. If it was my daughter here—my daughter is eight, her name is Madeleine—I'm telling you, I'd be doing exactly what you are doing. I'd put her in the hands of Dr. Mackenzie."

"Thank you," the mom says. "Thanks."

The nurse nods. "If you need anything, if you have any questions, just page me. I'll answer any I can, and if I can't"—she looks them in the eye, assuring them—"I will get Dr. Mackenzie to explain. In simple terms, if he can manage it," she says, making a joke.

The dad smiles. The mom, I notice, has stopped crying.

They end their conversation just as Gabby comes back with the map. Both Gabby and the nurse can now tell I've been eavesdropping. I quickly look away, but it doesn't matter. I've been caught.

Gabby pushes my chair down the hallway.

"I can do it," I say. I take the wheels. When we are far enough away, I ask her, "Was that the kids' cancer ward?"

"It says 'Pediatric Oncology Department,'" she says. "So yeah."

I don't say anything for a moment, and neither does she.

"We're actually not that far from your room," she says. "I just missed a left."

"Being a nurse . . . seems like a hard job. But fulfilling," I say.

"My dad has always said it's the nurses who provide the care," she says. "I always thought it was kind of a cheesy double entendre, but his point always made sense."

I laugh. "Yeah, he could just say, 'Nurses might not be the ones who cure you, but they certainly make you feel better.'"

Gabby laughs. "Tell him that, will you? Maybe he'll use that one from now on."

I don't know what you're supposed to wear to tell your new boyfriend, who used to be your ex-boyfriend and is the man you are pretty much convinced is the love of your life, that you are having a baby with another man.

I decide on jeans and a gray sweater.

I brush my hair so many times it develops a shine to it, and then I put it up in my very best high bun.

Before I head out the door, I offer, one more time, to stay home with Charlemagne and Gabby.

"Oh, no," Gabby says. "Absolutely not."

"But I don't want to leave you alone."

"I'll be fine," she says. "I mean, you know, I won't be fine. That was a lie. But I'll be fine in the sense that I'm not going to burn the house down or anything. I'll be just as sad when you get back. If it's any consolation."

"It is not," I say. I take my hand off the doorknob. I really don't feel good about leaving her by herself. "You shouldn't be alone."

"Who's alone?" she says. "I have Charlemagne. The two of us are going to watch television until our eyes fall out of our heads and then go to sleep. We might take an Ambien." She corrects herself. "I mean, I might take an Ambien." She continues to look at me. "Just to be clear," she says, "I'm not going to drug the dog."

"I'm staying," I say.

"You're going. Don't use me as an excuse to avoid your own problems. You and I have a lot of adjusting to do, and it's better for everyone if we know where things stand with Ethan as soon as possible."

She's right. Of course she's right.

"The new you tackles life head-on, remember?" she says. "The new you doesn't run from her problems."

"Ugh," I say, opening the front door. "I hate the new me."

Gabby smiles as I head out. It is the first smile I've seen in two days. "I'm proud of the new you," she says.

I thank her and walk out the door.

It's ten to seven when I park my car outside Ethan's apartment. It took me three times around the block before I found a spot, but then I saw a car pulling out of a space right in front of his place. I was both frustrated and thrilled at the experience. I suddenly wonder what driving in Los Angeles will be like with a child. Will it take me a half hour getting in and out of the car because I'll never truly figure out how to hook up a car seat? Will I have to circle the block over and over accompanied by the soothing sounds of a baby crying? Oh, God. I can't do this.

I have to do this.

What do you do when you have to do something you can't do?

I get out of the car and shut my door. I breathe in sharply, and then I breathe out slowly.

Life is just a series of breaths in and out. All I really have to do in this world is breathe in and then breathe out, in succession, until I die. I can do that. I can breathe in and out.

I knock on Ethan's door, and he opens it wearing an apron that says "Mr. Good Lookin' Is Cookin.'" It has a picture of a stick-figure man with a spatula.

I can't do this.

"Hey, you," he says. He grabs me in his arms, tightly, and I wonder if it's too tight for the baby. I don't know the first thing about being pregnant! I don't know anything about being a mom. What am I doing? This is all going to end in a terrible disaster. I am Hurricane Hannah, and everything I touch turns to shit.

"I missed you," he tells me. "Isn't that ridiculous? I can't go one day not seeing you, after years without you."

I smile at him. "I know what you mean."

He leads me into the kitchen. "I know we mentioned going out to dinner, but I decided to make you a proper meal."

"Oh, wow," I say, trying to muster up enthusiasm, but I'm not sure I'm doing a good job.

"I Googled some recipes at work and just got home from the store a few minutes before you got here. What you're look-ing at is chicken *sopa seca*." He pronounces it with an affected Spanish accent. He is silly and sweet and sincere, and I decide, right this second, that I'm not going to tell him tonight.

I love him. And I think I have always loved him. And I'm going to lose him. And just for tonight, I want to experience how it feels to be his, to be loved by him, to believe that this is the beginning of something.

Because I'm pretty sure it's the end.

Just like that, I become the version of myself that I was just two days ago. I am Hannah Martin, a woman who has no idea that she is pregnant, no idea that she is about to lose the one thing she might have wanted her entire adult life.

"Fancy!" I say to him. "It looks like it takes quite a bit of prep."

"Actually, I just have a few more steps, and then everything goes in the oven," he says. "I think. Yeah, I think it goes in the oven."

I start laughing. "You've never made this before?"

"Chicken *sopa seca*? When in my life would I have ever had reason to make chicken *sopa seca*? I didn't even know what it was until a few hours ago. I make grilled cheese. I bake potatoes. When I'm feeling really fancy, I'll make myself a pot of chili. I don't go around wooing girls with chicken *sopa seca*." He is chopping vegetables and putting them into a pot. I hang back and sit down on the stool by the kitchen.

"What is chicken *sopa seca*?" I ask him.

"I'm still a bit unclear on that," he says, laughing. "But it involves pasta, so . . ."

"You've never even had it?"

"Again, Hannah, I ask you, when do you think I have occasion to have chicken *sopa seca*?"

I laugh. "Well, why are you making it?" I ask. He is pouring broth into the pot. He looks like a natural.

"Because you are the kind of person who deserves a fuss made over her. That's why. And I'm just the guy to do that."

"You could have just made me a cinnamon roll," I tell him.

He laughs. "Considered and dismissed. It's too obvious. Everyone gets you cinnamon rolls. I wanted to do something unexpected."

I laugh. "Well, if you aren't making cinnamon rolls, then what's for dessert?"

"Ah!" he says. "I'm glad you asked." He pulls out a cluster of bananas.

"Bananas?"

"Bananas Foster. I'm gonna light these babies on fire."

"That sounds like a terrible idea."

He laughs. "I'm kidding. I bought fruit and Nutella."

"Oh, thank God," I say.

"How's Charlemagne?" Ethan asks. Charlemagne, the baby, Gabby and Mark—I want to leave all of it at the door. I don't want to bring any of that here.

"Let's not talk about Charlemagne," I say. "Let's talk about . . ."

"Let's talk about how kickass you are," Ethan says. "With a new job starting and a new car and a dog and a handsome boyfriend who makes world-class cuisine."

This is when I should say something. This is my opening.

But his eyes are so kind and his face so familiar. And so much else in my life is scary and new.

He kisses me. I immediately sink into him, into his breath, into his arms.

This is all going to be over. This is ending.

He picks me up off the stool, and I wrap my arms around him.

He brings me into the bedroom. He pulls my T-shirt off. He starts to unfasten my bra.

"Wait," I say.

"Oh, no, it's fine," he tells me. "The *sopa seca* has to simmer on low for a while. It's not going to burn."

"No," I say. I sit up. I look him in the eye. I put my shirt back on. "I'm pregnant."

D r. Winters comes in to check on me toward the end of the day. Gabby has gone home.

"So," she says, "I've heard you've been galavanting around the hospital in your wheelchair." She smiles. It's a reproach but a kind one.

"I'm not really supposed to be doing that, huh?" I ask.

"Not really," she says. "But I have bigger fish to fry, so to speak."

I smile, appreciative.

"You are healing nicely. We're almost out of the woods here, in terms of risk of complications."

"Yeah?"

"Yeah," she says, looking down at my chart. "We should talk about your next steps."

"OK," I say. "Tell me."

"One of our physical therapists is going to come in tomorrow, around eleven."

"OK."

"And he and I will assess what sort of mobility you have, what you can expect in a reasonable amount of time, what you should know going forward."

"Great."

"And we will come up with a program and a tentative time-line for when you can expect to begin walking unaided."

"Sounds good," I tell her.

"This is a long road ahead. It's one that can be very frustrating."

"I know," I say. I've been sitting in a bed for a week, leaving only rarely and only with help.

"It will only get more frustrating," she says. "You are going to have to learn how to do something you already know how to do. You will get angry. You will feel like giving up."

"Don't worry," I say. "I'm not going to give up."

"Oh, I know that," she says. "I just want you to know that it's OK to *want* to give up. That it's OK to reach a breaking point with this stuff. You have to have patience with yourself."

"You're saying I'm going to have to relearn how to walk," I tell her. "I already know that. I'm ready."

"I'm saying you're going to have to relearn how to live," she says. "Learn how to do things with your hands for a while instead of your legs. Learn how to ask for help. Learn when you have reached your limit and when you can keep going. And all I'm saying is that we have resources at your disposal. We can help you get through all of it. You will get through all of it."

I felt I had this under control, to a certain degree, before she walked in here, and now she's making me feel like everything is a disaster.

"OK," I say. "I'll let that marinate."

"OK," she says. "I'll come check on you tomorrow morning."

"Great," I say. I only half mean it.

It's four o'clock in the afternoon, but I know that if I go to sleep now, I'll wake up in time to see Henry. So that's what I do. I go to bed. I only have a few more nights in this hospital. I'd hate to waste one sleeping.

~

I'm awake by eleven, when he comes in. I'm prepared for him to make a joke about me being nocturnal or something, but he doesn't. He just says, "Hello."

"Hi," I say.

He looks down at my chart. "So you're going to be taking off pretty soon," he says.

"Yeah. I guess I'm just too healthy for this place."

"A blessing if I've ever heard one." He gives me a perfunctory smile and then checks my blood pressure.

"Would you want to help me practice standing?" I ask. "I want to show you how well I'm doing. I stood up almost entirely on my own this morning."

"I have a lot of patients to get to, so I don't think so," he says. He doesn't even look at me.

"Henry? What is going on with you?"

He looks up.

"Henry?"

"I'm being switched to days on another floor. You'll have a nice woman, Marlene, taking care of you for the remaining nights that you're here." He pulls the cuff off my arm and steps back from me.

"Oh," I say. "OK." I feel rejected, somehow. Rebuffed. "Can you still stop by just to say hi?"

"Hannah," Henry says. His voice is now more somber, more serious. "I shouldn't have been so . . . friendly with you. That is my fault. We can't keep joking around and goofing off."

"OK," I say. "I get it."

"Our relationship has to stay professional."

"OK."

"It's nothing personal." The phrase hangs there in the air.

I thought this *was* personal. Which I guess is the problem.

"I should go," he says.

"Henry, c'mon." I find myself getting emotional; I hear my voice cracking. I try desperately to get it under control. I know that letting him know how badly I want to see him again will only serve to push him further away. I know that. But sometimes you can't help but show the things you feel. Sometimes, despite how hard you try to fight your feelings, they show up in the glassiness of your eyes, the downward turn of your lips, the shakiness of your voice, and the lump in your throat. "We're friends," I say.

He stops where he is. He walks toward me. The look on his face is gentle and compassionate. I don't want gentle and compassionate. I am so goddamn sick of gentle and compassionate. "Hannah," he says.

"Don't," I say. "I get it. I'm sorry."

He looks at me and sighs.

"I probably misinterpreted everything," I say finally.

"OK," he says. And then he leaves. He actually leaves. He just turns on his heels and walks out the door.

I don't fall asleep, even though I'm tired. It's not that I can't fall asleep. I think I can. But I keep hoping he will check on me.

At two a.m., a woman in pale blue scrubs comes in and introduces herself as Marlene. "I'll be taking care of you at night from here on out," she says. "I'm surprised you're awake!"

"Yeah," I say somberly. "Well, I slept all afternoon."

She smiles kindly and leaves me be. I close my eyes and tell myself to go to sleep.

Henry's not coming. There's no reason to wait up.

You know what? I don't think I misinterpreted a goddamn thing.

I *like* him. I like being around him. I like being near him. I like the way he smells and the way he never shaves down to the skin. I like the way his voice is sort of rocky and deep. I like his passion for his job. I like how good he is at it. I just like him. The way you like people when you like them. How he makes me laugh when I least expect it. How my legs don't hurt as much when he's looking directly at me.

Or . . . I don't know. Maybe that's all nursing stuff. Maybe he makes everyone feel that way.

I turn off my side light and close my eyes.

Dr. Winters said earlier today that I might try to walk to-morrow.

I try to focus on that.

If I can survive being hit by a car, I will get over having a crush on my night nurse.

Hearts are just like legs, I guess. They mend.

It's not yours," I tell Ethan. He knows this, of course, based on timing alone. But I have to make it crystal clear.

"It could be, though, right?" he asks me. "I mean, maybe last week . . ."

I shake my head. "I'm eleven weeks. It's not yours."

"Whose is it?"

I breathe in and then out. That's all I have to do. In and then out. The rest is optional. "His name is Michael. He and I dated in New York. I thought it was more serious than it was. He and I were careless toward the end. He doesn't want another child."

"Another child?"

"He's married, with two children," I tell him.

He sighs loudly, as if he can't quite believe what I'm saying. "Did you know he had a family?"

"It's sort of hard to explain," I say. "I didn't know at first. For a long time, I assumed I was the only one he was with. But then I should have known better and, let's just say, I . . . made some mistakes."

"And now he doesn't care that you're pregnant?" Ethan stands up, furious. His emotions are just starting to set in, reality just starting to grab on to him. It's easier for him to be mad at Michael than it is to be mad at me or at the situation. So I let him, for a moment.

"He doesn't want the baby," I say. "And that's his right." I believe in a man's decision not to have a baby as much as I believe in a woman's.

"And you're just going to let this asshole treat you like this?"

"He doesn't want the baby. I do. I'm prepared to go it alone."

That word, the word *alone*, brings him back down to earth. "What does this mean for us?" he asks.

"Well," I say, "that's up to you."

He looks at me. His eyes find mine and hold on. And then he looks away. He looks down at his hands, which are placed firmly on his knees. "Are you asking me to be someone's father?"

"No," I say to him. "But I'm also not going to tell you that this doesn't change things. I'm pregnant. And if you're going to be with me, that means you'll be going through this with me. My body will be going through a lot. I'll have mood swings. When it gets time to have the baby, I'll be scared and confused and in pain. And then, once the baby is born, there will be a child in my life, at all times. If you want to be with me, you'll be with my child."

He listens, but he doesn't speak.

"I know you didn't ask for any of this," I say.

"Yeah, you can say that again," he snaps. He looks at me with remorse.

"But I wanted you to know so you could make a decision about your future."

"Our future," he says.

"I guess," I say. "Yeah."

"What do you want?" he asks.

Oh, boy. How do I even begin to answer that question? "I want my baby to be healthy and happy and have a safe, stable childhood." I suppose that's the only thing I know for sure.

"And us?"

"I don't want to lose you. I think you and I really have something, that this is the beginning of something with huge potential for us . . . But I would never want to put you in the position to do something you aren't ready for."

"This is a lot," he says. "To process."

"I know," I say. "You should take all the time you need." I stand up, ready to leave, ready to give him time to think.

He stops me. "You're really ready to be a single mother?"

"No," I say. "But this is the way life has worked out. And I'm embracing it."

"But I mean, this could be a mistake," he says. "What if you just made a mistake one night with this guy? Are you ready to live with the consequences of that for your entire life? Do I have to live with the consequences of that for mine?"

I sit back down. "I have to think that there is a method to all of this madness," I tell Ethan. "That there is a larger plan out there. Everything happens for a reason. Isn't that what they say? I met Michael, and I fell in love with him, even though I can clearly see now that he wasn't who I thought he was. And one night, everything happened just so, and I got pregnant. And maybe it's because I'm supposed to have this baby. That's how I'm choosing to look at it."

"And if I can't do it? If I'm not ready to take all of this on?"

"I suppose it would follow that if you and I come to a place we can't get past, then we aren't meant to be. Right? Then we aren't right for each other. I mean, I think I have to believe that life will work out the way it needs to. If everything that happens in the world is just a result of chance and there's no rhyme or reason to any of it, that's just too chaotic for me to handle. I'd have to go around questioning every decision

I've ever made, every decision I will ever make. If our fate is determined with every step we take . . . it's too exhausting. I'd prefer to believe that things happen as they are meant to happen."

"So you and I finally have the timing worked out, we can finally be together, be what we suspected we always were. And in the middle of that, it turns out you're pregnant with another man's baby, and you're saying *que será será?*"

I want to cry. I want to scream and shout. I want to beg him to stay with me during all of this. I want to tell him how scared I am, how much I feel I need him. I want to tell him how the night I reconnected with him, the night we spent together, was the first time I've felt at ease in years. But I don't. Because it will only drag this thing out further. It will only make things worse. "Yeah. *Que será será.* That's what I'm saying."

I get up and walk out into the living room. He follows me. I can smell dinner. I wish, just for a moment, that I hadn't told him. Right now, we'd be in his bedroom.

And then I think, if I'm wishing for things, maybe I should wish that I'm not pregnant at all. Or that it's his baby. Or that I never left Los Angeles. Or that Ethan and I never broke up.

But I wonder how different my world would be if any of those things had happened. You can't change just one part, can you? When you sit there and wish things had happened differently, you can't just wish away the bad stuff. You have to think about all the good stuff you might lose, too. Better just to stay in the now and focus on what you can do better in the future.

"Ethan," I tell him, "the minute I saw you again, I just knew that you and I were . . . I mean, I'm pretty sure you and I are . . ."

"Don't," he says. "Just . . . not right now, OK?"

"OK. I'll leave you with your *sopa seca*." I smile tenderly and then open the door to leave. He sees me out and shuts the door.

When I get to the last step, he calls my name. I turn around.

He's standing at the top of the stairs, looking down at me. "I love you," he says. "I don't think I ever really stopped."

I wonder if I'll be able to make it to my car before I burst into tears, before I cease to be a human being and become just a puddle with big boobs and a high bun.

"I was going to tell you that tonight," Ethan says. "Before all of this."

"And now?" I say.

He gives me a bittersweet smile. "I still love you," he says. "I've always loved you. I might never stop."

His gaze falls to the ground, and then he looks back up at me. "I just thought you should know now . . . in case . . ." He doesn't finish his sentence. He doesn't want to say the words, and he knows I don't want to hear them.

"I love you, too," I say, looking up at him. "So now you know. Just in case."

Luckily for everyone involved, my physical therapist is not my type.

"OK, Ms. Martin," he says. "We are—"

"Ted, just call me Hannah."

"Right, Hannah," Ted says. "Today we're going to work on standing with a walker."

"Sounds easy enough." I say it because that's what I normally say to everything, not because it actually sounds easy enough. At this stage in my life, it sounds quite hard.

He puts my feet on the floor. That part I've gotten good at. Then he puts the walker in front of me. He pulls me up onto him, resting my arms and chest on his shoulders. He is bearing my weight.

"Slowly, just try to ease the weight onto your right foot," he says. I hang on to him but try to back off just a little. My knees buckle.

"Slow," he says. "It's a marathon, not a sprint."

"I don't know if you should be using running terms to someone who can't walk," I tell him.

But he doesn't spit something back at me. Instead, he just smiles. "Good point, Ms. Martin."

When people are nice and sincere and they don't fire back with smart-ass remarks, it makes my harmless sarcastic words seem downright rude.

"I was just joking," I tell him, immediately trying to take it back. "Use all the sports analogies you want."

"Will do," he says.

Dr. Winters comes in to check on us. "Looking good," she says.

I'm half standing up in a hospital gown and white knee socks, leaning over a grown man, with my hands on a walker. The last thing I am is "looking good." But I decide to say only nice things, because I don't feel that Dr. Winters and Ted the physical therapist are up for my level of sarcasm. This is why I need Henry.

Dr. Winters starts asking questions directly to Ted. They are talking about me and yet ignoring me. It's like when I was little and my mom's friends would come over and say something like "Well, isn't she precious" or "Look at how cute she is!" and I always wanted to say, "I'm right here!"

Ted moves slightly, pushing more of my weight onto my own feet. I don't feel as if I have balance, per se, but I can handle it.

"Actually, Ted," I say, "can you . . ." I gesture at the walker, asking him to bring it right in front of me, which he does. I shimmy off him and put both arms on the walker. I'm holding myself up. I don't have my hands on a single person.

Dr. Winters actually claps. As if I'm learning how to crawl.

There is only so long you can be condescended to before you want to jump out of your skin.

"Let me know when you want to sit back down, Ms. Martin," Ted says.

"Hannah!" I say. "I said call me Hannah!" My voice is rough and unkind. Ted doesn't flinch.

"Ted, why don't you leave Hannah and me alone for a minute?" Dr. Winters says.

I'm still standing with the walker on my own. But no one is cheering anymore.

Ted leaves and shuts the door behind him.

Dr. Winters turns to me. "Can you sit down on your own?" she asks.

"Yeah," I tell her, even though I'm not sure it's true. I try bending at my hips, but I can't seem to get control properly. I land on my bed with more force and bounce than I mean to. "I should apologize to Ted," I say.

She smiles. "Eh," she says. "Nothing he hasn't heard before."

"Still . . ."

"This is hard," she says.

"Yeah," I tell her. "But I can do it. I just want to *do* it. I want to stop being treated with kid gloves or having people cheer because I can feel my toes. I know it's hard to do, but I want to do it. I want to start walking."

"I didn't mean it was hard to walk," she says. "I mean that it's hard not to be able to walk."

"You sort of tricked me," I tell her, laughing. "Your sentence was misleading."

Dr. Winters starts laughing, too. "I know what I'm talking about," she says. "This stuff is frustrating. But you can't rush it."

"I just want to get out of here," I tell her.

"I know, but we can't rush that, either—"

"Come on!" I say, my voice rising. "I've been lying in this bed for days. I lost a baby. I can't walk. The only time I can get up is when someone pushes me around the hideous hallways. Something as mundane as walking by myself to the other side of the room is unimaginable to me. That's where I'm at right now. The mundane is unimaginable. And I have absolutely no control over anything! My entire life is in a tailspin, and I can't do anything about it." And Henry. Now I don't even have Henry.

Dr. Winters doesn't say anything. She just looks at me.

"I'm sorry," I say, getting a handle on myself.

She hands me a pillow. I take it and look at her. I'm not sure I know where this is going.

"Put the pillow up to your face," she says.

I'm starting to think Dr. Winters is nuts.

"Just do it," she says. "Indulge me for a second."

"OK," I say, and put the pillow up to my face.

"Now, scream."

I pull the pillow away from my face. "What?"

She takes the pillow in her hand and gently puts it up to my face. I take it from her. "Scream as if your life depends on it."

I try to scream.

"C'mon, Hannah, you can do better than that."

I try to scream again.

"Louder!" she says.

I scream.

"C'mon!"

I scream louder and louder and louder.

"Yeah!" she says.

I scream until there is no more air in my lungs, no more force in my throat. I breathe in, and I scream again.

"You can't walk," she says. "And you lost a baby."

I scream.

"It's going to be months until you fully recover," she says.

I scream.

"Don't hold it in. Don't ignore it. Let it out."

I scream and I scream and I scream.

I'm angry that I can't walk yet. I'm angry that Dr. Winters is right to clap for me when I stand up with a walker, because standing up on my own, even with a walker, is really, really hard.

I'm angry about the pain.

And about that lady just driving away. As if I was nothing. Just kept on driving down the street while I lay there.

And I'm angry at Henry. Because he made things better, and now he's gone. And because he made me feel stupid. Because I thought he cared about me. I thought that maybe I meant something to him.

And I'm angry that I don't.

I'm angry that I ended up pregnant with Michael's baby.

I'm angry at myself for falling in love with him.

I'm angry that my parents come and go out of my life.

Right now, in this moment, it feels as if I'm angry at the whole goddamn world.

So I scream into the pillow.

When I'm done, I take the pillow away from my face, put it back on the bed, and turn to Dr. Winters.

"Are you ready?" she says.

"For what?" I ask her.

"To move forward," she says. "To accept that you cannot walk right now. And to be patient with yourself and with us as you learn how to do it again."

I'm not sure. So I take the pillow, and I put it up to my face. I scream one last time. But my heart's not in it. I don't have anything left to yell about. I mean, I'm still angry. But it's no longer boiling to the surface. It's a simmer. And you can control a simmer.

"Yeah," I say. "I'm ready."

She stands in front of me. She helps me stand up. She calls Ted into the room.

And the two of them stand with me, help me, coach me, walk me through the art of balancing on two feet.

When I get home, Charlemagne runs toward me, and I hear Gabby get out of her bed.

She comes down the stairs and looks at me. She can see from my face that it didn't go well. I can tell from hers that she's been crying.

"You're home early."

"Yeah," I say.

"You told him?"

"Yeah."

She gestures to the sofa, and we both walk over and sit down. "What did he say?"

"Nothing? Everything? He's going to think about it." Then I ask about her. "Did Mark call again?" Mark has called at least ten times since he left. Gabby hasn't answered any of them.

"Yeah," she says. "But I didn't answer again. It's not time to talk right now. I have to get myself together and get ready for it. I'll hear him out. I'm not writing him off entirely, I suppose."

"Got it," I say.

"But I'm also being realistic. He was having an affair for a long time. I can't think of an explanation he could have that would change my mind about getting a divorce."

"You're not tempted to answer the phone and scream at him?"

She laughs. "Definitely. I am definitely tempted to do that. I will probably do that soon."

"But not right now."

"What does it get me?" she says, shrugging. "At the end of the conversation, I'll still be me. He'll still be him. He'll still have cheated on me. I have to accept that."

"So at least we're facing our problems head-on," I tell her.

She looks at me and smiles sadly. "At least we have that."

"We make quite a pair, don't we?"

Gabby huffs. "I'll say."

"I couldn't do any of this without you."

"Ditto," she says.

"I kind of want to just feel sorry for myself and cry," I tell her. "Maybe for the foreseeable future."

She nods. "Honestly, that sounds great."

We both slump down on the couch. Charlemagne joins us.

The two of us quietly cry on and off for the rest of the night, taking turns being the one crying and the one consoling.

I think that through our wallowing, we are able to release some of our fear and pain, because when we wake up the next day, we both feel stronger, better, more ready to take on the world, no matter what it throws at us.

We go out for breakfast and try to make jokes. Gabby reminds me to take my prenatal vitamins. We walk Charlemagne and then go buy her a dog bed and some chew toys. We begin to potty train her by bringing her to the front door when she pees. Every time she looks as if she has to pee, we pick her up and bring her to the front door, where we have a wee-wee pad. Gabby and I high-five each other with an unmatched level of excitement when Charlemagne goes straight to the wee-wee pad on her own.

When Mark calls that night, Gabby answers. She calmly listens to what he has to say. I don't eavesdrop. I try to give her space.

It's hours until she comes to find me in my room.

"He apologized a million times. He says he never meant to hurt me. He says he hates himself for what he's done."

"OK," I say.

"He says he was going to tell me. That he was working up the courage to tell me."

"OK . . ." Her voice is shaky, and it's making me nervous.

"He loves her. And he wants a divorce."

I sit up straight in bed. "*He* wants a divorce?"

She nods her head, just as stunned as I am. "He says I can keep the house. He won't fight me on a settlement. He says I deserve everything he can give me. He says he loves me, but he's not sure he was ever in love with me. And that he's sorry he wasn't brave enough to face that fact earlier."

My mouth is agape.

"He says, looking back on it, he should have handled it differently, but he knows this is right for both of us."

"I'm going to kill him," I tell her.

She shakes her head. "No," she says. "I'm kind of OK."

"What?"

"Well, I think I'm in shock, first of all," she says. "So take this with a grain of salt."

"OK . . ."

"But I always just had this feeling that maybe there was someone better out there."

"Really?"

"Yeah," she says. "I mean, we've been together since we were in college, and then we both went on to more school, and who has time to really focus on dating then? Right? So I stayed with him because . . . I didn't really see a reason not to. We were comfortable around each other. We were happy enough. And then, you know, I got to the age where I felt I should get married. And things have been fine between us. Always fine."

"But just fine?"

"Right," she says.

"I mean, I don't know," she says. "I just sometimes hoped that I could have something more than just fine. Someone who made me feel like I hung the moon. But I sort of stopped believing that existed, I think. And I figured, why not marry a guy like Mark? He's a nice guy."

"Questionable."

She laughs. "Right. Now it's questionable. But at the time, I didn't think twice about it. You know? I was in a good relationship with a stable man who wanted to marry me and buy a house and do all the things you're supposed to do. I didn't see any reason not to take him up on that just because I felt like he was a B-plus. And I was perfectly happy. I mean, I doubt, if this hadn't happened, that I ever would have verbalized any of this. It just wasn't on my mind. I was happy enough. I really was." She starts crying again.

"Are you OK?" I ask.

"No," she says, getting hold of herself. "I'm absolutely devastated. But—"

"But what?"

"When he told me, I just kept thinking that if I met someone out there who was better for me, who I felt passionately for, I'd want to leave Mark. That's the truth. I'd want to leave. I don't think I would have done what he did. But I'd have wanted to."

Charlemagne comes into the room and curls up in a ball.

"So what now?" I ask.

"Now?" Gabby says. "I don't know. It's too hard to think long-term. I'm heartbroken and miserable and sort of relieved and embarrassed and sick to my stomach."

"So maybe we take it one step at a time," I say.

"Yeah."

"I'm really craving cinnamon rolls," I tell her.

She laughs. "That sounds great," she says. "Maybe with a lot of icing."

"Who wants a cinnamon roll with only a little icing?" I ask her.

"Touché."

"Maybe right now, all we have to do is go get cinnamon rolls with a lot of icing."

"Yeah," she says. "Me and the pregnant lady, putting back a half dozen cinnamon rolls."

"Right."

She leaves to go put on her shoes. I put on a jacket and flip-flops. You can do that in Los Angeles.

We get into the car.

"Ethan hasn't called you, right?" Gabby says.

I shake my head. "He will when he knows what he wants to do."

"And until then?" she asks.

"I'm not going to wait around for some man to call," I say, teasing her. "My best friend wouldn't stand for that."

She shrugs. "I don't know," she says. "Extenuating circum-stances."

"Still," I tell her, "if he wants to be with me, he'll be with me. If he doesn't, I'm moving on. I have a baby to raise. A job to start. I'm going through a lot. I don't know if I told you this, but my best friend is getting divorced."

Gabby laughs. "You're telling me! Mine is pregnant with a baby that isn't her boyfriend's."

"No shit!" I say.

"Yeah!" Gabby says. "And she came home the other day with a dog she decided to adopt out of the blue."

"Wow," I tell her. "Your friend sounds nuts."

"Yours, too," she says.

"Think they'll be OK?" I ask her.

"I know I'm supposed to say yes, but the truth is, I think they're doomed."

The two of us start laughing. It's probably much, much funnier to us than it would seem to anyone else. But the way she says we're doomed makes it clear just how *not* doomed we are. And that feels like something to let loose and laugh about.

After eleven days in this hospital, I'm leaving today. I'm going to end up right back here in forty-eight hours, albeit in the outpatient center. I'll be seeing Ted, the earnest physical therapist, several times a week for the foreseeable future.

Dr. Winters has been prepping me for this. She has gone over all the details with me, and I know them backward and forward.

Gabby is here helping me pack up my things. I've got enough on my plate just trying to get to the bathroom on my own. But I'm making my way there slowly. I want to brush my teeth.

I use my walker to get close enough to the sink.

I stand in front of the mirror, and I truly see myself for the first time in almost two weeks. I have a faint bruise on the left side of my face, near my temple. I'm sure it was a doozy when I got here, but now it's not too bad. I look pale, certainly. But if I had to guess, I'd say that's as much from being inside the same building day after day as it is from any health concerns. My hair is a mess. I haven't taken a proper shower in what feels like forever.

I'm looking forward to sleeping in a real bed and bathing myself, maybe blow-drying my hair. Apparently, preparations have to be made to make that work, too. Mark installed a seat in the shower. Oh, to clean myself unaided! These are the things that dreams are made of.

Now that I'm leaving the hospital, I am starting to realize just how much this has set me back. Weeks ago, I would have guessed that by now I'd at least have gone out and bought a car or started looking for a job. Instead, I'm not where I started but even further behind.

But I also know that I've come a long way in my recovery and as a person. I've faced things I might not have faced otherwise. And as I stare at myself in the mirror for the first time since I got here, I find myself ready to face the ugliest of truths: it might, in fact, be a merciful act of fate that I stand here, unencumbered by a budding life inside me.

I am not ready to be a mother.

I am nowhere near it.

I slowly brush my own teeth. They feel clean and slick when I am done.

"Why is there always pudding in your room?" Gabby asks me. I turn myself around in slow spurts of energy.

She has a chocolate pudding cup in her hand. I don't know when it got here. But I know it was Henry.

He left me pudding at some point in the past day. He left me chocolate pudding. Doesn't that *mean* something?

Gabby is over the pudding. She has moved on to other things. "Dr. Winters should be here soon to check you out," she says. "And I read all the documents. I've even been doing research on physical therapy rehabilitation—"

You don't just leave pudding for someone you don't care about.

"Can you get me the wheelchair?" I ask her.

"Oh," she says. "Sure. I thought you were going to try to use the walker until it was time to go."

"I'm going to find Henry," I tell her.

"The night nurse?"

"He started working days on another floor. I'm gonna find him. I'm going to ask him out on a date."

"Is that a good idea?" she says.

"He left me pudding," I say. That is my only answer. She waits, hoping I have more, but I don't. That's all I've got. *He left me pudding.*

"Should I come with you?" she asks me once she realizes I'm not going to change my mind.

I shake my head. "I want to do this on my own."

I sit down on my bed. The act takes a full thirty seconds to complete. But once I do, I instantly feel better. Gabby pulls the wheelchair around next to me.

"You're sure I can't come with you? Push you, maybe?"

"I'm already going to need you to help me into the shower. My level of dignity is fairly low, so I'm just hoping to spare myself the experience of you watching me tell someone I have feelings for him when, you know, he will probably turn me down."

"This seems like something that maybe you should wait and think about," she says.

"And tell him when? What am I gonna do? Call him on the phone? 'Hello, hospital. Henry, please. It's Hannah.'"

"That's a lot of *H*s," she says.

"You can only muster up this type of courage a few times in your life. I'm just stupid enough to have it now. So help me into the damn wheelchair so I can go make a fool out of myself."

She smiles. "All right, you got it."

She starts helping me into the chair, and pretty soon I'm rolling. "Wish me luck!" I say, and I head for the door and then brake abruptly, as I've learned to. "Do you think sometimes you can just *tell* about a person?"

"Like you meet them and you think, this one isn't like the rest of them, this one is something?"

"Yeah," I tell her. "Exactly like that."

"I don't know," she says. "Maybe. I'd like to think so. But I'm not sure. When I met Mark, I thought he looked like a dentist."

"He *is* a dentist," I tell her, confused.

"Yeah, but when we were in college, when I was, like, nineteen, I thought he looked like the kind of guy who would grow up to be a dentist."

"He seemed stable? Smart? What? What are you trying to say?"

"Nothing," she says. "Never mind."

"Did you think he looked boring?" I ask her, trying to get to the bottom of it.

"I thought he looked bland," she says. "But I was wrong, right? I'm just saying I didn't get those feelings you're talking about with my husband. And he's turned out to be a great guy. So I can't confirm or deny the existence of being able to just *tell*."

I think you can. That's what I think. I think I've always thought that. I thought it the first time I met Ethan. I thought there was something different about him, something special. And I was right. Look at what we had. It turned out not to be for a lifetime, but that's OK. It was real when it happened.

And I feel that way about Henry now.

But I don't know how to reconcile that with what Gabby is saying. I don't want to say that I believe you can tell when you meet someone who's right for you and then acknowledge that by that logic, Mark's not the one for her.

"Maybe some people can tell," I offer.

"Yeah," she says. "Maybe some people can. Either way, you believe you feel it. That's what's important."

"Yeah," I say. "Right. I gotta tell him."

"What are you gonna say?" she asks me.

"Yeah," I say, turning my wheelchair back to her. "What *am* I going to say?" I think about it for a moment. "I should practice. You be Henry."

Gabby smiles and sits down on the bed, taking on an affected manly pose.

"No, he's not like that," I say. "And he'd be standing."

"Oh," she says, standing up. "Sorry, I just wanted it to be easier because you're . . ."

"In a wheelchair, right," I say. "But don't coddle me. If I'm wheeling through the halls trying to find him, most likely he's going to be standing, and I'll be sitting."

"OK," she says. "Go for it."

I breathe in deeply. I close my eyes. I speak. "Henry, I know this sounds crazy—"

"Nope," she says. "Don't start with that. Never start with 'I know this sounds crazy.' Come from strength. He'd be lucky to be with you. You've got an extraordinary attitude, a brilliant heart, and an infectious optimism. You are a dream woman. Come from strength."

"OK," I say, and then I look down at my legs. "I don't know, Gabby. I'm crippled. This isn't my strongest moment."

"You're Hannah Martin. Your weakest moment is a strong moment. Be Hannah Martin. Let's hear it."

"OK," I say, starting over. And then it just comes out of me. "Henry, I think we have something here. I know I'm a patient and you're a nurse, and this is all very against the rules and everything, but I truly believe we could mean something to each other, and we owe it to ourselves to see. How often can you say that about somebody and really mean it? That the two of you have potential for something great? I want to see where we end up. There's something about you, Henry. There's something about us. I can just tell." I look at Gabby. "OK, how was that?"

Gabby stares at me. "Is that how you really feel?"

I nod. "Yeah."

"Go find him!" she says. "What the hell are you doing practicing on me?"

I laugh. "What do you think he'll say?"

"I don't know," she says. "But if he turns you down, he's such a massive idiot that I'm pretty sure you'll have dodged a bullet."

"That doesn't make me feel better."

She shrugs. "Sometimes the truth doesn't," she says. "Now, go."

And so I do.

I wheel myself out of my room and speed down the hall to the nurses' station. I ask where Henry is, and they tell me they don't know. So I get into the elevator, and I go to the top floor, and I start wheeling the halls. I won't stop until I find him.

It's Saturday night. Gabby and I are watching a movie. Charlemagne is lying in her dog bed at our feet. We ordered Thai food, and Gabby is eating all the pad Thai before I can even get my hands on it.

"You know I'm pregnant, right? I should at least get a chance to eat some of the food."

"My husband cheated on me and then left me," she says. She's not even looking up. She's just shoveling noodles into her mouth with her eyes glued to the television. "I don't have to be nice to anyone right now."

"Ugh, fine, you win."

The phone rings, and I look at the caller ID, stunned. It's Ethan.

Gabby pauses the movie. "Well, answer it!" she says.

I do. "Hi," I say.

"Hey," he says. "Is now a good time?"

"Sure. Yeah."

"I was thinking I would come over," he says. "Now, if that's OK. I can stop by."

"Yeah," I tell him. "Absolutely. Come by."

I hang up the phone and stare at Gabby. "What is he going to say?" I ask her.

"I was just going to ask you. What *did* he say?"

"He said he wants to come over. He said he'll stop by."

"Which was it? Come over or stop by?"

"Both. First he said one, then the other."

"Which one was first?"

"Come by. I mean, come over. Yeah, then he said 'stop by.'"

"I don't know if that's good or bad," she says.

"Me, neither." Suddenly, I am overwhelmed by desperation. What is about to happen? "Do you think it's possible he's up for all of this? That I might not lose him?"

"I don't know!" she says. She's just as stressed out about this as I am.

"People shouldn't be possibly breaking up with their boy-friends while they are pregnant," I say. "All of this anxiety can't be good for the baby."

"Are you gonna change?" Gabby asks.

I look down at myself. I'm wearing black leggings and a huge sweatshirt. "Should I?"

"Politely, yes."

"OK," I say. "What do I wear?" I get up and head to my room, thinking of what to put on.

"How about that red sweater?" she calls up the stairs. "And just jeans or something. Super casual."

"Yeah, OK," I say, peeking my head back out to talk to her. "Casual but nice."

"Right," she calls to me. "Also, fix your bun. It's falling over."

"OK."

The doorbell rings when I'm putting on mascara. I feel so fat lately. No telling if it's because I'm actually fat, just think I'm fat, or both.

"I'll get the door!" Gabby says, and I hear her run up the stairs, away from the front door and toward me. "Before I do, though . . ." she says when she's standing outside my room.

"Yeah?"

"You're amazing. You're smart, and you're loving, and you are the best friend I've ever had, and you are just the best best best person in the universe. Don't ever forget that."

I smile at her. "OK," I say.

And then she turns away and runs down to get the door. I hear her greet him. I come out of my room and down the stairs.

"Hi," I say to him.

"Hi," he says. "Can we talk?"

"Sure."

"You guys take the living room," Gabby says. "I was going to take Charlemagne for a walk anyway."

Ethan bends down and pets Charlemagne as Gabby grabs the leash and slips on a pair of shoes. Then she and Charlemagne are out the door.

Ethan looks at me.

We don't have to talk about anything. I can tell just by the sorrowful look on his face what he's here to say.

It's over.

All I have to do is get through this. That is all I have to do. And when he's gone, I can cry until I'm a senior citizen.

"We can sit down," I tell him. I am proud of how even my voice sounds.

"I can't do it," he says, not moving.

"I know," I tell him.

His voice breaks. His chin starts to spasm, ever so slightly. "I've thought, for so many years now, that I just needed to get you back, and everything would be fine." He's so sad that I don't have any room to be sad.

"I know," I say. "Come sit down." I lead him over to the sofa. I sit so he will sit. Sitting helps sad people, I think. Later, when he is gone, when I am the sad one again, I will sit. I will sit right here.

"I messed this all up. We never should have broken up in college. We should have stayed together. We should have . . . we should have done this all differently."

"I know," I say.

"I'm not ready for this," he says. "I can't do it."

I knew this was what he was going to say, but hearing the words still feels like I'm being punched in the lungs.

"I completely understand," I tell him, because it's true. I wish I didn't understand. Maybe then I could be angry. But I've got nothing to be angry about. All of this is my doing.

"I've been trying for days now to get on board with the idea. I keep thinking that I'll get used to it. That it will all be OK. I keep thinking that if someone is right for you, nothing should get in the way of that. I keep trying to convince myself that I can do this."

"You don't have to—"

"No," he says. "I love you. I meant that when I said it, and I mean it now. And I want to be with you through everything in your life. And I want to be the kind of man who can say, 'OK, you're pregnant with someone else's baby, and that's OK.' But I am not that man, Hannah. I'm not ready to have my own child yet. Let alone raise someone else's. And I know you say that I wouldn't be the dad. I know that. But how can I love you and not share this with you? How could I not be there for all of it? It would drive a wedge between us before we've even gotten this thing off the ground."

"Ethan, listen, I get it," I tell him. "I am so sorry to have put you in this position. I never wanted to do this to you. To make you choose between the life you want and being with me."

"I want a family of my own someday. And if I say yes to you right now, if I say I think we can be together when you're having this baby, I feel like I'd be committing to a family with you. I absolutely believe that we could have a great future together. But I don't think we are ready for this, for having a baby together. Even if it *were* mine."

"Well, you never know what you're ready for until you have to face it," I say. I'm not trying to convince him of anything. It's just something I've learned recently.

"If I had come to you last week and said, 'Hannah, let's have a baby together,' what would you have said?"

"I would have said that was insane." I hate that he's right. "I would have said I'm not ready."

"I'm not prepared to take on another man's baby," he says. "And I'm ashamed of that. I truly am. Because I want to be the man you need. How many times have I told you that there was nothing we could do to mess this up?"

I nod knowingly.

"I want to be the right man for you," he continues. "But I'm not. I can't believe I'm saying this, but . . . I'm not the right man for you."

I look at him. I don't say anything. Nothing I could say would change the way either of us feels. I much prefer problems with solutions, conflicts where one person is right and the other is wrong, and all you have to do is just figure out which is which.

This isn't one of those.

Ethan reaches his hand out and grabs mine. He squeezes it.

And in that one motion, he is no longer the sad one. I am the sad one.

"Who knows?" he says. "Maybe I'll end up a single dad in a

couple of years, and we'll find each other again. Maybe it's just the timing. Maybe now is not our time."

"Maybe," I say. My heart is breaking. I can feel it breaking.

I swallow hard and get hold of myself. "Let's leave it at this," I say. "Just like in high school, this isn't our time. Maybe one day, we'll get the timing right. Maybe this is the middle of a longer love story."

"I like that idea."

"Or maybe we just weren't meant to be," I say. "And maybe that's OK."

He nods, ever so slightly, and looks down at his shoes. "Maybe," he says. "Yeah. Maybe."

Henry's not on my floor or any of the floors above mine. I checked in with nurses, administrators, three doctors, and two visitors of patients whom I mistook for staff. I rolled over three different feet on two different people, and I knocked over a trash can. I'm not sure that pushing yourself around in a wheelchair is that difficult. I think I might just be that uncoordinated.

When I give up on the sixth floor, I get back into the elevator and head down to the fourth, the floor below mine. It's my last shot. According to the elevator buttons, the first three floors hold the lobby, the cafeteria, and administrative offices. So he's got to be on the fourth. It's the only one left.

The elevator opens, and there's a man waiting for it. I start to roll myself out, and he holds the elevator open for me as I pass by. He smiles and then slips into the elevator. He's handsome in an unconventional way, maybe in his late forties. For a moment, I wonder if he smiled at me because he thinks I'm cute, but then I remember that I'm an invalid. He just felt bad for me, wanted to help me out. The realization stings. It is not unlike the time I thought people were checking me out at the grocery store because I was having a great hair day, only to realize later that I'd had a booger. Except this is worse, to be honest. The booger incident was less condescending.

I shake it off the way I shake off everything else that plagues me, and I breathe in deeply, ready to roll my way to Henry. I'm stopped in my place by a nurse.

"Can I help you?" she asks me.

"Yes," I tell her. "I'm looking for Henry. He's a nurse here."

"What's the last name?" she asks. She is tall and broad-shouldered, with short, coarse hair. She looks as if she's been doing this job for a long time and might be sick of it.

I don't actually know Henry's last name. None of the other nurses brought it up, but that's probably because there were no Henrys on that floor anyway. The fact that she's asking is a pretty good indication that he's here.

"Tall, dark hair, brown eyes," I tell her. "He has a tattoo. On his forearm. You know who I'm talking about."

"I'm sorry, Miss, I can't help you. What floor are you a patient on?" She hits the up button on the elevator. I think it's for me.

"What? The fifth floor," I say. "No, listen to me. Henry with the tattoo. I need to speak to him."

"I can't help you," she says.

The elevator in front of us dings and opens. She looks at me expectantly. I don't move. She raises her eyebrows, and I raise mine back. The elevator closes. She rolls her eyes at me.

"Henry isn't here today," she says. "He starts on my service tomorrow. I've never met him, so I'm not sure that it's the Henry you're talking about, but the Henry I know was transferred to me because his boss felt he was getting too close to a patient." She can see my face change, and it emboldens her. "You can see my hesitance," she says. She hits the button again.

"Did he get in trouble?" I ask her, and the minute it comes out of my mouth, I know it's the wrong thing to say.

She frowns at me, as if I have confirmed her worst fears about myself and that I also just don't seem to get it.

"I retract my question," I tell her. "You're probably not open to helping me find him outside of the hospital, right? No last name, no phone number?"

"That's correct," she says.

I nod. "I hear you," I say. "Could I leave a message? With my phone number?"

She's stoic and stone-faced.

"I'm gonna guess that even if I did, you'd probably just throw it away."

"I wouldn't waste much thought about it," she says.

"OK," I say. I can finally see now that it's not going to happen today. Even if I could get past this woman, he's still not here. Unless . . . maybe she's lying? Maybe he is here after all?

I hit the up button on the elevator. "OK," I say. "I read you loud and clear. I'll get out of your hair."

She looks at me sideways. The elevator dings and appears again. I start rolling myself into it and wave good-bye. She walks away. I let the elevator doors close, and then I hit the button for the same floor I'm on.

The doors open, and I take off. I wheel myself in the opposite direction from where she's looking, past the nurses' station. I'm at the corner before she sees me.

"Hey!" she says. I take the corner and push with all of my might toward the end of the hall. My arms feel weak, and my heart is pumping faster than it has in days, but I keep going. I turn back to see her briskly walking toward me. Her face looks pissed, but I get the impression she's trying not to cause a scene.

In front of me are two double glass doors. They don't open from my side, so I'm stuck. I'm dead-ended. The evil nurse is coming for me. On the opposite side of the doors, I see a doctor coming through. Any second now, he's going to open the doors, and I can roll in. Maybe.

I'm not sure what's possessed me to do this. Maybe it's my desire to find Henry. Maybe it's the fact that I've been cooped up in a room for so long with everyone on the planet telling me what to do. Maybe it's the fact that I almost died, and on some level, that has to make you fearless. Maybe it's all three.

The door opens, and the doctor walks by me. I roll myself through, praying the doors close before Nurse Ratched gets to me. But I don't have time to stop and look. I keep rolling, looking in each room for Henry. I get right to the end of the hall. I turn left around the corner, and then I feel the grip of two hands on the back of my chair. Abruptly, I come to a complete stop.

Caught.

I turn and look at her. "What can I say so that you don't arrest me?"

She pushes me forward, but she doesn't answer my question. Suddenly, with my adrenaline now fading, I'm realizing that my stunt was stupid and fruitless. He's really not here. And unless I come back to this hospital tomorrow and try this again, I'm probably never going to find him.

"I can push myself," I tell her.

"Nope," she says.

I laugh nervously. "This sort of thing probably happens all the time, I bet," I say, trying to lighten the mood.

"Nope."

We get to the elevator. She hits the button. I can't look at her. The elevator opens.

"Well," I say, "I guess this is good-bye."

She stares at me and then puts her hands back on my chair. "Nope."

She pushes the two of us into the elevator and hits the button for the fifth floor.

I sit in silence, staring forward. She stands next to me. When the elevator opens, she pushes me toward the nurses' station.

"Hi, Deanna," she says. "Can you tell me what room this patient belongs in?"

"I can tell you," I say to her. "I'm right over here."

"If it's all right with you, Wheels, I'd like to hear it from Deanna," she says to me.

Deanna laughs. "Hannah's right. She's just right there." Deanna points to my door, and Nurse Ratched pushes me all the way to my room, where Gabby is waiting.

Gabby sees the two of us and isn't quite sure what to make of it. "What happened?"

Nurse Ratched pipes up before I can. "Look," she says directly to me, "everyone makes bad decisions sometimes, and this is probably a crazy time in your life, so I'm going to let this go. But you will not come down to my floor again. Are we clear?"

I nod, and she starts to leave.

"Nurse," I say, and then I realize I shouldn't call her Nurse Ratched to her face. "Sorry," I say. "What was your name?"

"Hannah," she says.

"For heaven's sake! I'm trying to apologize. I'm just asking your name."

"I know," she says. "My name is Hannah."

"Oh," I say. "Sorry."

Hannah looks at Gabby. "Is she always this charming?"

"This appears not to be her best day," Gabby says. I think

that's as close as she can come to defending me. So I appreciate it.

"I just wanted to say I'm sorry for giving you trouble. I was wrong to do it."

"Well, thank you," she says. She turns to leave.

"Hannah," I say.

She turns back to me.

"I'm a stalker."

"Excuse me?"

"It's not Henry's fault," I tell her. "That we got too close, I mean. He was nothing but professional, and I basically stalked him. He kept making it clear that we had a professional relationship and nothing more. And I kept pressing the issue, trying to get him to change his mind. It's me. He's not . . . I'd hate for him to be considered unprofessional because of the way I behaved. It was me."

She nods and leaves. I'm not entirely sure if she believes me, but my actions today sort of support the claim that I'm at least a little delusional. So I have that going for me.

I turn to Gabby. "He wasn't there, and I caused a scene."

"No big speech?"

I shake my head. "There was a chase, though."

"Well, I guess that's enough drama for one day. Dr. Winters came while you were gone. She says we're good to go."

"So we're leaving?" I ask her.

"Yep."

"What do I do about Henry?" I ask her. "I can't leave knowing I'll never see him again."

"I don't know," she says. "Maybe you'll run into him sometime? Here at the hospital, during a physical therapy appointment?"

"Maybe," I say.

"If it's meant to be, you'll find each other," she says. "Right?"

"Yeah," I tell her. "I don't know. I guess."

Instinctually, from muscle memory, I put my hands on the armrests of the wheelchair, as if I think I'm going to stand up. And then I remember who I am. And what is going on.

Deanna comes in. "You ready to go?" she says.

"Yes, ma'am," I tell her.

Gabby has my things. Deanna pushes me to the elevator. She stays with us as we start to move down. I wonder if Deanna is doing this because it's protocol or because I'm a flight risk. The elevator opens for a minute on four, as an older woman gets in. I can see Nurse Hannah standing at the nurses' station talking to a patient. She looks at me and then looks away. I swear I see a smile crack on her face, but I see what I want to see sometimes.

When we get to the lobby, Deanna tells me that the wheelchair is mine to keep. For a moment, I think, *Cool, free wheelchair*, and then I remember that I am a person other people give wheelchairs to. *Shake it off.*

"Thanks, Deanna," I say as we exit onto the street. She waves and heads back in.

Mark pulls up with the car. He gets out and runs toward me. I realize it's the first time I've seen him since the accident. And that's sort of weird, isn't it? Shouldn't he have visited me? I would have visited him.

Gabby and Mark put my stuff into the car, and I wheel myself to the door. I try to open it myself, but it's harder than I think. I wait patiently for one of them to come around to the side, and as I do, I look up at the building.

I may never see Henry again.

Gabby opens my door and helps me into the backseat. Mark puts my wheelchair into the trunk. We drive away.

If I'm meant to find him, I'll find him. I guess I do believe that.

But sometimes I wish *I* got to decide what I was meant to do.

Gabby left early this morning to go spend the day with her parents. Mark is coming later to pick up the rest of his things, and she doesn't want to be here.

Mark has only come by one other time since he left, to grab a few suits and some odds and ends. Neither Gabby nor I was here, and it was a bit creepy, to be honest, coming home to see the house picked through. Gabby changed the locks after that. So now Mark needs one of us to be here while he moves his stuff out. It seems quite obvious that I am the woman for the job.

In his e-mail, he said he'd be here by noon, but it's early enough that I figure I've got some time to kill. I decide now is the time to call my parents and tell them the news. At this hour, I can probably grab them before they head out for dinner in London.

I dial their landline, prepared to tell them I'm pregnant the moment one of them picks up. I'm just going to blurt it out before I start to worry what they will say.

But the voice I hear on the other end of the line, the voice that says "Hello?" isn't my mother or my father. It's my sister.

"Sarah?" I ask. "What are you doing at Mom and Dad's?"

"Hannah!" she says. "Hi! George and I are here for the week-end." She pronounces it "wee-KEND." I find myself rolling my eyes. I can hear my dad in the background, asking who is on the phone. I hear my sister's voice turn away from the handset. "It's Hannah, Dad. Chill out . . . Dad wants to talk to you," she says.

"Oh, OK," I say back, but she doesn't give up the phone.

"I want to know when you're coming to visit," she says. "You didn't come last Christmas like you normally do, so I think we're owed."

I know she's joking. But it irritates me that she assumes I should always go there. Just once, I'd like to be important enough to be the visited instead of the visitor. Just once.

"Well, I'm in L.A. now," I tell her. "So the flight is a bit longer. But I'll get there. Eventually."

"OK, OK," she says to my dad. "Hannah, I have to go." She's gone before I can even say good-bye.

"Hannah Savannah," my dad says. "How are you?"

"I'm good, Dad. I'm good. How are you?"

"How am I? How am I? That is the question."

I laugh.

"No, I'm fine, sweetheart. I'm fine. Your mother and I are just sitting here discussing whether we want to order Italian or Thai takeaway for dinner. Your sister and George are trying to get us to go out someplace, but it's pouring out, and I'm just not in the mood."

My plan to blurt it out has failed.

Or has it?

"That's nice. So, Dad, I'm pregnant."

. . .

. . .

. . .

I swear to God, it sounds as if the line has gone dead. "Dad?"

"I'm here," he says, breathless. "I'm getting your mother."

I hear another voice on the phone now. "Hi, Hannah," my mom says.

"Can you repeat what you said, Hannah?" my dad says. "I'm afraid that if your mother hears it from me, she will think I am playing a joke on her."

I have to blurt it out twice?

"I'm pregnant."

. . .

. . .

. . .

Silence again. And then a high-pitched squeal. A squeal so loud and jarring that I pull the phone away from my ear.

And then I hear my mother scream, "Sarah! Sarah, get over here!"

"What, Mom? Good Lord. Stop screaming."

"Hannah is pregnant."

I hear the phone being rustled from person to person. I hear them all fighting over the handset. I hear my mother win.

"Tell us everything. This is marvelous. Tell us about the father! I didn't know you were seeing someone serious."

Oh, no.

My mom thinks I got pregnant on purpose.

My mom thinks I'm ready to have a baby.

My mom thinks there's a father.

My mom, my own mother, is so unaware of who I truly am and what my life is like that she thinks I planned this baby.

That is one of the funniest things I have ever heard. I start laughing, and I keep laughing until the tears in my eyes fall to my cheeks.

"No father in the picture," I say between fits of laughter. "I'll be a single mother. Entirely accidental."

My mother quickly adjusts her tone. "Oh," she says. "OK."

My dad grabs the phone from her. "Wow!" he says. "This is shocking news. But great news! This is great, great news!"

"It is?" I mean, it is. It is. But they think it is?

"I'm going to be a grandpa!" he says. "I am going to be a phenomenal grandfather. I'm going to teach your kid all kinds of grandpa things."

I smile. "Of course you will!" I say it, but I don't mean it in the slightest. He's not here. He's never here.

Sarah grabs the phone from my dad and starts talking about how happy she is for me and how it doesn't matter that I'm raising the baby on my own. And then she corrects herself. "I mean, it matters. Of course it *matters*. But you're going to be so great at it that it won't *matter*."

"Thanks," I say.

And then my mother steals the phone from Sarah, and I can hear the background din changing as she moves into another room. I hear the door shut behind her.

"Mom?" I say. "Are you OK?"

I hear her brace herself. "You should move home," she says.

"What?" I ask her. I don't even understand what she's talking about.

"We can help you," she says. "We can help you raise a baby."

"You mean I should move to London?"

"Yeah, here with us. Home with us."

"London is not my home," I tell her, but this doesn't faze her in the slightest.

"Well, maybe it should be," she says. "You need a family to

raise a baby. You don't want to do it on your own. And your father and I would love to help you, love to have you here. You should be here with us."

"I don't know . . ." I say.

"Why not? You just moved to Los Angeles, so you can't tell me you've built a life there. And if there is no father in the picture, there is no one to hold you back."

I think about what she's saying.

"Hannah," she says. "Let us help you. Let us be your parents. Move into the guest room, have the baby here. I've always said you should have moved to London with us a long time ago." She has never said that. Never once said that to me.

"I'll think about it," I tell her.

I hear the door open. I hear her talk to my father.

"I'm telling Hannah it's time for her to move to London."

"Absolutely, she should," I hear him say. Then he grabs the phone. "Who knows, Hannah Savannah, maybe you were always meant to live in London."

Until this very moment, it never even occurred to me that I might belong in London. The city my own family lives in, and I never considered moving there.

"Maybe, Dad," I say. "Who knows?"

By the time I get off the phone, my parents are convinced I'm moving there as soon as possible, despite the fact that I very clearly promise only that I will consider it. In order to get them off the phone, I have to promise to call them tomorrow. So I do. And then they let me go.

I lie there on my bed, staring at the ceiling for what feels like hours. I daydream about what would happen if I left Los Angeles, if I moved to London.

I consider what my life might look like if I lived in my parents' London apartment with a new baby. I think about my child growing up with a British accent.

But mostly, I think about Gabby.

And everything I'd miss if I left here.

It's noon before Mark shows up.

I answer the door quickly, my hands jittery and nervous. I'm not nervous because he intimidates me or I don't know what to say to him. I'm nervous because I'm scared I might say something I'll regret.

"Hi," he says. He's standing in front of me, wearing jeans and a green T-shirt. As I hoped, he's alone. He has broken-down boxes under his arm.

"Hi," I say. "Come on in."

He steps into the house, lightly, as if he doesn't belong here. "The moving van is coming in a half hour," he says. "I got a small one. That's sounds right, right? I don't have a lot of stuff, I guess."

"Right," I tell him.

I watch as his gaze travels down to Charlemagne, the two of them foes in the most conventional sense of the word. The house isn't big enough for the two of them.

Mark rubs his eyes and then looks at me. "Well," he says, "I'll get to packing, I guess. Excuse me."

He's more uncomfortable about this than I am. His vulnerability eases me. I'm less likely to scream at a repentant man.

I sit on the sofa. I turn on the TV. I can't relax while he's here, but I'm also not going to stand over him.

The movers ring the bell soon after, and he rushes to answer the door.

"If you guys are going to be in and out," I tell him, "I'll keep Charlemagne in the bedroom."

"Great," he says. "Thanks." The movers come in, and Charlemagne and I stay in my room.

I feel like crying for some reason. Maybe it's my hormones. Maybe it's because I never wanted Gabby to have to go through this. I don't know. Sometimes it's hard to tell anymore what's my real reason for crying, laughing, or standing still.

When he's done, he knocks on my door. "That's the last of it," he says.

"Great," I say back.

He looks down at the floor. Then up at me. "I'm sorry," he says. "For what it's worth."

"It's not worth very much," I tell him. Maybe it's because he has the audacity to try to apologize that I no longer feel for him.

"I know," he says. "This situation isn't ideal."

"Let's not do this," I tell him.

"She's going to end up with someone better for her than me," he says. "You, of all people, should know that's good news."

"Oh, I *know* she's going to end up with someone better than you," I tell him. "But that doesn't change the fact that you acted like a chickenshit about it, and instead of being honest, you lied and you cheated."

"You know, when you meet the love of your life, it makes you do crazy things," he says in his own defense. As if I couldn't possibly understand what he's been through because I haven't met my soul mate. As if being in love is an excuse for anything. "I didn't want to love Jennifer this way. I didn't mean for it to happen. But when you have that kind of connection with someone, nothing can stand in its way."

I don't believe that being in love absolves you of anything. I no longer believe that all's fair in love and war. I'd go so far as to say your actions in love are not an exception to who you are. They are, in fact, the very definition of who you are. "Why are you trying to convince me you're a good guy?"

"Because you're the only one Gabby will listen to."

"I'm not going to defend you to her."

"I know that—"

"And more to the point, Mark, I don't agree with you. I don't think meeting the love of your life gives you carte blanche to ruin everything in your path. There are a lot of people out there who find the person they believe they are supposed to be with, and it doesn't work out because they have other things they have to do, and instead of being a liar and running from their responsibilities, they act like adults and do the right thing."

"I just want Gabby to know that I never meant to hurt her."

"OK, fine," I tell him, so that he will leave. But the truth is, it's not OK. It's not OK at all.

It doesn't matter if we don't mean to do the things we do. It doesn't matter if it was an accident or a mistake. It doesn't even matter if we think this is all up to fate. Because regardless of our destiny, we still have to answer for our actions. We make choices, big and small, every day of our lives, and those choices have consequences.

We have to face those consequences head-on, for better or worse. We don't get to erase them just by saying we didn't mean to. Fate or not, our lives are still the results of our choices. I'm starting to think that when we don't own them, we don't own ourselves.

Mark moves toward the front door, and I follow him out.

"So I guess that's it, then," he says. "I guess I don't live here anymore."

Charlemagne comes out of the bedroom and runs over to him. He's skittish around her, scared. Maybe that's why she pees on his shoe. Or maybe it's because he's standing at the door, where we normally put her wee-wee pads.

Either way, I watch as she squats down and pees right on him.

He makes a face of disgust and looks at me. I stare back at him.

He turns around and walks out.

When Gabby comes home later that day, Charlemagne and I rush to the door. I greet her by telling her what Charlemagne did.

Gabby laughs a full belly laugh and leans over to give Charlemagne a hug.

The three of us stand there, laughing.

"My parents want me to move to London," I say. "They said they'll help me with the baby."

Gabby looks up at me, surprised. "Really?" she says. "What do you think of that? Think you'll go?"

And then I say something that I've never said before. "No," I say. "I want to stay here." I start laughing suddenly.

Gabby looks at me as if I have three heads. "What is so funny?" she says.

Between the laughter, I say, "It's just that I ruined things with the only man I think I've ever really loved. I'm pregnant with a baby I didn't plan for, as a result of sleeping with a married man, who won't even be in my child's life. I'm fatter than I've ever been. And my dog is still peeing inside the house. And yet, somehow, I feel like my life here is so good I couldn't possibly leave it. For the first time in my life, I have someone I feel like I can't live without."

"Is it me?" Gabby says suspiciously. "Because if it's not, this is a weird story."

"Yeah dude," I say to her. "It's you."

"Awww, thanks, bro!"

I'm sitting in the backseat of the car, looking out the open window. I'm inhaling the fresh air as we drive through the city. It's possible that from an outside perspective, I look like a dog. But I don't care. I'm so happy to be out of the hospital. To be living out in the real world. To see sunshine without the filter of a windowpane. Everything in the world has a smell to it. Outside isn't just the smell of fresh-cut grass and flowers. It's also smoke from diners and garlic from Italian restaurants. And I love all of it. It's probably just because I've spent so much time inhaling inorganic scents in a sterile hospital. And maybe a month from now I won't appreciate it the way I do right now. But that's OK. I appreciate it now.

I turn my head away from the window for a moment when I hear Mark sigh at a red light. I notice now that it is eerily quiet in the car. Mark seems to be getting more and more nervous the closer we get to their house. As I pay more attention, I can tell that he's out of sorts.

"Are you OK?" Gabby asks him.

"Hm? What? No, yeah, I'm fine," he says. "Just focusing on the road."

I can see his hands twitching. I can hear the shortness of his breath. And I'm starting to wonder if I'm missing something, if maybe he really doesn't want me living with them, if he sees it as a burden.

If he did, if he told Gabby that he didn't want to take on the responsibility, she'd fight him on it. I know that. And she'd never let on to me. I know that, too. So it's entirely possible that I'm imposing and I don't even know it.

We pull up to the side of the road in front of their place, and I can see that Mark installed a ramp for me to get up the three small steps to their door. He gets out of the car and immediately comes around to my side to help me out. He opens my door before Gabby can even get to me.

"Oh," he says. "You need the chair." Before I can answer, he's opened the trunk and is pulling it out. It drops to the ground with a thud. "Sorry," he says. "It's heavier than I thought."

Gabby moves toward him to help him open it up, and I see him flinch at her touch.

It's not me he's uncomfortable around. It's her.

"Are you sure you're OK?" she asks.

"Let's just get inside, OK?" he says.

"Um, OK . . ."

The two of them help me into the chair, and Mark grabs my bags. I wheel myself behind Gabby as she makes her way to the front door.

When she opens it and the three of us walk through the door, the tension is palpable. There is something wrong, and all three of us know it.

"I installed a seat in the shower and took the door off. It's just a curtain now. That should make it easy for you to get in and out on your own," Mark says.

He's talking to me, but he's looking at Gabby. He wants her to know all the work he did.

"I also moved all of your things into the first-floor office.

And put the guest bed in there so you don't have to go up and down the stairs. And I lowered the bed. You can try it."

I don't move.

"Or later, I guess."

Gabby looks at him sideways.

"You should be able to rest down on it to sit and then swing your legs over, as opposed to having to use your pelvis to sit or stand."

"Mark, what is going on?" Gabby asks.

"I bought a two-way pager system, so if you're in bed, you can just talk into it, and Gabby will know to come get you. And the dining-room table was too high, so this morning I had one delivered that is lower to the ground so your chair can reach."

Gabby whips her head around the corner, surprised. "You did that this morning? Where did our table go?"

Mark breathes in. "Hannah, could you give us a minute? Maybe you could confirm that your bed is the right height?"

"Mark, what the hell is going on?" Gabby's voice is tight and rigid. There is no bend in it, no patience.

"Hannah," he pleads.

"OK," I say, and I start wheeling myself away.

"No!" Gabby says, losing her patience. "She can barely move herself from place to place. Don't ask her to leave the room."

"It's fine, really," I say, but just as I say it, Mark blurts it out.

"I'm leaving," he says. He looks at the ground when he says it.

"To go where?" Gabby asks.

"I mean I'm leaving you," he says.

She goes from confused to stunned, as if she's been slapped across the face. Her jaw goes slack, her eyes open wide, her head shakes subtly from side to side, as if incapable of processing what she's hearing.

He fills in the gaps for her. "I've met someone. And I believe she is the one for me. And I'm leaving. I've left you with everything you two could need. Hannah is taken care of. I'm leaving you the house and most of the furniture. Louis Grant is drafting the paperwork."

"You called our attorney before you talked to me?"

"I was just asking him for a referral when he explained he could do it himself. I didn't mean to go behind your back."

She starts laughing. I knew she was going to start laughing when he said that. I wonder if the second it came out of his mouth, he thought, *Oh, crap, I shouldn't have said that.* I want to wheel out of the room very badly, but I also know that my wheelchair squeaks, and we are three people in one room. If one of us leaves, the other two are going to notice. And I'm not even sure they are registering that I'm here. I don't want to bring attention to the fact that I'm here by not being here anymore.

"You have got to be kidding me," she says.

"I'm sorry," he says. "But I'm not. We should talk about this in a few days, when you've had time to adjust to the information. I'm truly sorry to hurt you. It was never my intention. But I am in love with someone else, and it no longer seems fair to keep going the way we have been."

"What am I missing?" she asks. "We were talking about having a baby."

Mark shakes his head. "That was a . . . that was wrong of me. I was . . . pretending to be someone I'm not. I have made mistakes, Gabrielle, and I am now trying to fix them."

"Leaving me is fixing your mistakes?"

"I think we should talk about this at a later date. For now, I have moved my clothes and other things to my new place."

"Did you take my dining-room table?"

"I wanted to make sure you and Hannah had what you needed, so I took the table to my new home and bought you both a table that would work better for Hannah's situation."

"She's not an invalid, Mark. She's going to be walking eventually. I want my table back."

"I did what I thought was best. I think I should go now."

She stares at him for what feels like hours but is probably only thirty seconds. And then she erupts like I have never seen her before.

"Get out of my house!" she screams. "Get out of here! Get away from me!"

He heads for the door.

"I never should have married you," she says, and you can tell she means it. She deeply, deeply means it. She doesn't say it as if it's just occurring to her or as if she wants to hurt his feelings. She says it as if she is heartbroken that her worst fears came true right in front of her very eyes.

He doesn't look back at her. He just walks out the door, leaving it open behind him. It strikes me as cruel, that small gesture. He could have shut the door behind him. It's almost instinctual, isn't it? To shut the door behind you? But he didn't. He let it hang open, forcing her to close it.

But she doesn't. Instead, she crumples to the ground, yelling from the base of her lungs. It's throaty and deep, a grunt more than a scream. "I hate you!"

And then she looks up at me, remembering that I am here.

She gathers herself as best she can, but I wouldn't say she succeeds. Tears are falling down her face, her nose is running, her mouth is open and overflowing. "Will you get his key?" she says. She whispers it, but even in attempting to whisper, she cannot control the edges of her voice.

I spring into action. I wheel myself out the front door and down the ramp. He's getting into the car.

"The key," I say. "Your key, to the house."

"It's on the coffee table," he says. "With the deed. I signed over the townhouse," he says, as if it is a secret he has been waiting to tell, like a student excited to tell the teacher he did the extra credit.

"OK," I say, and then I turn my chair around and head back toward the front door.

"I want her to be OK," he says. "That's why I gave her the house."

"OK, Mark," I say.

"It's worth a lot of money," he says. "The equity in the town-house, I mean. My parents helped us with the down payment, and I'm giving it to her."

I turn the chair around. "What do you want me to say, Mark? Do you want a gold medal?"

"I want her to understand that I'm doing everything in my power to make this easier on her. That I care about her. You get it, don't you?"

"Get what?"

"That love makes you do crazy things, that sometimes you have to do things that seem wrong from the outside but you know are right. I thought you'd understand. Given what Gabby told me happened between you and Michael."

If I hadn't just been in a car accident where I almost lost my life, maybe I'd be hurt by something as small as a sentence. If I hadn't spent the past week learning how to stand up on my own and use a wheelchair, maybe I'd let myself fall for this sort of crap. But Mark has the wrong idea about me. I'm no longer a person willing to pretend the things I've done wrong are justifiable because of how they make me feel.

I made a mistake. And that mistake is part of what has led me to this moment. And while I neither regret nor condone what I did, I have learned from it. I have grown since. And I'm different now.

You can only forgive yourself for the mistakes you made in the past once you know you'll never make them again. And I know I'll never make that mistake again. So I let his words rush past me and off into the wind.

"Just go, Mark," I tell him. "I'll let her know the house is hers."

"I never meant to hurt her." He opens his car door.

"OK," I say, and I turn away from him. I roll myself up the ramp. I hear his car leave the street. I'm not going to tell her any of that. She can see the deed to the townhouse on her own and form an opinion about it. I'm not going to try to tell her he didn't mean to hurt her. That's absurd and meaningless.

It doesn't matter if we don't mean to do the things we do. It doesn't matter if it was an accident or a mistake. It doesn't even matter if we think this is all up to fate. Because regardless of our destiny, we still have to answer for our actions. We make choices, big and small, every day of our lives, and those choices have consequences.

We have to face those consequences head-on, for better or worse. We don't get to erase them just by saying we didn't mean to. Fate or not, our lives are still the results of our choices. I'm starting to think that when we don't own them, we don't own ourselves.

I roll back into the house and see Gabby, still lying on the floor, nearly catatonic. She's staring at the ceiling. Her tears spill from her face and form tiny puddles on the floor.

"I don't know if I've ever felt pain like this," she says. "And I think I'm still in shock. It's only going to get worse, right? It's only going to get deeper and sharper, and it's already so deep and so sharp."

For the first time in what feels like a long time, I'm higher up than Gabby. I have to look down to meet her eyeline. "You won't have to go through it alone," I tell her. "I'll be here through every part of it. I'd do anything for you, do you know that? Does it help? To know that I'd move mountains for you? That I'd part seas?"

She looks up at me.

I move one foot onto the ground and lean over. I try to get my hands onto the floor in front of me.

"Hannah, stop," she says as I push my center of gravity closer to her, trying to lie down next to her. But I don't have the mechanics right. I don't have the right strength just yet. I topple over. It hurts. It actually hurts quite a bit. But I have pain medication in my bag and things to do. So I move through it. I scoot next to her, pushing the wheelchair out of the way.

"I love you," I tell her. "And I believe in you. I believe in Gabby Hudson. I believe she can do anything."

She looks at me with gratitude, and then she keeps crying. "I'm so embarrassed," she says between breaths. She's about to start hyperventilating.

"Shhh. There's no reason to be embarrassed. I can't go to the bathroom on my own. So you have no right to claim embarrassment," I tell her.

She laughs, if only for the smallest, infinitesimal second, and then she starts crying again. To hear it makes my heart ache.

"Squeeze my hand," I tell her as I take her hand in mine. "When it hurts so bad you don't think you can stand it, squeeze my hand."

She starts crying again, and she squeezes.

And at that moment, I realize that if I have taken away a fraction of her pain, then I have more purpose than I have ever known.

I'm not moving to London. I'm staying right here.

I found my home. And it's not New York or Seattle or London or even Los Angeles.

It's Gabby.

That night, Gabby and I decide to take Charlemagne for a long walk. At first, we were just going to walk around the block, but Gabby suggests getting out of the neighborhood. So we get into the car and drive to the Los Angeles County Museum of Art.

Gabby says it's beautiful at night. There is a light installation that shines brightly in the dark. She wants to show me.

We stop at Coffee Bean and get tea lattes. Mine is herbal because Gabby read an article that said pregnant women shouldn't have any caffeine. There are about ten others that say caffeine is fine in moderation but Gabby is very persuasive.

We park the car a few blocks from the museum, put Charlemagne on the sidewalk, and start walking. The air is cool; the sun set early tonight, and it's quiet on the streets of L.A., even for a Sunday night.

Gabby doesn't want to talk about Mark, and I don't really want to talk about the baby. Lately, it seems as if all we do is talk about Mark and the baby. So we decide instead to talk about high school.

"Freshman year, you had a crush on Will Underwood," Gabby says. She sips her drink right after she says it, and I look at her to see her eyes giving a mischievous glance. It's true, I did have a crush on Will Underwood. But she also knows that just mentioning it is enough to make me mortified. During our freshman year, Will Underwood was a senior who was completely cheesy and dated freshman girls. When you are a freshman girl, you don't understand what's so unlikable about guys who are interested in freshman girls. Instead, I very much hoped he'd notice me. I wanted to be one of those girls. He's now a shock jock on an FM station here. He dates strippers.

"Well, I've never had good taste," I say, laughing at myself, and then I point at my belly. "As evidenced here by my baby with no daddy."

Gabby laughs. "Ethan was a good one," she says. "You were smart enough to choose Ethan."

"Twice," I remind her as we keep walking. Charlemagne pulls on the leash, leading us toward a tree. We stop.

"Well, I'm no better at choosing, clearly," Gabby says, and it occurs to me that when you're going through a divorce or when you're having a baby, there is no not talking about it. It shades everything you do. You have to talk about it, even when you aren't talking about it. And maybe that's OK. Maybe what's important is that you have someone to listen.

Charlemagne pees beside the tree and then starts scratching away at the grass, trying to cover it up. This is a pet peeve of Gabby's, because Gabby appreciates a nicely landscaped curb.

"Charlemagne, no," Gabby says. Charlemagne stops and looks up at her, hoping to please. "Good girl," Gabby says, and then she looks at me. "She's so smart. Did you think dogs were this smart?"

I laugh at her. "She's not that smart," I tell her. "Earlier today, she ran into the wall. You just love her, so you think she's smart. Rose-colored glasses and what have you."

Gabby cocks her head to the side and looks at Charlemagne.

"No," she says. "She's really smart. I just know it. I can tell. I mean, yes, I do love her. I love her to pieces. I honestly don't know what I was doing without a dog this whole time. Mark ruined all the good stuff."

Obviously, Mark didn't actually ruin every good thing in the world, but I don't contradict her. Anger is a part of healing. "Yeah," I say. "Well, actually, you did have good taste in men once. Remember how in love you were with Jesse Flint all through high school? And then senior year? You guys went out on the one date?"

"Oh, my God!" Gabby says. "Jesse Flint! I could never forget Jesse Flint! He was an actual dream man. I still think he's the most handsome guy I've ever seen in my life."

I laugh at her. "Oh, come on! He was tiny. I don't even know if he was taller than you."

She nods. "Oh, yes, he was. He was one inch taller than me and perfect. And then stupid Jessica Campos got back together with him the day after our date, and they ended up getting married after college. The major tragedy of my young life."

"You should call him," I say.

"Call Jesse Flint? And say what? 'Hey, Jesse, my marriage is over, and I remember one nice date with you when we were seventeen. How's Jessica?'"

"They got divorced, like, two years ago."

"What?" Gabby says. She stops in place. "No more Jesse and Jessica? Why did I not know about this?"

"I assumed you did. It was on Facebook."

"He's divorced?"

"Yeah, so maybe you two can talk about what divorce is like or something."

She starts walking again. Charlemagne and I walk with her. "You know something embarrassing?"

"What?"

"I thought about Jesse on my wedding day. How lame is that? As I was walking down the aisle, I specifically thought, *Jesse Flint is already married. So he isn't the one you were meant to be with.* It made me feel better about my decision. I think I figured, you know, Mark really was the best one out there for me that was available."

I can't help it. I start laughing. "It's like you really wanted to get Count Chocula, but someone took the last box, and all they had was Cheerios, so you told yourself, 'OK, Cheerios is what I was meant to have.'"

"Mark is totally Cheerios," Gabby says. But she doesn't say it as if she's in on the joke. She says it as if it's a Zen riddle that has blown her mind. "Not Honey Nut, either. Straight-up, heart-healthy Cheerios."

"OK," I tell her. "So one day, when you're ready, probably a bit far off into the future, you call Count Chocula."

"Just like that?" she asks.

"Yep," I say. "Just like that."

"Just like that," she says back to me.

We walk for a little while, and then she points to a series of lights shining in long rows.

"That's the Urban Light installation I was telling you about," she says.

We walk closer to it and stop just in front of it, across the street. I have a wide view.

It's made up of old-fashioned streetlights, the kind that look as if they belong on a studio lot. The lights are beautiful, all clustered together in rows and columns. I'm not sure I understand the meaning behind it, exactly. I don't know if I get the artist's intention. But it is certainly striking. And I'm learning not to read too much into good things. I'm learning just to appreciate the good while you have it in your sights. Not to worry so much about what it all means and what will happen next.

"What do you think?" Gabby asks me. "It's pretty, right?"

"Yeah," I say. "I like it. There's something very hopeful about it."

And then, as quickly as we came, we turn around and walk back toward the car.

"You're going to find someone great one day," I say to Gabby. "I just have this feeling. Like we're headed in a good direction."

"Yeah?" she says. "I mean, all signs sort of point otherwise."

I shake my head. "No," I say. "I think everything is happening exactly as it's supposed to."

It's early in the morning, and Gabby and I have been lying on the floor all night. The sun is starting to break through the clouds, into the windows, and straight onto my eyes. It gets bright so early now.

"Are you awake?" I whisper. If she's sleeping, I want her to sleep. If she's awake, I need her to help me get up and pee.

"Yeah," she says. "I don't think I slept all night."

"You could have woken me up," I tell her. "I would have stayed up with you."

"I know," she says. "I know you would have."

I turn my head toward her and then push my torso up using my arms, so I'm sitting down. My body feels tight, tighter than it ever felt in the hospital.

"I have to pee," I tell her.

"OK," she says, getting up slowly. It's clumsy, but she's up. I can see now that her eyes are red, her cheeks are splotchy, her skin looks sallow and yellow. She's not doing well. I suppose that's to be expected.

"If you can get me up and bring me my walker, I can do it," I tell her. "I want to do it on my own."

"OK," she says. She gets the walker from where we left it by the front door yesterday. She unfolds it and locks it into place. She puts it in front of me. And then she puts her arms under mine and lifts me. It's sounds so simple, standing up. But it's incredibly hard. Gabby bears almost my entire weight. It can't be easy for her. She's so much tinier than I am. But she manages to do it. She leans me on my walker and then lets go. Now I'm standing on my own, thanks to her.

"OK," I say. "I'll just be anywhere from three to sixty minutes. Depending on whether I manage to fall into the toilet."

She tries to laugh, but her heart isn't in it. I move myself slowly, step by step, in the right direction. "You're sure you don't want help?" she asks.

I don't even turn around. "I got it," I tell her. "You just take care of you."

It feels as if the bathroom is a million miles away, but I get there, one tiny, tentative step at a time.

When I get back to the living room, I'm feeling cold, so I shuffle over to my things that Gabby brought home from the hospital. I rummage through the bag, looking for my sweatshirt. When I finally see it and pull it out, an envelope drops to the floor. The front simply says "Hannah." I don't recognize the handwriting, but I know who it's from.

Hannah,

I'm sorry I had to trade your care to another nurse. I can't keep treating you. I enjoy your company too much. And my coworkers are starting to take notice.

I'm sure you know this, but it's highly unprofessional of any of us on the nursing staff to have a personal relationship with a patient, no matter the scope. I'm not allowed to exchange any personal contact information with you. I'm not allowed to try to contact you after you leave the hospital. If we were to run into each other on the street, I'm not even supposed to say hello to you unless you say hello first. I could be fired.

I don't have to tell you how much this job, this work, means to me.

I've been thinking about breaking the rules. I've been thinking about giving you my number. Or asking for yours. But I care too much about my work to compromise it by doing something I've sworn not to do.

All of this is to say that I wish we had met under different circumstances.

Maybe one day we will end up at the same place at the same time. Maybe we'll meet again when you aren't my patient and I'm not your nurse. When we are just two people.

If we do, I really hope you say hello. So that I can say hello back and then ask you out on a date.

Warmly,
Henry

"He left me the house," I hear from the couch. I tuck the letter away in my bag and turn to see Gabby crying, looking at the coffee table. She has the deed to the house in her hands.

"Yeah," I say.

"His parents paid for the down payment. A lot of his own money went into the mortgage."

"Yeah."

"He feels bad," she says. "He knows what he's doing is screwed up, and he's still doing it. That's what's so strange about this. That's not like him."

I set the walker in front of the couch and slowly let myself down. I really hope we aren't moving from this couch anytime soon, because I think that's all the energy I have for a while.

Gabby looks at me. "He must really love her."

I look at her and frown. I put my hand on her back. "It

doesn't justify what he did," I tell her. "His timing, his selfishness."

"Yeah," she says. "But . . ."

"But what?"

"He did everything he could except stay."

I hold her hand.

"Maybe he just has a feeling about her," Gabby says, echoing my sentiments from yesterday morning. Although, I'll tell you, it feels like a decade ago. "Maybe he can just *tell*."

I don't know what to say to that, so I don't say anything.

"I was never sure he was the one. Even when you asked me the other day, I could sort of feel myself sugarcoating what I really thought. I just thought Mark was a smart decision. We'd been together for a long time, and I just figured that's what you do. But I never had the moment when I just *knew*. You," she says to me, "have that feeling."

I dismiss her. "I've had that feeling before, though. For a long time, I had that feeling about Ethan. Now I have it about Henry. I mean, maybe it doesn't count, if you have it for more than one person."

"But I *never* had it. About him. He never had it about me. And maybe he has it now. It makes me feel a little better," she says. "To think that he left me because he met the one."

"Why does that make you feel better?" I cannot possibly conceive of how that could make her feel better.

"Because if I'm not his soul mate, then that means he's not mine. There's someone else out there for me. If he found his, maybe I'll find my own."

"And that makes you feel better?"

She holds her index finger and thumb together to form the

smallest gap. "Ever so slightly," she says. "So much it's almost nonexistent."

"Invisible to the naked eye," I add.

"But it's there."

I rub her back some more as she digests all of this.

"You know who I thought of yesterday? When you were talking about that feeling? The only one I think I might have felt that with?"

"Who?"

"Jesse Flint."

"From high school?"

She nods. "Yeah," she says. "He ended up marrying that girl Jessica Campos. But I—I don't know, until then, I always figured we would have something."

"They got divorced," I tell her. "A few years ago, I think. I saw it on Facebook."

"Well, there you go," she says. "Just that little piece of information gives me hope that there's somebody out there who makes me feel the way Henry makes you feel."

I smile at her. "I can promise you, there is someone better out there. I'd write it in stone."

"You have to find Henry," she says. "Don't you think? How do we do it? How are you going to find Henry?"

I tell her about the letter and then I shrug. "I might not find him," I say. "And that's OK. If you'd told me a month ago that I was going to get hit by a car and Mark was going to leave you, you'd never have been able to convince me that things would be OK. But I got hit by a car, and Mark left you, and . . . we're still standing. Well, you can stand. I'm sitting. But we're still alive. Right? We're still OK."

"I mean, things are pretty crappy, Hannah," she says.

"But they are OK, aren't they? Aren't we OK? Don't we both still have hope for the future?"

"Yeah." She nods somberly. "We do."

"So I'm not going to go around worrying too much," I tell her. "I'm just going to do my best and live under the assumption that if there are things in this life that we are supposed to do, if there are people in this world we are supposed to love, we'll find them. In time. The future is so incredibly unpredictable that trying to plan for it is like studying for a test you'll never take. I'm OK in this moment. To be with you. Here. In Los Angeles. If we're both quiet, we can hear birds chirping outside. If we take a moment, we can smell the onions from the Mexican place on the corner. This moment, we're OK. So I'm just going to focus on what I want and need *right now* and trust that the future will take care of itself."

"So what is it, then?" Gabby asks.

"What is what?"

"What is it you want out of life *right now*?"

I look at her and smile. "A cinnamon roll."

THREE WEEKS LATER

I am now firmly in my second trimester. I've gained enough weight that I look big but not enough that it's clear I'm pregnant. I'm just big enough to look like I have a beer belly. I'm sure I'll be complaining when I'm the size of a house, but I'm inclined to think this part is worse, at least for my ego. Some days, I feel good. Other days, I have a backache and eat three sandwiches for lunch. I'm convinced that I have a double chin. Gabby says I don't, but I do. I can see it when I look in the mirror. There's my chin and then a second chin right there below the first one.

Gabby comes to a lot of my doctor's appointments and birthing classes. Not all of them but most of them. She has also been reading the books with me and talking things through. Will I have a natural birth? Will I use cloth diapers? (My instinct tells me no and no.) It's nice to have someone in my corner. It makes me more confident that I can do this.

And I am finally finding my confidence. Sure, this is all very scary, and sometimes I want to crawl under the blankets and never come out. But I'm a woman who has been desperately looking for purpose and family, and I found both. Never has it been more clear to me that I have family around me in unconventional places, that I have always had more purpose than I have ever known.

I no longer feel a rush to leave this city and head for greener pastures, because there are no greener pastures and there is no better city. I am grounded here. I have a support system here. I have someone who needs me to put down roots and pick a place.

My parents were disappointed to learn that I wasn't going to join them in London, but the moment they resigned themselves to my decision, they suggested that the two of them and Sarah come out to L.A. when the baby is born. *They* are going to come and visit *me*. Us.

I just started working at Carl's office, and it has been both hugely stabilizing and really eye-opening. I see mothers and fathers every day who are in our office because they have a sick kid or a new baby or they are worried about one thing or another. You see how deeply these parents love their children, how much they would do for them, how far they are willing to go to make them happy, to keep them healthy. It's really made me think about what's important to me, what I'd be willing to lose everything for, not just as a friend or as a parent but also as a person.

I'm enjoying it so much that I'm thinking about working in a pediatrician's office long-term. Obviously, this is all very new, but I can't remember the last time a job made me this excited. I like working with kids and parents. I like helping people through things that might be scary or new or nerve-racking.

So this morning, while Gabby is taking Charlemagne to the vet, I have found myself Googling nursing schools. I mean, it seems completely absurd to have a job, go to nursing school, and have a child, but I'm not going to let that stop me. I'm looking into it. I'll see if there is any way I can make it work. That's what you do when you want something. You don't look for reasons why it won't work. You look for reasons why it will. So I'm searching, I'm digging, for ways to make it happen.

I'm looking into the local community college when my phone rings.

It's Ethan.

I hesitate for a moment. I hesitate for so long that by the time I decide to answer, I've missed the call.

I stare at the phone, stunned, until I hear his voice.

"I know you're home," he says, teasing me. "I can see your car on the street."

I whip my head toward the entry, and I can see his forehead and hair through the glass at the top of the door.

"I didn't get to the phone in time," I tell him as I stand up and walk to the door.

There is a part of me that doesn't want to open it. I've been thinking lately that maybe I am meant to raise this baby on my own, to be on my own, until my kid is in college and I'm pushing fifty. Sometimes, when I'm lying awake at night, I imagine a middle-aged Ethan knocking on my door, years in the future. He says he loves me and can't live without me anymore. And I tell him I feel the same way. And we spend the second half of our lives together. I have told myself on more than one occasion that the timing will work out one day. I've told myself this so many times that I've started to believe it.

And now, knowing he's on the other side of the door, it feels wrong. This wasn't a part of my new plan.

"Will you open the door?" he asks. "Or do you hate me that much?"

"I don't hate you," I say. "I don't hate you at all." My hand is on the knob, but my wrist doesn't turn.

"But you're not going to open the door?"

It's polite to open the door. It's what you do. "No," I say, and then I realize the real reason I don't want to open it, and I figure the best thing to do is to tell him. "I'm not ready to see you," I say. "To look at you."

He's quiet for a moment. Quiet so long that I think he might have left. And then he speaks. "How about just talking to me? Is that OK? Talking?"

"Yeah," I say. "That's OK."

"Well, then, get comfortable," he says. "This may take a minute." I see his hair disappear from view, and I realize he's sitting down on the front stoop.

"OK," I say. "I'm listening."

He's quiet again. But this time, I know he hasn't left. "I broke up with you," he says.

"Well, I don't know about that," I tell him. "I didn't leave you much choice. I'm having a baby."

"No," he says. "In high school."

I smile and shake my head, but then I realize he can't see me, so I give him the verbal cue he's looking for. "No shit, Sherlock."

"I think I wanted to pin it on you because I didn't want to admit that I might have avoided this whole thing if I'd acted differently back then."

"Avoided what? Me being pregnant?" I don't want to avoid being pregnant. I like where life has led me, and if he can't handle it, that is not my problem.

"No," he says. "Being without you for so many years."

"Oh," I say.

"I love you," he says. "I'm pretty sure I loved you from the moment I met you at Homecoming and you told me you listened to Weezer."

I laugh and work my way down to sit on the floor.

"And I broke up with you because I thought I was going to marry you."

"What do you mean?"

"I was nineteen and a freshman in college, and I thought, I have already met the girl I'm going to marry. And it scared me, you know? I remember thinking that I'd never sleep with anyone else. I'd never kiss another girl. I'd never do any of the things my friends at school were doing, things I wanted to do. Because I'd already met you. I'd already met the girl of my dreams. And you know, for one stupid moment in college, I thought that was a bad thing. So I let you go. And if I'm being completely honest, even though it makes me sound like a total jerk, I always thought I'd get you back. I thought I could break up with you and have my fun and be young, and then, when I was done, I'd go get you back. It never occurred to me that you have to hold those things sacred."

"I didn't know that," I tell him.

"I know, because I never told you. And then, of course, I realized that I didn't want any of those stupid college things, I wanted you, but when I came home for Christmas to tell you, you were already dating someone else. I should have blamed myself, but I blamed you. And I should have fought for you, but I didn't. I felt rejected, and I turned to someone else."

"I'm sorry," I say.

"No," he says. "You shouldn't be sorry. I'm sorry. I'm sorry I keep chickening out. I see what I want, and I'm too scared to do what it takes to have it. I'm too much of an idiot to sacrifice the small stuff in order to have the big stuff. I love you, Hannah. More than I have ever loved anyone else. And I told you, when I got you back, that I would never again let anything get in the way."

I nod to myself, even though I know he can't see me.

"And what do I do? At the first sign of trouble, I back out."

"It's not that simple, Ethan. We started dating again, and within two weeks, I told you I was having another man's baby. These are extenuating circumstances."

"I don't know," he says. "I'm not sure I believe in extenuating circumstances, not when it comes to this."

"You said it yourself," I tell him. "Sometimes the timing just doesn't work out."

"I'm not sure I believe in that anymore, either," he says. "Timing seems like an excuse. Extenuating circumstances is an excuse. If you love someone, if you think you could make them happy for the rest of your life together, then nothing should stop you. You should be prepared to take them as they are and deal with the consequences. Relationships aren't neat and clean. They're ugly and messy, and they make almost no sense except to the two people in them. That's what I think. I think if you truly love someone, you accept the circumstances; you don't hide behind them."

"What do you mean?"

"I mean I love you, and I want to be with you, and if you want to be with me, then nothing is going to stop me. Not timing, not babies, nothing. If you want to do this, if you want to be with me, I will take you in whatever form I can have you. I will love you just as you are. I won't try to change a single thing about you."

"Ethan, you don't know what you're saying."

"I do," he says. With my back against the door, I can feel that he has stood up. I stand up with him. "Hannah, I believe you are the love of my life, and I'd rather live a life with forty babies that aren't mine than be without you. I have missed you every day since I last saw you. I've missed you for years. I'm not saying this is an ideal situation. But I am saying that it's one I'm on board for, if you'll have me."

"What happens when my baby is born?" I ask him.

"I don't know," he says. "I know I said that I wasn't ready to be a father. But I keep thinking to myself, what if it was my baby? Would I behave differently? And I would. If you were pregnant by me, accident or not, I'd *get* ready."

"And now?" I ask him through the door. "When it's not your kid?"

"I'm not sure I see much of a difference anymore," he says. "What you love, I love."

I stare down at the floor. My hands are shaking.

"We can figure out how you want to play it," he says. "I can be a dad or a stepdad or a friend or an uncle. I can help with all the classes and be there when you give birth, if you'll let me. Or I can hang back, if that's what you want. I'll follow your lead. I'll be the person you need me to be. Just let me be a part of this, Hannah. Let me be with you."

I put my hands on the door to steady them. I feel as if I might fall down. "I don't know what to say," I tell him.

"Say how you feel," he says.

"I feel confused," I say. "And surprised."

"Sure," he says.

"And I feel like maybe we can do this."

"You do?"

"Yeah," I say. "I feel like maybe this was how it was supposed to go all along."

"Yeah?" he says. I can feel the joy in his voice as it vibrates through the door.

"Yeah," I say. "Maybe I was meant to have this baby. And I was meant to be with you. And everything is happening the way it's supposed to." What I believe to be fated seems to fall perfectly in line with what I want to be true at any given moment. But I think that's OK. I think that's hope. "It's messy," I tell him. "You said earlier that it's messy, and you're right. It's messy."

"Messy is OK," he says. "Right? We can do messy."

"Yeah," I say, tears now falling down my face. "We can do messy."

"Open the door, sweetheart, please," he says. "I love you."

"I love you, too," I say. But I don't open the door.

"Hannah?" Ethan says.

"I'm fat now," I tell him.

"That's OK."

"No, really, I'm growing a double chin."

"I have back acne," he says. "Nobody's perfect."

I laugh through my tears. "Are you sure you can be with a fat lady?"

"What did I tell you?" he says. "I told you that you could gain four hundred pounds and I'd want to be with you."

"And you meant it?"

"I meant it."

I open the door to see Ethan standing on the stoop. He is wearing a light blue T-shirt and dark jeans. His eyes are glassy, and his mouth is smiling wide. He has a box of cinnamon rolls in his hand.

"You're the most gorgeous woman I've ever seen," he says, and then he steps into the house, and he kisses me. And for the first time in my life, I know I have done everything right.

THREE MONTHS LATER

I can walk now. Without a walker. On my own. I use a cane sometimes, when I'm tired or sore. But it never holds me back. Sometimes I walk to the convenience store down the street to get a candy bar, not because I want the candy bar but because I appreciate the walk to get one.

Gabby's still not ready to date, still skittish from the shock of it all, but she's moving on. She's happy. She got us a dog. A Saint Bernard just like Carl and Tina have. She named him Tucker.

The woman who hit me proved also to be responsible for another hit-and-run two years ago. She didn't hit a person then, but she did hit a car and drive off. Between insurance payouts and the lawsuit, I'll have enough money to be comfortable on my feet.

When I got to the point where I could get myself from place to place, I bought a car. It's a cherry-red hatchback. You can see me coming from miles away, which I like. I think it's a very "me" car.

Then, once I had a car, I started looking for a job.

I told Carl and Tina that I've been thinking about going to nursing school. After the money comes in, I'll be able to afford it, and I keep thinking about the nurses who helped me during my hospital stay. In particular, I think of Nurse Hannah and how well she handled me at my most annoying. And I think of

Deanna and that pediatric nurse who helped those parents on the oncology floor.

And of course, I think of Henry.

Nurses help people. And I'm starting to think there's nothing more important I can do with my time than that.

When you almost lose your life, it makes you want to double down, to do something important and bigger than yourself. And I think this is my thing.

Carl offered me a job at his pediatric office until I figure out what I want to do. He says that his practice has a program to help staff members go to night school if they meet certain financial criteria. When I reminded him that I probably won't meet those criteria, he laughed at me and said, "Good point! Just come take the job for the experience and living wage, then. Spend your money on school."

So I took him up on it. It's early still, I've only been working there a few weeks, but it's confirming what I already know: I'm headed in the right direction.

I told my parents that I wasn't moving to London, and they were sad but seemed to take it well. "OK," my mom said, "we get it. But in that case, we need to talk about a good time for us to visit."

And then my dad pulled the phone away from her and said he was coming in July, whether I liked it or not. "I don't want to wait until Christmas to see you again, and to be honest, I'm starting to miss Fourth of July barbecues."

A few weeks later, my mom called to say they were considering buying a condo in Los Angeles. "You know, just a place where we could stay when we come to visit from now on," she said. "That is, if you're staying in Los Angeles . . ."

I told her I was. I said I wasn't going anywhere. I said I was here to stay. I didn't even think twice about it. I just said it.

Because it was true.

Ethan has started dating a really nice woman named Ella. She's a high school teacher and a pretty intense cyclist. He bought a bike last month, and now they are on some three-day trek raising money for cancer research. He seems incredibly happy. The other day, he told me that he can't believe he's gone so many years living in Los Angeles without seeing it from a bike. He has bike shorts now. Hilariously tight little bike shorts that he wears with a bike shirt and a helmet. We had dinner the other night, and he biked there from his place, a thirty-minute drive away. The smile on his face when he walked in the door rivaled the sun.

And he's been great to me. He texts me whenever he sees a place with a cinnamon roll that I haven't tried. When I could walk upstairs on my own, he came over and helped Gabby and me move my stuff back up to the second floor. Even he and Gabby have become close in their own right. The point is, Ethan is a great friend. And I'm glad I didn't ruin it by thinking we had anything left between us. We are better this way.

I'd be lying if I said I never think about the child I might have if I hadn't been hit. Occasionally, I'll be doing something completely arbitrary, like taking a shower or driving home, and I'll think about it, the baby. The only way I can make any peace with it is to know that I wasn't ready to be a mother then. But one day, I will be. And I try not to busy my mind with too many thoughts about the past or what could have been.

I wake up most mornings feeling refreshed and well rested,

with an excitement about the day. And as long as you can say that, I think you're doing OK.

I woke up early this morning, so I figured I'd get into the car and head to Primo's. It's a habit I've started for myself, a small treat when I find the time. I often call my dad while I'm there. It's not the same as when he would take me as a child, but it's close. And I'm finding that, at least with my parents, the more we talk on the phone, the better I feel.

I call him now as I'm driving, but he doesn't pick up. I leave a message. I tell him I'm on my way to Primo's and I'm thinking of him.

I pull into the crowded Primo's parking lot and park the car. I grab my cane from the backseat and walk around to the front of the store. I stand in line and order a cinnamon roll and a buttermilk doughnut for Gabby.

I pay, and I'm handed an already-greasy bag.

And then I hear a familiar voice speak to the cashier. "A cinnamon roll, please."

I turn and look. For a moment, I don't recognize him. He's wearing jeans and a T-shirt. I've only seen him in navy-blue scrubs.

I look down at his arm, to make sure I'm not crazy, to confirm that I'm not seeing things.

Isabella.

"Henry?" I say. But of course it's him. And I'm surprised just how familiar he looks, how natural it seems that he would be standing in front of me.

Henry.

"Hello," I say to him. "Hello, hello. Hi."

"Hi," he says, smiling. "I thought I might see you here one of these days."

The man behind the counter gives Henry his cinnamon roll, and Henry hands over some cash.

"All the cinnamon roll joints in all the world, and you had to walk into mine," I say.

He laughs. "By design, actually," he says.

"What do you mean?"

"I figured if I was ever gonna meet you again, run into you, and start a conversation like two normal people, I knew my best bet was a place with good cinnamon rolls."

I blush. I know I'm blushing, because I can feel the warmth on my cheeks.

"Can we talk outside?" he says. The two of us are holding up the line.

I nod and follow him out. He sits down at one of the metal tables. I put down my food. Both of us pull out our cinnamon rolls. Henry takes a bite of his first.

"Did you get my letter?" he asks me when he's done chewing.

I chew, closing my eyes and nodding. "Yeah," I say finally. "I looked for you for a while. On street corners and in stores. I kept looking at men's arms."

"For the tattoo?" he asks.

"Yeah," I say.

"And you never found me."

"Until today," I say.

He smiles.

"I'm sorry if I caused any problems for you at work," I say.

He waves me off. "You didn't. Hannah didn't love the stunt you pulled after I left, though," he says, laughing. "But she also said you seemed like a stalker. And that I was clearly not to blame."

I blush so hard I have to put my head in my hands. "Oh, I'm so embarrassed," I say. "I was on a lot of medication."

He laughs. "Don't be embarrassed," he says. "It made my day when I found out about it."

"It did?" I ask him.

"Are you kidding me? Prettiest girl you've ever seen rolls herself through a hospital desperately trying to find you? Made my week."

"Well," I say. "I . . . wanted to say a proper good-bye, I guess. I felt like we . . ."

Henry shakes his head. "You don't need to explain anything to me. Are you free tonight for dinner? I want to take you on a date."

"You do?" I say.

"Yes," Henry says. "What do you say?"

I laugh. "I say yeah. That sounds lovely. Oh, but I can't tonight. I have plans with Gabby. But tomorrow? Could you do tomorrow?"

"Yep," he says. "I can do whenever you can do. What about now? What are you doing now?"

"Now?"

"Yeah."

"Nothing."

"Will you go for a walk with me?"

"I would love that," I tell him. I wipe the sugar off my hands and grab my cane. "I hope you don't mind that I have to use my cane."

"Are you kidding me?" he says. "I've been going to bakeries for months hoping to find you. Something as small as a cane isn't going to put me off."

I smile. "Plus, if I didn't need this cane, I probably would never have met you. Although, who knows, maybe we could have met another way."

"As a man who has been trying to run into you for months, let me assure you how rare it is that two specific people's paths will cross."

He takes my hand in his, and I have waited for it for so long, have believed so strongly that it may never happen, that it proves as intimate a gesture as any I have ever experienced.

"To car accidents, then," I say.

He laughs. "To car accidents. And to everything that has led up to this."

He kisses me then, and I realize I was wrong about the hand holding. It now feels teenager-ish and quaint. This is what I'd been waiting for.

And as I stand there, in the middle of the city, kissing my night nurse, I know, for the first time in my life, that I have done everything right.

After all, he tastes like a cinnamon roll, and I've never kissed anyone who tasted like a cinnamon roll.

THREE YEARS LATER

Gabby hates surprises, but Carl and Tina insisted that it had to be a surprise party. I told them I would go along with their plan, and then I spilled the beans to Gabby last week so she'd know what to expect. I just knew that if it were me, I'd want the heads-up. So here we are, at her thirty-second birthday, me, Ethan, and fifty of her closest friends, huddled in her parents' living room, completely in the dark, waiting to surprise someone who won't be surprised.

We hear her parents' car pull into the driveway. I give one last warning to everyone to be quiet when I see their headlights go out.

We hear them walk up to the door.

We see the door open.

I turn on the lights, and the entire room of us yells, "Surprise!" just as we are supposed to.

Gabby's eyes go wide. She's a good faker. She looks genuinely terrified. And then she turns immediately into Jesse's chest. He laughs, holding her.

"Happy birthday!" he says, and then he spins her back around to look at all of us.

Tina decorated the room tastefully. Champagne and a dessert bar. White and silver balloons.

Gabby makes her way to me first. "Thank God you told me,"

she whispers. "I don't know if I could have handled all of this without a warning."

I laugh. "Happy birthday!" I tell her. "Surprise!"

We laugh.

"Where's Gabriella?"

"I left her with Paula," I say. Paula is our go-to babysitter, maybe more of a nanny. She's an older woman I worked with in Carl's office. She retired and then found herself really bored, so she looks after Gabriella during the day when I am at work or anytime Gabby, Ethan, and I aren't around. Gabriella loves her. Ethan and I have always jokingly called Gabby the third parent, so it was only natural that we started calling Paula the fourth. For a woman who felt as if her parents weren't around, I've certainly given my kid a plethora of them.

"Did you tell Paula yet?" Gabby asks in a clandestine whisper. "About the *thing*?" I can only assume that she's referring to the fact that Ethan and I have, just this month, started trying to have a second child.

"No," I whisper. "You're still the only one who knows."

"Seems better just to let everyone know once we've succeeded," Ethan says. "But Hannah has forgotten to tell you the best part about tonight."

"I have?"

"Paula said she'd spend the night, so it's party time, as far as I'm concerned!" Ethan says, standing beside me. "And happy birthday! That, too." He hands Gabby a bottle of wine that we picked up for her.

"Thank you!" she says. She gives him a big hug. "I love you guys. Thank you so much for all of this."

"We love you, too," I say. "Have you seen the Flints? They're in the back." I point, but she's already moving toward them. I watch her as she hugs her soon-to-be in-laws. You can tell they love her.

"Nice try, kiddo," Carl says, coming up to me. "You two almost fooled me."

I act mock-confused. "I have no idea what you're talking about."

"She knew. I know my daughter, and she knew. And I know Jesse didn't tell her, because he's still too scared of me. You're the only one brave enough to defy me."

I laugh. "She hates surprises," I say in my own defense.

Carl shakes his head and then looks at Ethan. "Is this what serves as an apology with your wife?"

Ethan laughs and puts his hands up in surrender. "I'm staying out of it."

"I'm sorry," I say to Carl sincerely.

He waves me off. "I'm teasing. As long as she's happy, I don't care. And it appears she is."

Tina fights her way through the crowd to talk to us. She gives me a big hug and then goes straight for the kill. "When are you leaving the office to start school full-time?"

"Next month," I say. "But I'm still not sure about this."

I look to Carl. So far, I have put myself through school by working just under full-time for him and taking advantage of his practice's tuition-reimbursement program. It's been an amazing opportunity, but with Gabriella and the possibility of a second child, I want to finish my certification faster. Ethan and I discussed it, and I'm leaving my job to go to school full-time. But if Carl wants me to stay longer, I'll stay longer. I'd do anything for him. Without him, without the Hudsons in general, I don't know where I'd be.

"Would you stop? Get your certification. And when you're done, at least give me the first option to hire you. That's all I can ask."

"But you two have done so much for me. I don't know how I could ever repay you."

"You don't *repay* us," Tina says. "We're your family."

I smile and put my head on Carl's shoulder.

"I do need a favor of you tonight, though," Carl says. "If you'll oblige me."

"Of course," I say.

"Yates has been on me to hire someone from his old office. A nurse, I guess, who's here with him. I swear, Yates is like a dog with a bone. He just will not let up when he wants something."

Dr. Yates is a new doctor at the practice. Carl and Dr. Yates don't see eye to eye on a lot of stuff, but he's a good guy. I invited him to the party even though Carl thought it wasn't necessary. But Carl also wanted to invite the entire office *except* Yates. So . . . I think I was right about this.

"And you know me," Carl continues. "I'm not good talking business at a party. Or, rather, I hate talking business at a party." Carl is perfectly fine talking business anywhere. He just doesn't want to talk to Yates.

"I'll do a quick screening for you if I run into them," I say.

"I'm going to go check on Gabriella," Ethan says. He steps into the kitchen, and I watch as he calls Paula. He always does this. He talks a big game about leaving her for a night, and then he calls every two hours. He has to know how she is, what she's eaten. For someone who didn't know if he was ready to be a parent, he is the most conscientious parent I've ever seen.

He officially adopted Gabriella last year. Ethan wanted us all to have the same name. "We're a family," he says. "A team."

She is now Gabriella Martin Hanover. We are the Martin Hanovers.

And sure, maybe Gabriella and Ethan aren't related by blood, but you'd never know it to look at them, to hear them talk to each other. They are family as much as any two people can be. The other day at the grocery store, the cashier said Gabriella and Ethan had the same eyes. He smiled and said thank you.

"I know, sweetheart, but Daddy needs to talk to Paula," I can hear him saying into the phone. "If you go to bed when Paula asks you to, Mama and I will come in and give you a kiss when we get home, OK?" Gabriella must have given the phone back to Paula, because the next thing I hear out of Ethan's mouth is "OK, but you got the marble out of her nose?"

We are tired a lot of the time. We don't go on dates as often as we'd like. But we love each other madly. I'm married to a man who became a father because he loved me and now loves me because I made him a father. And he makes me laugh. And he looks handsome when he dresses up, which he has done tonight.

He comes back into the room, and soon the place is so loud we can barely hear each other speak. Just when the party seems to hit its peak, someone asks Jesse to tell the story of how he and Gabby met. Slowly but surely, the entire house quiets down to listen. Jesse stands at the base of the fireplace so he can be seen and heard by everyone. He's too short to be seen on his own.

"First day of geometry class. Tenth grade. I looked to the front of the classroom and saw the most interesting girl I'd ever laid eyes on."

Jesse has told this story so many times I could tell it myself at this point.

"And, to my delight, she was shorter than me."

Everyone laughs.

"But I didn't ask her out. I was too nervous. Three weeks into school, another girl asked me out, and I said yes because I was fifteen and was going to take it wherever I could get it."

The crowd laughs again.

"Jessica and I dated for a long time and then broke up senior year. And of course, when we broke up, I immediately found Gabby and asked her out. And we had this great date. And then, the next morning, my girlfriend called me, and she wanted to get back together. And . . . we did. Jessica and I spent college together, got married after, yada yada yada . . ."

He always says "yada yada yada."

"Jessica and I split up after two years of marriage. It just wasn't working. And then, a few years later, I get a Facebook request from Gabby Hudson. *The* Gabby Hudson."

That's my favorite part. The part where he calls her *the* Gabby Hudson.

"And I got really nervous and excited, and I started Facebook-stalking her and wondering if she was single and if she would ever date me. And the next thing I know, we're out to dinner at some hip restaurant in Hollywood. And I just had this feeling. I didn't tell her then, because I didn't want to be creepy, but I felt like I finally understood why people get married a second time. When I got divorced, I wasn't sure if I'd ever be up for it again. But then it all clicked into place, and I understood that my marriage failed the first time because I picked the wrong person. And finally, the right person was standing in front of me. So I waited the appropriate amount of months of dating, and I told her how I felt. And then I asked her to marry me, and she said yes."

That's usually the end of his story, but he keeps talking.

"I was reading a book about the cosmos recently," he says, and then he looks around and goes, "Hold on, trust me, this relates."

The crowd laughs again.

"And I was reading about different theories about the universe. I was really taken with this one theory that states that everything that is possible happens. That means that when you flip a quarter, it doesn't come down heads *or* tails. It comes up heads *and* tails. Every time you flip a coin and it comes up heads, you are merely in the universe where the coin came up heads. There is another version of you out there, created the second the quarter flipped, who saw it come up tails. This is happening every second of every day. The world is splitting further and further into an infinite number of parallel universes where everything that could happen *is* happening. This is completely plausible, by the way. It's a legitimate interpretation of quantum mechanics. It's entirely possible that every time we make a decision, there is a version of us out there somewhere who made a different choice. An infinite number of versions of ourselves are living out the consequences of every single possibility in our lives. What I'm getting at here is that I know there may be universes out there where I made different choices that led me somewhere else, led me to *someone* else."

He looks at Gabby. "And my heart breaks for every single version of me that didn't end up with you."

I'm embarrassed to say that I start crying. Gabby catches my eye, and I can see she's teary, too. Everyone is staring in rapt attention. Jesse is done speaking, but no one can turn away. I know that I should do something, but I'm not sure what to do.

"Way to make the rest of us look bad!" a guy shouts from the back of the room.

The crowd laughs and disperses. I turn and look behind me, trying to find the man who spoke, but I don't see him. Instead, I see Dr. Yates. I turn to Ethan.

"Dr. Yates is back there," I say. "I'm going to go say hi. I'll be back in a second."

He nods and walks over to the desserts. "I'll get you some cheesecake," he says. "Unless I see a cinnamon roll."

I head over to Dr. Yates.

"Hannah," he says. "Quite a party."

I laugh. "So it is."

"Listen, I want to introduce you to someone." He gestures to the man standing next to him. The man has a large tattoo on his forearm. I can't quite make out what it is. I think it's some sort of cursive script. "This is Henry. I'm trying to persuade him to leave Angeles Presbyterian and come work with us."

"Well, it's a great place to work," I say.

"And Henry is one of the best nurses I've ever worked with," Dr. Yates says.

"Quite a recommendation!" I say to Henry.

"Well, I paid good money for him to say that," he says.

I laugh.

"Would you two excuse me?" Dr. Yates says. "I want to say hello to Gabby."

He walks off, and I am left with Henry, unsure what to say.

"Did you see the dessert bar?" I ask.

"Yeah," he says. "I was gonna grab something, but honestly, I like breakfast sweets much better. Cheese danishes, for instance. Or cinnamon rolls."

"I am obsessed with cinnamon rolls," I say.

"Rightfully so," he says. "They are delicious. I'd take a cinnamon roll over a brownie any day."

I laugh. "It is like you are stealing the words right out of my mouth."

He laughs, too. "Are you from around here?"

"Yeah," I say. "I am. You?"

He shakes his head. "No, I moved out from Texas about eight years ago."

"Oh, whereabouts in Texas?" I ask.

"Just outside of Austin."

I smile. "I lived in Austin for a little while," I say. "Great area."

"Yeah," he says. "Hot as hell, though."

"Yes," I say. "Amen to that."

"So are you a nurse, too?" he asks me.

"Trying to be," I say. "I'm about to leave the practice to go to school full-time. I'm eager to be done with school and start working."

"I remember when I officially became an RN." He laughs to himself. "Seems like ages ago."

"Well, I'm a little bit behind," I say.

"Oh, no," he says. "That's not what I meant at all. I just meant I feel like eons have passed since I started."

"Did you always want to work in health care?" I ask him. Since we're on the subject, no sense in wasting the opportunity to find out more about him and see if he's right for the office.

He nods. "Yeah, more or less. My sister died when I was young."

"I'm so sorry," I say.

He waves me off. "Not necessary, but thank you. I just remember being in the hospital as a kid and seeing how much the nurses were doing to take care of her, to make her comfortable, to make all of us comfortable, and, I don't know, I guess I just always wanted to do that." Aaaaaand there's no way I would ever say no to this guy, with a story like that.

"For me, it was when I was pregnant with my daughter and I had just started working in the office," I say. "I could see how scared some of the parents were sometimes and how much they needed someone who understood what they were going through, and I just really wanted to be that person. And then, once I had my daughter, I felt that fear. I felt how much you ache at the thought of anything happening to them. I just wanted to help soothe the anxiety, you know?"

He smiles. It's a nice smile. There's something very calming about it. "Yeah, I hear you," he says.

If Jesse is right and there are other universes out there, I've probably met Henry before in one of them. We might work together somewhere. Or we would have met in Texas years ago. Maybe in line for a cinnamon roll.

"Well, I'm sure I'll be seeing you," I say. "Some way or another."

"Yeah," he says. "Or maybe in another life."

I laugh and excuse myself as Ethan comes and finds me. He brings me a bite-sized cheesecake.

"What do you say we leave early?" he says.

"Early?" I say. "I thought we were partying all night. Paula will sleep at our place."

"Yeah," he says. "But what if we left the party and went . . . to a *hotel*?"

My eyebrows go up. "Are you suggesting what I think you're suggesting?"

"Let's make a baby, baby."

I put down my glass of water and pop the cheesecake into

my mouth. I scoot over to the corner of the room, where I see Carl, Tina, Gabby, and Jesse talking.

"Carl, he seems great. Henry, I mean. You should hire him. For sure. Gabby, I love you. Happy birthday. If you'll excuse Ethan and me, we have to go home."

Gabby and Tina give me a hug. Ethan shakes hands with Carl and Jesse.

Ethan and I walk out the front door. It started to rain sometime during the evening. I'm chilly, and Ethan takes off his jacket and puts it around my shoulders.

"We could stay up all night, you know," he says, teasing me. "Or we could have sex once, turn on the TV, and fall asleep peacefully."

I laugh. "That last one sounds great," I say.

I get into the car, and I am overwhelmed by gratitude.

If there are an infinite number of universes, I don't know how I got so lucky as to end up in this one.

Maybe there are other lives for me out there, but I can't imagine being as happy in any of them as I am right now, today.

I have to think that while I may exist in other universes, none is as good as this.

Gabby hates surprises, but I couldn't persuade Carl and Tina to go about this any other way, and I wasn't going to be the one who told her. So here we are, at her thirty-second birthday, me, Henry, and fifty of her closest friends, huddled in her parents' living room, completely in the dark.

We hear her parents' car pull into the driveway. I give one last warning to everyone to be quiet when I see their headlights go out.

I hear them walk up to the door.

I see the door open.

I turn on the lights, and the entire room of us yells, "Surprise!" just as we are supposed to.

Gabby's eyes go wide. She's genuinely terrified for a moment. And then she turns immediately into Jesse's chest. He laughs, holding her.

"Happy birthday!" he says, and then he spins her back around to look at all of us.

The living room is full of beautiful decorations. Champagne flutes and Moët. A dessert bar. Henry and I went all over Los Angeles today to find linen tablecloths to match the décor. Henry loves Gabby. Would do anything for her.

Gabby makes her way to me first. "Are you mad?" I ask as she hugs me. "I toyed with the idea of telling you."

She pulls away from me. You can tell from her face that she's still startled. "No," she says. "I'm not mad. Overwhelmed, maybe. I'm sort of shocked that between you and Jesse, no one let it slip."

"We made a pact," I tell her. "Not to say anything. It was really important to your parents."

"They did all this?" she says.

I nod. "All their idea."

"Happy birthday," Henry says. He hands her a glass of champagne. She takes it and gives him a hug.

"And I suppose you won't be having any?" Gabby says, looking at my belly. I'm seven months pregnant. It's a girl. We're naming her Isabella, after Henry's sister. Gabby doesn't know that we've talked about naming her Isabella Gabrielle, after her.

"Nope," I say. "But I'll be drinking with you in spirit. Have you seen the Flints?" I ask her. "They are . . ." I look around until I find them in the back, waving at her and talking to Jesse. She's already moving toward them.

I watch her as she hugs her soon-to-be in-laws. They love her—that much is clear.

"Well done, kiddo," Carl says to me. "I wasn't sure you'd be able to pull it off."

"I'm not great with keeping secrets," I tell him. "But I figured this was an important one. So . . . ta-da!" I lift my hands up in the air, as if I've performed a magic trick.

Carl looks at my hands and then at Henry. "You let your wife attend parties without a wedding ring, son?"

Henry laughs. "You can get into that with her," he says. "I don't tell her what to do."

"I had to take it off," I tell Carl, defending myself. "My fingers are the size of sausages."

Carl shakes his head, teasing me. "Not even married a year, and already she's coming up with reasons to take off the ring. Tsk-tsk."

"You're right. I'm liable to run off at any minute," I say, pointing down to my belly.

Carl laughs, and Tina fights her way through the crowd to talk to us.

"Look at you. About to be a mother and a nurse," she says, by way of hello.

I will finish my nursing degree in a year or so, but that seems like a lifetime from now. All I can think about these days is the baby I'm about to have.

"I'm starting to get nervous about juggling it all when the baby comes," I tell her. "I mean, I know I can do it. Plenty of women do it. I think I'm just anxious about everything changing."

"You're gonna be great," Tina says, smiling at me.

"How many times do I have to ask you to come back and work for me once you're done with school?" Carl says.

"I don't want you to feel like you have to offer me a nursing spot," I say. "I want to earn it on my own."

"I'd give you the shirt off my back if you needed it," Carl says. "But that's not why I'm offering you a job."

"It isn't?"

"No. I think you're going to be a great nurse, and I want you at my office."

"Plus, this little baby girl is the closest thing we've got to a grandchild," Tina says. "I'd like to keep you as close by as possible."

"Everybody wants access to the kid," Henry says.

"When you two have been married as long as we have," Carl tells him, "and your children are grown, and you're bored as hell, you're gonna want access to grandkids, too. Trust me. Do you know how much television I watch? It's shameful. I need a distraction."

Gabby and Jesse come back and join us.

"What are we talking about?" Gabby asks.

"Grandchildren," Tina says, looking at Gabby and Jesse with intent.

"Oh, no!" Jesse jokes. "Gabby, turn away slowly, and maybe they won't see us."

Gabby mimes trying to leave, but Tina pulls her and Jesse back.

"Hannah and Henry seem to have found a way to have a baby," Tina says. "And I'm not getting any younger. It wouldn't kill you to *try*."

"Tina," Jesse says, "I promise you, the minute your daughter and I are happily wed, it will be the first thing on my To Do list."

Ethan and Ella join us. They must have just come through the door.

"Sorry we're late," Ella says. "I was stuck at work, and you know how it is! Happy birthday!" she says to Gabby. She hugs her and then turns to Ethan, who hugs Gabby and smiles. He shakes Henry's hand, gives Jesse a pat on the back, and then hugs me.

"We did bring a present," Ethan says. "To make up for it."

It's a box of Godiva chocolates. The moment I see them, I want to shove them all into my mouth. I figure I can take them from Gabby later if I really want them. Or get some of my own. I know that if I say I want them, Henry will stop on the way home. He always gets me any food I want, at any time of night. He says that's his job. He says it's the least he can do. "You carry the baby. I'll get the food." His morning breath is terrible, and he's cheap as hell, but I feel like the luckiest woman in the entire world.

The party goes on, all of us hopping from person to person, talking and sharing stories about Gabby. Just when the party seems to hit its peak, someone asks Jesse to tell the story of how he and Gabby met. Slowly but surely, everyone quiets down to listen in. Jesse stands at the base of the fireplace so he can be seen and heard by everyone. I asked him his height once. He's five-foot-six.

"First day of geometry class. Tenth grade. I look to the front of the classroom and see the prettiest girl I've ever laid eyes on." Jesse has told this story about nine thousand times, and each time starts the same. "Although Gabby would say that's not the first thing that I should have noticed about her." He looks over at her, and she smiles. "But you'd have to notice it about her. She was gorgeous. And, to my delight, she was also short. So I figured I had a shot."

The whole crowd laughs.

"But I didn't ask her out, because I was a chicken. Three weeks into school, another girl asked me out, and I said yes, because when you're fifteen and a girl asks you out, you say yes."

The crowd laughs again.

"Jessica and I dated all through high school, and we broke up senior year. So what do I do? I go right out and find Gabby and ask her out. And we have this great date. And then the next morning, my ex-girlfriend calls me, and she wants to get back together. And . . . long story short, I married Jessica. Anyway, eventually, Jessica and I split up. We had to split up. We weren't right for each other. And once I could see that, there was no turning back. So we divorced. And then, a few years later, I get a Facebook request from Gabby Hudson. *The* Gabby Hudson."

That's my favorite part. The part where he calls her *the* Gabby Hudson.

"And I get way ahead of myself, and I start Facebook-stalking her and wondering if she's single and if she'd ever date me, and yada yada yada, the next thing I know, we're at lunch on the beach in Santa Monica. She refused to let me pay and said going dutch was the most appropriate thing to do. And we started walking back to my car, and I didn't tell her this then, because I knew it would freak her out, but I felt like I finally understood why people get married again. You get your heart broken, you fail at marriage, you're not sure you'll ever be up for it a second time. And then it all clicks into place, and you see that you failed the first time because you picked the wrong person. And now the right person is standing in front of you. So I waited the appropriate amount of months of dating, and then I told her how I felt. And she said she felt the same way. And now we're getting married. And I'm the luckiest guy alive."

That's usually the end of his story, but he keeps talking.

"I was reading a book about the cosmos recently," he says, and then he looks around and goes, "Hold on, trust me, this relates."

The crowd laughs again.

"And I was reading about different theories about the uni-

verse. I was really taken with this theory that some very cred-
ible physicists believe in called the multiverse theory. And it
states that everything that is possible happens. That means that
when you flip a quarter, it comes down heads *and* tails. Not
heads *or* tails. Every time you flip a coin and it comes up heads,
you are merely in the universe where the coin came up heads.
There is another version of you out there, created the second
the quarter flipped, who saw it come up tails. Every second of
every day, the world is splitting further and further into an infinite number of parallel universes, where everything that could
happen is happening. There are millions, trillions, or quadril-
lions, I guess, of different versions of ourselves living out the
consequences of our choices. What I'm getting at here is that I
know there may be universes out there where I made different
choices and they led me somewhere else, led me to *someone*
else." He looks at Gabby. "And my heart breaks for every single
version of me that didn't end up with you."

Maybe it's the moment. Maybe it's the hormones. But I start
crying. Gabby catches my eye, and I can see that she's teary,
too. Jesse is done speaking, but no one can turn away. Everyone
is staring at Gabby. I know I should do something, but I'm not
sure what to do.

"Way to make the rest of us look bad," Henry says loudly.

The crowd laughs and disperses. I look at him, and he wipes
the tears from my eyes.

"I love you as much as that show-off loves her," he jokes. "I
just didn't watch the same *Nova* special."

"I know," I tell him. "I know." Because I do know. "Do you
think that theory is true?" I ask Henry. "Do you think there are
versions of us out there who never met?"

"Maybe one where you didn't get into an accident and you ended up married to a cinnamon roll chef?" he says.

"Everything that is possible happens . . ."

"Do you wish you were married to a cinnamon roll chef?"

"I certainly wish you were better at making cinnamon rolls," I say. "But no, this universe is OK with me."

"You sure? We can try to defy space and time and go find another for you."

"No," I tell him. "I like this one. I like you. And her." I point to my belly. "And Gabby. And Jesse. And Carl and Tina. I'm excited to get my nursing degree. And I'm OK with the fact that sometimes when it rains, my hip aches. Yeah," I say. "I think I'll stay."

"OK," he says, kissing me. "Let me know if you change your mind."

He slips off to the bathroom, and I start to head toward Gabby and Tina, standing by the mini-cheesecakes. I'm mostly interested in the mini-cheesecakes, but I am stopped in place behind a linebacker of a man. I ask him to move, but he doesn't hear me. I am about to give up.

"Sir," I hear from behind me. "Can she get through?"

The linebacker and I both turn around to see Ethan standing there.

"Oh, I'm so sorry," the linebacker says. "I'm a glutton for cheesecake. When I'm in front of it, everything around me is a blur."

I laugh and fumble through. Ethan steps up with me.

"Six months now?" he asks. He takes a piece of banana cream pie.

"Seven," I say, taking a piece of cheesecake.

"What is this? No cinnamon rolls for you?"

"It is a nighttime party," I say. "So it's OK. But I've been eating them pretty much nonstop lately. Henry says you can smell cinnamon in my hair."

Ethan laughs. "I believe it. I'm sure I told you that after we broke up, I couldn't smell a cinnamon roll without getting depressed."

"You never told me that," I say, laughing. "How long did that last? Until Thanksgiving break?"

He laughs back. "Fair enough," he says. "It is true, though."

"Well, you shouldn't have broken up with me, then," I tell him.

He guffaws. "You broke up with me, OK?"

"Oh, please," I say. "Go sell it to somebody else."

"Well," he says, "whoever broke up with whom, my heart was broken."

"Ditto," I tell him.

"Yeah?" he says, as if this information makes him feel better.

"Are you kidding? I didn't sleep with anyone else for years afterward, because I kept thinking of you. I bet you can't say the same."

He laughs. "No," he says. "I definitely slept with people. But that's . . . that didn't mean anything."

"I always thought we'd get back together at some point," I say. "It's funny how the teenage brain works."

He shrugs, eating his pie. "Not that funny. I thought it, too. From time to time. I almost . . ."

"What?" I ask.

"When you came back to L.A., right before the accident, I thought maybe . . ."

I think back to that time. That was a rough period. I kept a happy face through all of it. I tried really hard to keep it together, but looking at it now, I think of how heartbreaking it all was. I think of the baby I lost, and I wonder if . . . I wonder if I had to lose that baby to get to where I am now. I wonder if I had to lose that baby to have this one.

"I think I thought maybe, too," I say.

"Just didn't work out that way, I guess," he says.

"I guess not." I see Henry coming back from the bathroom. I see him stop and talk to Carl. He loves Carl. If we could have a bronze bust of Carl in our living room, he'd do it. "Who knows?" I tell Ethan. "If Jesse's theory is right, about the universes, maybe there's one out there where we figured out a way to make it work."

Ethan laughs. "Yeah," he says. "Maybe." He lifts his pie as if to make a toast. I lift my cheesecake to meet it. "Maybe in another life," he says.

I smile at him and leave him by the dessert table.

I miss my husband.

He's now standing in a circle with Gabby, Jesse, Carl, and Tina. I join them.

"I see you found the cheesecake," Gabby says.

"The pregnant lady always finds the cheesecake," I tell her. "You know that."

Henry moves closer to me as he continues to talk to Carl. He puts his arm around me. He gives me a squeeze. He opens his mouth wide, and I smile at him. I feed him the cheesecake.

It's on his face.

"I love you," he says with his mouth full. I can barely make out the words individually. But there's no doubt what he said.

He kisses me on the forehead and grazes his hand against my belly.

One Saturday night in my late twenties, I was hit by a car, and that accident led me to marry my night nurse. If that's not fate, I don't know what is.

So I have to think that while I may exist in other universes, none of them are as sweet as this.

ACKNOWLEDGMENTS

I am fortunate enough to have more than one Gabby in my life, and for that I am grateful every day. Thank you to Erin Fricker, Julia Furlan, Sara Arrington, and Tamara Hunter for being such phenomenal people and close friends. This book is dedicated to you, because your friendship has kept me going at times when I wasn't sure I could take another step. And to Bea Arthur, Andy Bauch, Katie Brydon, Emily Giorgio, Jesse Hill, Phillip Jordan, Tim Paulik, Ryan Powers, Jess Reynoso, Ashley and Colin Rodger, Jason Stamey, Kate Sullivan, and all the rest of my incredibly supportive and wonderful friends, I am so lucky to know all of you and have you in my life.

To Carly Watters, the world's most wonderful agent, I often thank the fates (or mere chance) for bringing me to your blog back in 2012 and driving me to query you. That I got so lucky as to be repped by someone I *like* so much is either the very definition of destiny or a wonderful coincidence. I am equally thankful to Brad Mendelsohn and Rich Green. Thank you, Brad, for understanding me and getting my work the way you do, and Rich, I'm so excited about what we've done.

Greer Hendricks, it's impossible to imagine a universe where you are any more lovely. Thank you for being such a pleasure to talk to and for being so incredibly good at what you do. My work could not be in better hands. The same goes to Sarah Cantin, Tory Lowy, and the rest of the Atria team.

To the Hanes and Reid families, thank you. To Rose and Warren, Sally and Bernie, Niko and Zach: When I tell my friends how much I love my in-laws, I'm pretty sure they all roll their eyes at me as if I'm a student reminding the teacher that she forgot to assign homework—but I'll keep saying it until I'm blue in the face. I'm lucky to have married into such a wonderful family. I love you all.

To the Jenkins and Morris families, thank you. To my mother, Mindy, and my brother, Jake, I love you. I am so fortunate to have you in my corner. Thank you for always believing in me and for always being game to talk through ideas about life and humanity.

To my grandmother, Linda, words will never express what you mean to me. I feel humbled just to have known you, let alone to have been so lucky as to be your granddaughter. Thank you for every single moment of our time together. I am who I am because I have grown up trying to make you proud. Consider this my solemn promise to remember to stop and smell the roses.

And finally, to Alex Reid: This book isn't about us. But there's one line that I wrote just for you. "I know there may be universes out there where I made different choices and they led me somewhere else, led me to *someone* else. And my heart breaks for every single version of me that didn't end up with you."

MAYBE IN ANOTHER LIFE

TAYLOR JENKINS REID

A Readers Club Guide

At the age of twenty-nine, Hannah Martin still has no idea what she wants to do with her life. She has lived in six different cities and held countless meaningless jobs since college, but on the heels of a disastrous breakup, she has finally returned to her hometown of Los Angeles. To celebrate her first night back, her best friend, Gabby, takes Hannah out to a bar—where she meets up with her high school boyfriend, Ethan.

It's just past midnight when Gabby asks Hannah if she's ready to go. Ethan quickly offers to give her a ride later if she wants to stay.

Hannah hesitates.

What happens if she leaves with Gabby?

What happens if she leaves with Ethan?

In concurrent storylines, Hannah lives out the effects of each decision. Quickly, these parallel universes develop into surprisingly different stories with far-reaching consequences for Hannah and the people around her, raising questions including: Is anything meant to be? How much in our life is determined by chance? And perhaps most compellingly: Is there such a thing as a soul mate?

Hannah believes there is. And, in both worlds, she believes she's found him.

QUESTIONS AND TOPICS OF DISCUSSION

1. Hannah opens the novel needing to find a sense of home, and a renewed, stronger sense of self. Does she find both of these things by the novel's conclusion? Are they different in each ending, or more or less the same?

2. Hannah has a complicated and somewhat distant relationship with her family after they move to London. Hannah's dad admits, "Your mother and I realized we had made a huge mistake not bringing you with us. We never should have let you stay in Los Angeles. Never should have left you" (page 125). What do you think about this statement? What does Hannah's reaction to this confession indicate to you?

3. Why do you think Gabby makes such an effort to spell out her feminism?

4. There are some choices that Hannah faces in both of her stories. Can you identify these? Discuss whether her ultimate decisions differ or are the same in each plot thread. What is their significance?

5. Turn to p. 194 and reread the conversation Hannah has with Ethan from her hospital bed. What do you make of her statement, "Whatever would have happened wasn't *supposed* to happen" (page 165)? Do you agree with Hannah that believing we're all destined for something makes it easier to bear the harder moments?

6. Hannah says, "I'm starting to think maybe you just pick a place and stay there. You pick a career and do it. You pick a person and commit to him" (page 210). Is this idea—that sometimes, you just have to make a decision and stick with it—mutually exclusive with any notion of fate or destiny?

7. Reread Gabby and Hannah's conversation about soul mates (pages 208–210). Do you agree with Hannah when she says that sometimes you can just *tell* about a person? Have you ever had a person about whom you felt you could just *tell*?

8. While on the surface, the novel may seem to focus on which man Hannah will end up with, there are several types of love explored in *Maybe in Another Life*. Discuss these as a group. Which of the many relationships depicted was your favorite? How did they change and grow in each storyline?

9. Mark tries to defend his decision to leave Gabby by saying, "I didn't mean for it to happen. But when you have that kind of connection with someone, nothing can stand in its way" (page 273). What do you think about this? Do you agree with Hannah's belief that "your actions in love are not an exception to who you are. They are, in fact, the very definition of who you are" (page 274)? How does this jibe with the idea that sometimes you can just *tell* someone is right for you?

10. Did you believe in fate when you started the novel? Did the novel change, challenge, or uphold your opinion?

11. Certainly some of the characters, including Hannah at times, believe in fate. Do you think the book itself suggests that fate exists? What about soul mates?

12. Did you find yourself rooting for one ending versus the other? Do you have an opinion on whether Hannah should have ended up with Henry or with Ethan? If you were Hannah, which ending would you have wanted for yourself?

13. Think about the statement that Jesse makes at the end of the novel: "Everything that is possible happens" (page 330). If that's true, what do other versions of your life look like?

ENHANCE YOUR BOOK CLUB

1. Hannah has a special love for cinnamon rolls. In honor of her, make (or buy from your favorite bakery) some cinnamon rolls for your book club.

2. The 1998 movie *Sliding Doors* (starring Gwyneth Paltrow) takes a similar premise as *Maybe in Another Life*, and examines how one woman's life differs based on whether or not she catches a train. Watch the film as a group, and discuss how its portrayal of two possible outcomes for one woman's life differs from Hannah's story. Are the two projects making the same point or contrasting ones?

3. Taylor Jenkins Reid is the author of two other novels, *Forever, Interrupted* and *After I Do*. Pick one to read as a group and compare and contrast it with *Maybe in Another Life*. What do Reid's earlier books have to say about fate and soul mates?